Prai

"*Thirst* sails quickly over half-glimpsed depths, making you want to go back and explore them more. This slim volume of 100 pages is a haven of both comedy and horror."

—*The Telegraph* (UK)

"Gelasimov's spare prose and pointed dialogue make this tale of drinking, disfigurement, and self-discovery a memorable one; Kostya's unique voice may particularly resonate with readers dealing with postcombat adjustment issues in their own lives."

—*Booklist*

"Andrei Gelasimov writes lean prose, and the pace never slows. The plot of *Thirst* is fairly simple, essentially a Moscow road trip, but the complicated and secretive characters are cunningly revealed in each step of their quest. Never asking for pity, Konstantin makes it clear that not all scars are visible and that his identity is not found merely in his reflection."

—*Rain Taxi*

"It is not often that on finishing a novel the reader feels compelled to go back to the beginning and start reading it again. But Gelasimov, whose unadorned prose and youthful, troubled narrative has invited comparisons with Salinger and Hemingway, is that kind of writer."

—*Russia Now*

# Also by
# Andrei Gelasimov

*Thirst*
*Gods of the Steppe* (forthcoming)
*Rachel* (forthcoming)

# THE LYING YEAR

## Andrei Gelasimov

Translated by Marian Schwartz

**amazon** crossing

The characters and events portrayed in this book are fictitious. Any similarity to real persons, living or dead, is coincidental and not intended by the author.

Text copyright © 2003 by Andrei Gelasimov
English translation copyright © 2013 by Marian Schwartz

All rights reserved.
Printed in the United States of America.

No part of this book may be reproduced, or stored in a retrieval system, or transmitted in any form or by any means, electronic, mechanical, photocopying, recording, or otherwise, without express written permission of the publisher.

*The Lying Year* was first published in 2003 by Eksmo Publishers, Moscow, as Год обмана *(God obmana).*
Translated from Russian by Marian Schwartz.
Published in English by AmazonCrossing in 2013.

Published by AmazonCrossing
P.O. Box 400818
Las Vegas, NV 89140

ISBN-13: 9781611090710
ISBN-10: 1611090717
Library of Congress Control Number: 2012913713

# THE LYING YEAR

## Spring: Mikhail

Then I started thinking who I could hit up to tide me over for a week. No one, it turned out. When they took me on at the firm, everyone was pretty easy about loans. A solid business. Partners in the States and all over Europe, an office with all the perks, and a boss with his own helicopter. Who knew cutbacks were in the offing? How was I going to repay my debts now? They kicked me out on my ass like a dog. Now go sit on the street in the middle of this slush and wipe your snot on your fist. Spring's come, damn it. Open the gates!

---

After dinner I sat on Gogolevsky Boulevard for a while, then by Christ the Savior Church, then on the library steps near the Dostoevsky monument, and when I was chilled through I made my way over to the Alexandrovsky Garden, which had the most comfortable benches. Downy soft, they even seemed warm. By that time my ass could easily distinguish between a bench on Tverskaya and a bench near the Kremlin gates. It was a professor, not an ass. It was just too bad they didn't take that kind at Moscow State. Though what do they get there, those professors?

"You wouldn't happen to have a light, would you?"

A pretty little lady had appeared out of nowhere. As if she'd popped out of the ground. How was it I hadn't noticed her? She probably had an eye on that nice bench too.

"Please." I suavely flicked my Zippo. I liked the real thing.

She didn't look like she'd been chucked out of her job. A cheerful look, chic à la Nina Ricci, or who was I thinking of? Lately I'd barely been keeping up. So I had no idea why she was slumming on benches.

I scanned for her goons. There had to be some kind of driver hovering around such a fortunate soul.

This one was alone.

"How much?" She leaned toward me, and I thought, She's wearing two-hundred-buck perfume.

"A hundred," I said without thinking.

I just said it. I was joking. I didn't even know what she was asking me.

She opened her purse and pulled out two fifties. Greenbacks.

Just like in the movies. And put them in my hand.

I said, "What for?"

She said, "You know."

I looked at her a moment and said, "No-o-o, I don't think so."

She said, "Not enough, is it? Here, another fifty."

I said, "I just don't want to, keep your fifty."

And she said, "Well then, let's say two hundred."

And she put more cash in my hand.

Damn it, I thought, I've landed in it. She's a crazy lady! Meanwhile, I kept giving it back.

Suddenly she said, "You mean you just happened to sit down on this bench?"

"Uh-huh," I said. "My butt was freezing sitting on stone."

She burst out laughing.

"Well then, give me another light."

Now she said it in a normal voice.

I flicked my Zippo again, she took a drag, and we started sitting in silence. It was like we'd just sat down on a bench and were enjoying ourselves. Whose business was that? Tourists were strolling past. There are lots of them on Manezhnaya now since they built that stupid underground place. Little fountains and animals; kids like that.

Suddenly she started laughing quietly.

"But why did you refuse, actually?"

I shrugged.

"I don't know. It felt wrong for money."

"And you pushed my hand away so seriously." She bubbled up with laughter. "Shy, are you? You actually turned pale."

"Of course not," I said. "It's just at first I didn't catch on."

"You really sat down here by accident?"

"You mean you can't just sit here?"

She took a deeper drag.

"Well, it's kind of a special spot."

"Yeah, I got that."

"Clever boy."

She fell silent and, squinting from the smoke, kept looking at me.

"But maybe you didn't like me. I must be a little old for you, right?"

She looked to be about thirty. Naturally, a little younger would be better, but she was good-looking. Pretty. Attractive, no question. Age was no barrier here.

"Of course not," I said. "Age has nothing to do with it. I just can't for money."

"Well, you know best."

She leaned back a little and rested her arm on the back of the bench.

"This is great. Spring's finally come," she said, heaving a sigh. "Are you doing all right?"

"Oh, yeah, peachy. How about you?"

"Then why are you sitting here alone? You're blue from cold."

"Oh, that's nothing. I just have a lot of time."

"People who have a lot of time don't sit on benches in this kind of weather."

"Where do they sit?"

"In all kinds of nice places."

"Places like that take decent cash."

She tossed her cigarette away and smiled.

"Now you know where to get it."

"In principle, naturally…," I began.

"Well, if you change your mind, give me a call."

She stood up and handed me her card.

"You're terrific, only you're all blue. Go home or you'll freeze solid. So what's your name?"

"Misha."

I held the card and thought that I should have agreed on principle. That was the cash I'd been thinking about since morning. But how could I run after her now? Like, "Wait up, can we talk some more?" Damn it, it's always like that! You're forever coming up with something too late. I'd clicked on the same spot for the umpteenth time.

I stuck her card deep in my pocket and decided I'd go home.

What else was left?

The next morning I scraped everything out of my pockets and the result was not very inspiring. To keep from getting too upset, I ran out to the bakery and grocery store. I ate my fill of poppy-seed rolls. I had enough left for milk, but only day-old. I was consoled by the fact that it could be made to last three days. My refrigerator was still working. After deducting a pack of Marlboros and a box of Tic Tacs, I had a little change left. I could take two trips somewhere on the metro. Preferably where there was cash. Once there and once back. If there really was cash there, I wouldn't have to worry about the return fare. That was small potatoes.

I sat down next to the phone and tried to think. Nothing came to mind other than angry friends and offended relatives. They were constantly pouting at me, and when we met on the street, they'd turn away or step into some store. They all considered me a bad person. They were irritated that I managed my financial affairs so badly, I could never hold on to money. What irritated them most of all was that I could never hold on to their money. All these thoughts made me hungry again. I had to make some decision. If we were Americans, it occurred to me, they would bring cash if you called 911. In neat little stacks wrapped in gold foil. Like a fairy tale. And they'd sing "Heppi byozdei tu yu" in quiet voices.

Finally, I took yesterday's card out of my pocket and stared at it. I couldn't say I'd forgotten about her, of course, but still there had to be some way to cadge some cash the tried-and-true way. Actually, to hell with it!

I was reaching for the phone when it rang so abruptly itself that my heart nearly skipped a beat.

"Yes?" I nearly shouted after picking up.

"This is the receptionist for the general director of Red Star Industries. Is this the Vorobyov apartment?"

"Yes, that's me!" I shouted even louder. "Not the apartment, I mean…but Mikhail Vorobyov. That's me!"

"You have an appointment scheduled today at twelve o'clock. Please arrive five minutes early."

"But…I was let go in the cutbacks. I already got my last paycheck the day before yesterday." And spent it, a second voice said in my head.

"At five to twelve. Please don't be late. All the best."

"Wait up! Wait!" I yelled. "Who is the appointment with? What's it for?"

"With the general director. Good-bye."

The receiver started beeping, but I kept holding it up to my ear. In all the time I'd worked at the company, I'd never had occasion to see anyone higher than my department head. None of our people had ever seen the big boss himself.

The gods had taken an interest in me.

This change for the metro is going to come in handy, I thought. Finally, I hung up.

---

There were half a dozen other people sitting in the waiting room besides the secretary. Laid off too, probably, I thought. And now they've been called in like me. Maybe it's some mistake. What if they give me back my job? My guess was too good to be true. Just in case, though, I privately gave them the finger in my pocket.

"My name is Vorobyov," I had begun when suddenly the speaker on the secretary's desk started talking.

"Hasn't Vorobyov arrived?" it asked.

"He just walked up, Pavel Petrovich."

The secretary looked at me.

"You may go in."

"Fine."

"Zinaida…"

"Yes, Pavel Petrovich."

"What else do I have before lunch?"

"A meeting with representatives from the board of directors."

"What time?"

"Twelve thirty."

"Cancel it. They can come tomorrow."

"Before lunch?"

"You sort it out."

"Fine, Pavel Petrovich."

The speaker fell silent, and the secretary looked at me again.

"Well, what are you standing there for? Go on. He's waiting."

"Aha," I said.

---

The boss's office wasn't all that big. Not all that big, but way cool.

I wouldn't mind one like it. A white laminate floor.

The boss looked up from his papers and regarded me carefully. He looked at my Docs longest of all. I lowered my eyes to my boots too. A chain of dirty footprints from my shitkickers stretched across the white floor.

The thought flashed through my mind that I should run to the secretary for a rag.

"Yes, we're in the throes of spring," the boss said thoughtfully.

He was silent a moment, then got up from his desk and walked toward the window.

"But there's still no greenery."

"It'll show up soon," I interjected.

He kept looking out the window. We were both silent. Two minutes must have passed. I'd already begun to think he was lost in his own thoughts.

"How old are you?"

He asked me so suddenly that I startled. It was good he was facing the window.

"Twenty-three."

"And how long did you work for my company?"

"Four months."

"Not long."

He grinned and finally turned his head away from the window.

"I was laid off."

"Yes? And why was that?"

There was sympathy in his voice. This encouraged me.

"They said I wasn't handling the job."

"And you?"

"Oh, I was."

He smiled and shook his head.

"A month and a half ago, the company failed to meet its obligations to the Italians. We failed to supply them with enough raw materials. Wasn't your department handling that?"

My heart sank. That was, in fact, my fault. We'd caroused for two days at this dog's dacha, and I never completed the packet of documents.

"But they never did demand a penalty."

"I gave the president of their company a fishing boat."

To this I said nothing and started looking at my boots. Black puddles were spreading around them.

"Two weeks ago," the boss continued, "we started having problems with law enforcement."

This was flat-out my fault. On February 23, I assembled my fellow classmates right in my office. No one else in our class had landed such a great job. There's always that urge to keep score, damn it.

When the alarm went off at two in the morning and the cops suddenly showed up, for some reason our gang started resisting. I tried to calm them down, but I got punched so hard in the face that when I woke up, I was in the slammer. The next day, as I was later told, they kept coming across bras all over the department. One ended up in the supervisor's desk.

"Did you fight with the police that time too?"

"They started it."

"All in all, do you fight often?"

"Well, not that much…"

"But still?"

He narrowed his eyes and looked straight into mine.

"It happens."

I dropped my head.

"And you drink?"

"Uh-huh."

"And you have lots of girlfriends?"

I realized resistance was futile.

"Even a few prostitutes," I admitted with a sigh.

"As you see, you're a worthless employee. How much was I paying you?"

"Nine hundred dollars."

"Quite a lot for work like that."

He grinned again. Obviously, my train had left the station. I sighed deeply and we were both silent for a long time.

He was the first to speak up.

"Would you like to make twice as much?"

I thought he'd misspoken. He'd meant to say "half as much" but accidentally said "twice." Even on those terms, though, I came out smelling like a rose. You aren't going to find four hundred and fifty bucks lying around.

"Excuse me?"

"Twice as much."

For a minute I lost the gift of speech.

"But who's going to pay me?"

"I am."

Suddenly it occurred to me that this was a dream. This happens to me sometimes.

"What for?"

"That's a separate topic. So, are you interested? Or should I find someone else?"

"No, no! I'm interested! What do I have to do?"

"Don't worry, you don't have to kill anybody. Have a seat, I need to tell you a few things."

We sat down at his desk, and he offered me something that made my jaw drop all the way to the floor.

The way Pluto's does in the Disney cartoons when he stops somewhere and witnesses some extreme outrage: Mickey Mouse is up to something, or the spiteful chipmunks have come running in. Basically, it doesn't matter. In short, the job suited me. To be honest, it was pretty cushy.

I had to look after his son.

I understood that the boss was seriously upset over his dear son. The kid had either gone to hell or was just plain weird. In short, his dear papa was afraid he might be gay or, God forbid, he'd been dragged into some sect. Not that there were any actual homos hanging around, but the boy was not behaving quite normally. He sat home for days at a time, didn't socialize with people his age, didn't party, had no girlfriends—nothing but the computer, searching for something there, who the hell knew what, on the Internet. Or else he would go away for a long time, but he always came back sober and alone. What worried his dear papa most of all was that he came back sober. For him, this was the most suspicious part.

In short, he wanted me to teach him to drink.

He wanted me to teach him to fight.

He wanted me to teach him to chase women.

Basically, his papa wanted me to make a man of him.

"Here's money for expenses."

He laid fifteen hundreds down in front of me. Greenbacks, naturally.

"It won't be deducted from your salary. You'll just tell me later what you spent it on."

This was heaven. The seventh day of creation. It was all there, but there were still no problems with the snake. All the apples were hanging where they were supposed to.

"Now go down to the garage and choose a car. Do you have a driver's license?"

"International."

"Good. Then drive to this address. They'll be expecting you."

I jumped up from the desk and dashed for the door.

"Hold up!"

I braked like a racing dog.

"You didn't ask me his name."

"Whose?"

"My son's."

"Yeah? So what is it?"

"His name is Sergei."

"Very nice!"

---

The cars in the garage looked like playthings. I could take any one I wanted. All I had to do was point, and they were supposed to give me the keys immediately. Fords, BMWs, Fiats, even one Mercedes.

Up until this moment I'd believed heaven had been invented by the popes. Now I saw—they could never invent anything like this.

"This one here." I finally stopped, unable to move any farther.

It was simply a miracle. I'd dreamed of it so many times that now, like Joan of Arc, I distinctly heard a voice from the heavens: "Misha! This is your destiny! Please help the king!"

The big old English Land Rover's chrome details flickered dimly in the dark garage. It was a real beast. An aircraft carrier on dry land. They're made for safaris in Africa. For really rich people. Even a rhinoceros couldn't overturn a car like that right away. The best was to use it for hunting antelope. Cruising speed like a cheetah's, and no roads required.

"And gas?" I could barely exhale.

"A full tank." The mechanic on duty smiled. "And another couple of containers in back."

We could go after lions. All that was missing was an old .505 Gibbs rifle, or at least a Springfield. On the other hand, instead, to the right of the driver's seat, in a convenient little pocket, lay a cool cell phone and, directly in front of it, a Sony television. I really did have no need for change for the metro back.

I turned the key and the engine started purring discreetly, like a sated cat. It too was happy we had met at last.

As I pulled out of the garage, I took tremendous pleasure in soaking a dawdling idiot with a file under his arm, splashing a dirty puddle on him.

I was in a remarkable mood. The sun was tearing along as hard as it could. The sparrows were hollering like crazy.

"It's spring!" I shouted, and I turned the radio up all the way.

---

They really were expecting me at the boss's house. They greeted me, invited me in, and explained. Their place was in the fanfuckingtastic style. I liked that style. Compared with what I saw there, Euro renovations are lame. It stands in the corner pathetically snuffling into a rag.

My guy was sitting in his room. Concocting something or other on his PC. Just a guy. Ordinary enough. Sitting and looking. About seventeen. Obviously not a homo. Though lately, fuck-all if I can tell. Lots have started looking like ordinary guys too.

"Hi," I said. "My name's Mikhail."

"The archangel?"

I didn't get it. I answered, "I don't get it."

And he replied, "Don't shed any tears over it. It'll all be fine."

"Awesome," I told him.

Then he offered me a chair.

I sat down and laid out papa dear's program. This pale teen didn't so much as blink. When I finished, he said, "Well, okay, if Papa wants it, like, where do we start?" I was kind of surprised. I thought, He's an okay guy, you've got to give him that, emancipated. Young people have it fucking going on! In his place I'd definitely be pissed off. But he was sitting there looking at me very seriously.

"Maybe you didn't understand what you and I are supposed to do," I said.

"No," he said. "It's perfectly clear. When do we start?"

I was thinking, Well now I'm going to surprise you. We'll see just how imperturbable you are!

I got out yesterday's card and said, "Where's your phone?"

He pulled a cell phone out from behind the computer.

"Know how to use it?"

That was him talking to me.

I quickly dialed.

"Hello?"—she picked up almost immediately.

"Hi. It's me, Misha. From the Alexandrovsky Garden. Remember, you and I were talking there yesterday?"

"Ah, splendid man! How are you doing?"

"I'm fine. I'm calling you about yesterday's—"

"Ah, so you gave it some thought after all? Well, good for you. Clever man—"

"No, no," I quickly interrupted her. "It's not me. It's this other person. Someone else. Not me."

"What someone else?"

"He's good. Really excellent. Even younger."

She was silent for a moment.

"How much?"

"Looks to be seventeen."

"I don't mean that."

Now I was silent for a moment.

"A hundred will probably do it."

"Agreed. Bring him to the same place. I'll pick him up in forty minutes."

"Excellent!"

I clicked the phone off and turned to this papa's boy. He was looking me calmly in the eye.

Fine, then. Let's see what you have to say now!

———

She brought him back an hour and a half later. In the meantime I'd run back to the car to warm up five times. The day had turned windy. It was crazy cold. There was a crime show on TV. If I hadn't been afraid of missing them, I'd have been happy to sit there in the SUV.

Basically, I didn't notice when they arrived. She probably parked her car somewhere else. When I saw them they were on our bench. Fuck if I knew how long they'd been sitting there. When I walked up they were yakking away about something. And it would have been fine if they'd just been yakking. It had the feel of an aunt discussing how school was going with her nephew.

"Ah, Misha," she said. "Join us. We'll be just a minute."

She might as easily have said in this same tone of voice, "Oh, look, what a sweet little dog!"

I sat down and, like an idiot, started listening to them.

"Basically, you should have told her everything right away," she was saying. "Do you understand me?"

My guy nodded.

"And everything would have been clear immediately," she went on.

What's going on here? I thought, sitting. Or am I the one who's lost his mind?

"Basically, it's up to you." She sighed and rose from the bench. "Misha, you're a wonder!"

She took a hundred bucks from her purse. The kid gave me a careful look.

"Maybe you'll think better of it somehow? You're such a dear. I've been driving myself crazy over who you resemble."

"Who?"

"Johnny Depp. Such a darling."

"No, I'll pass," I said, stashing the money in my pocket.

Especially since I had no idea who this Johnny was.

The kid still couldn't take his eyes off me. Evidently he meant to burn a hole right through me.

"You know best."

She leaned toward him, gave him a smack on the cheek, and ruffled his head with her beringed left hand.

"Bye, Seryozha. Think about what I told you."

"Okay," he replied, straightening his hair. "I will. Good-bye."

"All the best, boys."

We sat there like idiots for about ten minutes, in silence. My feet were blocks of ice.

"Well, what are we going to do with the money?" I finally asked.

"A hundred bucks isn't money."

"To some it is."

"Let's spend it," he said.

"Let's. What on?"

"How much does a prostitute cost?"

I realized I wasn't going to surprise him today. Papa's Seryozha was a special case.

———

Basically, the girl's name was Olesya. Probably from somewhere in Ukraine. They say there's nothing at all to eat there now. Or maybe she was longing for the beautiful life. There's lots of them, Ukrainian girls, hanging around Tverskaya. We ended up with a decent one, attractive. True, she talked too much.

"If you want, I can do you both at once. But that would cost more."

"You don't have to do us both," I said.

"Who then?"

"Him."

"What if I'd rather do you? You're so cute."

"No, only him," I answered.

My kid was sulking.

"So where are we going?"

"We're going to my place."

"I don't go to houses."

"Look at him. He's just a kid. You mean you're scared of him?"

"No, not him."

"Oh, I'm not even going to go upstairs. I'll wait for you in the car."

"You know how awful these kids are. The younger they are, the worse. Give me a puff."

She took a greedy drag on my cigarette.

"What if I'd rather do you? He's not saying anything for some reason. You sure he's all there? I don't need any stupid-ass adventures."

"Don't be scared. I'll come running if need be."

"Don't be scared! You're kidding. Does the guy need to part with his virginity at last?"

This Seryozha looked at me like a wolf.

There, I thought, I got you this time. And he's sitting there like the prince of Denmark. This is Russia, brother! There are no fucking Hamlets here!

They did it fast. The girl came down first and asked me to turn on the TV.

"My favorite soap is on TV Center right now. It's like it's all about me. Don't laugh if I start bawling. Give me a cigarette."

"So where's my kid?"

"I don't know. He stayed behind. He said he wanted to be alone for a while. Kind of a strange one. You know, your apartment's shit."

"I know. Is he going to be there long?"

"You're asking me? I told you, I wish you'd have gone with me. I'd fuck you for free. Not many good-looking guys in Moscow, you know. It's so much better back home!"

"In Ukraine?"

"Why Ukraine? Krasnoyarsk."

Well, what could I say to that?

I turned the television on for her.

―――

After we took the girl back, my Sergei suddenly got talkative.

"What do you think you'll die of?"

I realized he'd decided to shock me silly. Evidently he hadn't finished with his agenda for today.

"Why don't you watch television?"

"People die for different reasons." He just wouldn't let it go.

"Yeah?" I responded just to say something. I did get this job because of him, after all.

"Mayakovsky's father died after pricking his finger with a pin."

"Is that right?"

"Krylov died of gluttony. And Giordano Bruno was burned alive."

I chimed in, "Joan of Arc too."

"Exactly. And Anacreon choked on a grape seed."

"It happens," I agreed, braking at a traffic light and pondering who this Anacreon might be. "My neighbors' child suffocated after eating foxberries. Their relatives sent the berries from Siberia. After that, his mother slit her veins. She said he was sad there without her. They brought her body back."

"There, you see?"

He fell silent and stared at me.

"What? Why 'There, you see?' "

"It's different for everyone."

"So what? Naturally it's different for everyone."

"How are you going to?"

"To hell with you! I'm not!"

He turned toward the window and said softly, "Yes, you are…How can you escape it?"

A minute later he added, "But don't be afraid. Dying is like going home. You know, to your grandmother's in the country. A big country house. Woven floor mats and fresh milk in the morning…The main thing is that it not be over something silly…"

I had nothing more to say. I just turned the volume up on the television.

When he got out of the car near his house, I leaned over the wheel and shouted at his back, "I'll be by tomorrow at ten in the morning."

He turned around.

"Tell my father I did what I was supposed to. Papa will be proud of me. And of you too, of course."

He didn't say "wanker," but I guessed it, in principle.

The next morning I was at his house at ten on the dot. Again, my Sergei was sitting at his computer cooking something up.

"Hi," I said to the back of his head.

He turned around right away and stood up as soon as he saw me. I looked at the monitor, but he'd quickly switched everything off.

So it begins, I thought.

"You know," he said, "I barely slept all night."

"Curious."

"No, it's not about that. I was just thinking about our conversation in the car yesterday."

"Okay, let's have it," I said quietly, realizing he'd decided to keep bugging me. It wasn't that I didn't care at all, but that wasn't what they were paying me for. So what if he was farting around? With that kind of money, he could.

Or rather, with his father's.

"I realized I should apologize to you."

"What?" I wasn't sure I'd heard him right.

"Can you accept my apology?"

"What?" I said again.

"Let's shake hands."

He held out his white palm and I automatically took it with my right hand.

"Well then, that's good. Have you had breakfast?"

"Yes."

"Then let's go. What are we waiting for?"

"Where to?"

"I'll explain later."

He jabbered nonstop the whole way. First about transmigration of souls, then about cloning. He cited various names and terms. He even got red in the face. As if he hadn't been as pale as death that morning. We really have to forbid today's kids from fooling around on the Internet so much. It can easily send them around the bend. It would be all right if they were just looking for pornography. As it is, they're reading all kinds of trash.

"Where to now?" I asked when we hopped on Volgogradka.

"Go straight. I'll tell you where to turn."

"Are we going to Lyubertsy or something?"

"You'll find out soon enough."

At Kuzminki, he told me to turn after the Budapest department store and park.

"Now we have to go on foot. Coming with me?"

"You bet," I said. "You think I'm some fool who goes somewhere this remote without finding out why?"

Actually, I could tell he wanted me to. He was aching to show me something. That was obviously why we'd come.

I locked the car and we walked past the market and deep into a complex of five-story tenements. The mud all around was impassable.

Couldn't we have driven up in the car? I thought.

At that moment, someone called out behind us, "Seryozha!"

My guy stopped dead in his tracks, and his face looked as distraught as a kid's. Just like a little boy's.

He turned around and said in an idiotic voice, "Oh, it's you, Marina."

I looked too and thought, So this is Marina, and what a Marina! Cool dame. I could do her. I wouldn't say no!

This Marina walked up and looked at us. Her cheeks were blazing. She was smiling. Really cool. Black eyebrows, sly eyes. I could eat her up.

"You promised to come yesterday."

Even her voice was remarkable.

"Yeah, you know…Yesterday I was busy," my Seryozha stammered. "I was doing some work…around the house… My mother told me…"

He's lying, I thought. It was his dear papa's little idea. Though it wasn't exactly around the house…

Meanwhile Marina had started darting her little eyes at me. She could tell.

They can always feel it.

"And this is Mikhail," he said finally.

Then he stammered again and added, "He's no angel."

That is so true, I thought. You're going to be a real believer very soon.

"Hello." I held out my hand to her. "Very pleased to meet you."

"Me too," she said, and she let her hand linger in mine for a few seconds. "I was on my way to the institute. Our boys have a stage-direction test today. I thought I'd watch."

"So, we're actresses, I see," I guessed.

"I won't go." She smiled. "I didn't get into a single scene anyway."

My Sergei stood there like a statue until I intervened.

"Well, so, I guess we're coming to see you, Marina? If that's not too forward?"

"Of course not"—and her eyes flashed briefly—"not too forward at all."

Her little apartment was no great shakes, of course. A cramped vestibule, low ceilings, pretty dark—about what you'd expect from genteel poverty. I had no idea how my kid ever found his way here. You couldn't call the neighborhood prestigious. The folks here weren't exactly loaded. I wondered what papa's Seryozha wanted here. Were they smeared with honey or something?

"Oh, Seryozha's here!" The papa came out of his room. These papas evidently are born in tracksuits and wife beaters. And they always have a paunch and two days' stubble.

"Hello, Ilya Semyonich," this Sergei said.

"We waited for you all day yesterday. Marina never stepped away from the windows. She didn't even go to the institute."

I looked at her, but she said nothing. Only her eyes flashed briefly in the dark vestibule.

"And this is...my friend Mikhail," my kid stammered a little again.

"Well, come in, we'll have tea," her papa responded.

"How was your transit here?" he continued after we'd all sat down around a very modest table.

"Fine," Sergei answered. "The metro, as always."

I looked at him, but he turned away immediately.

Fuck if I know why he lied. But I decided to sit there and keep my mouth shut. What business was it of mine? The main thing was, they paid. For cash I could confirm that we'd crawled here on all fours.

Marina was keeping her mouth shut too. She sat looking at us with those eyes. First at me, then at this Seryozha.

"Did it take long?" Papa would not let up about the metro.

"Oh, no," Sergei said. "It's just so muddy. Spring. I got my boots all dirty."

"So that's why we walked from the department store," I guessed.

Though I still didn't get why he was lying.

"So what station did you take?" the father continued aggressively.

"The same as always—" Sergei began, but the other quickly interrupted him.

"—since Kuzminki's closed today. They're doing repairs there."

I nearly choked on my tea.

"—at Volgogradsky Prospect," Sergei finished in a different voice.

The look on his face now! I thought merrily. I wonder how he's going to get out of this one.

"I always come from there," he went on. "It's very healthy… and…and…most of all…"

He couldn't find anything more to say. You could tell he was totally flustered. His face was just pathetic. I could barely keep from laughing out loud. At this, Papa decided to deal the final blow.

"You should have got out at Tekstilshchiki. That would have been much closer. Tekstilshchiki comes right before Kuzminki. Volgogradsky comes even before that!"

Naturally! How could this Seryozha know the sequence of stations on one lousy branch of our beloved metro? It was a rout. Ten to nothing in favor of the poor.

"I often walk…a few stations at a time…"

He was still trying to save face, but Papa had already turned to me.

"Mikhail, more tea for you?"

And his face was oh so cunning.

Ten minutes later I was in the kitchen alone. Marina had dragged my Sergei to her room, and her dear papa had decided to duck out for cigarettes. He'd refused my Marlboros. "Thanks, we don't smoke Jew cigs." He stated his preference for "ours." Most of all, he respects Yava. Give him Yavas any time. Oh well, to each his own. I stayed and sat, waiting.

---

About a minute after dear papa ran out, somewhere in the apartment I heard quick steps, and a sleepy little butterball appeared at the kitchen door. He stood there swaying, facing me, and rubbed his face with his chubby little fists.

"Who are you?" he said finally, yawning with his pink mouth.

"I'm Misha. And who are you?"

"I'm the Misha. You're some stranger."

"I'll be leaving soon."

"Good," he said. "But where's my papa?"

"He went out for cigarettes. He'll be right back. How old are you, Misha?"

"Five. How old are you?"

"I'm twenty-three."

"You're all grown up." He yawned again and shuddered like a kitten.

"You should put on your pants," I said. "Where did you take them off?"

"Marina did it. She always puts me to bed."

"She'll be here soon too. Want some tea?"

"With sugar," he said firmly.

After drinking a whole mug straight down, he regarded me with interest.

"Do you know why you have a beard?"

"Why?"

"Because you ate lots of fish. The bones got stuck in your throat and then they poked out on your face."

"You think so?"

"Of course. Papa always has that too."

I decided to keep the conversation going.

"Do you like buckwheat groats?"

"Not with milk," the child replied. "Just with sugar."

"And do you know what they're made from?"

"No."

"They're made from bucks. They catch them when they're small, before they've grown up, and make groats out of them."

"But what are bucks?" he asked.

I realized I'd lost.

"Two to nothing, your favor, Mikhail. But you still should find your pants."

He hopped off the stool and shuffled out of the kitchen. A minute later he came back, still without his pants, but he did bring a big Lego model.

"What's that mausoleum you've got there?"

"It's a house."

"And who lives in it?"

He let five or six plastic figures drop to the floor.

"Soldiers," I said. "Then what you have is a barracks, not a house."

"It's Heracles and Hercules," he objected. "Those aren't soldiers, they're strong men. Like Schwarzenegger."

At that moment, Marina appeared. Her hair was a mess. She was fastening her robe with one hand and holding the neck together with the other.

"Did we wake you up?" she said quickly. "Let's go. Don't bother our guest. Where are your pants?"

"It's not a guest, it's Misha," the child said loudly. "I want to play with him."

"Don't worry." I smiled at her. "We're getting along fine here. Go on, go on. Your father will be back soon."

She looked at me closely and gave me a slow smile. My Sergei's red face flashed behind her back. He peeked into the kitchen too, and then locked himself in the bathroom. Marina was still smiling, not taking her eyes off me, silent.

"Don't worry," I repeated. "I get along well with children."

---

The next day I decided not to let the initiative slip from my hands. I got down to business, the way it's supposed to be done. "Study, study, and study," as our great leader bequeathed. Pedagogy is a serious thing. It takes a deep approach using the scientific method.

"Today we're going to study boozing," I told my pupil, tearing him away from his computer again. "What are you doing there all the time?"

"Oh, this stupid thing," he responded. "I already know how to booze."

"No." I drew the word out and smiled enigmatically. "Getting drunk a couple of times at some druggie party is not the same as boozing. From this day on, it's a new life for you. Rejoice, you're in the hands of a professional. I'm the Moscow middleweight champion."

"Why not heavyweight?"

"I'm working on that. But there's no middleweight to compare with me."

"Fine," he said with a smile. "When do we start?"

"First you have to undergo theoretical training."

"Yeah? How's that?"

"You need to learn the rules for champion boozers."

"What do champion boozers have to do with it?"

"Those who don't booze it up according to the science are just amateurs. Out-and-out amateur hour. Champion boozers, my dear boy, are the elite."

"I see." He smiled again.

"Rule number one: If you're going to booze, then booze. You can't be a real champion boozer if you have any doubts. The main thing is for there to be a sincere desire in your heart to be a drunk little piglet. Will has nothing to do with it. You have to really want it. Then something may come of you. Nowadays there are hardly any true masters left, just amateurs. But I'll teach you."

My guy was grinning from ear to ear, but silent.

"Rule number two: A champion boozer has to be an artist. Without a poetic attitude toward the whole thing, nothing ever comes of it. Do you like the sea?"

"Yeah."

"Think about it when you drink."

"I get seasick."

"Then think about a woman."

"Marina?"

"Anyone you want. It just has to be poetry. Whose poems do you like?"

"Yesenin."

"Excellent. He was a boozer too. You have to assign a poet to each drink. Let Yesenin be vodka."

"Preferably rowanberry vodka."

"Good boy. Who else?"

"Pushkin."

"That's champagne. Another?"

"Byron."

"Haven't read him. Think up something yourself."

"Brandy, probably…"

"You have to be sure."

"Yeah, brandy, for sure."

"We still have wine. First red."

He didn't answer right away.

"Blok maybe?"

"How am I supposed to know?"

"No, Blok is white wine."

"Then who's red?" I asked.

"François Villon," he thought again. "Yeah, for sure! François Villon."

"Hungarian?"

"No, French. He was hanged for looting and pillaging."

"Good poet. Give him to me to read later. Who are you putting in charge of the port?"

"I don't know. I've never drunk port."

"That means there are gaps. All right, we're going to eliminate those. Here's your homework assignment. Today, port, and tomorrow dive into your papa's books."

"He doesn't have poetry."

"Well then go to the library. That's all for now, basically. All the whisky-shishkies we'll leave for another assignment. You shouldn't mix them all in one heap."

"No more rules?" he asked, disappointed.

"At least two more. But first a quiz. Who was the most faithful Leninist, who we should all emulate?"

His face expressed powerful amazement. Then he thought hard and, finally, smiled.

"Boozarin?"

"Five points. You're starting to catch my drift. The next rule says: Never forget your boozekeeping. If you've stopped keeping track, you're just a boozer, not the head boozekeeper. You always have to know how much you've drunk. Then you can think strategically and allocate your remaining resources correctly. Is that clear?"

"As mud."

"And finally, the golden rule of head boozekeepers: No throwing up. Under any circumstances. It demeans human dignity."

After discussing a few other details with him, I sat down at the telephone and started searching for an appropriate drinking party.

As usual, we had lots of options. Two weddings, one stag party, a class reunion, a presentation at a tour company, a bachelorette party, and a few drinking parties for no occasion at all. All this was fine, but it lacked style. The whole composition demanded an inner tension.

Finally, I came across what I'd been looking for. A couple of months ago, four guys I knew were kicked out of the institute. Apparently they'd been going heavy on the alcohol and mischief. Today was their send-off: they were going into the army. This was exactly what we needed. Discreet male grief and heartfelt sympathy for one's comrades.

———

When we walked in, everyone gave us a look of disapproval.

I introduced my pupil and pulled out a package with three bottles of Finlandia.

Their faces brightened.

After this, Seryozha took a large pack of Carlsberg beer out of his bag.

Their eyes warmed with respect.

Finally I announced that I had five more packages like that in my car, and strong male hands were extended to us on all sides.

After greeting everyone there, we got a spot at the end of the couch. I moved the opened bottle of vodka closer and the practical part of our assignment began.

A problem was being discussed at the table—draft dodging. The two draftees were already so drunk that they'd dropped out of the discussion. However, two others were listening avidly to the advice from these men of the world. Speaking loudest of all was one guy who'd been discharged from the military. I didn't know him, and he was drunk as a skunk. He'd just returned to civilian life and was used to thinking everyone should listen to him. The army spoils people, instilling delusions of grandeur in them.

"You've got to dodge smart, guys," he shouted with such tension that his neck and part of his face turned red.

"You have to dodge so it isn't agonizingly painful," my neighbor on the left said as he chased his vodka with a green onion.

"It's pointless pissing yourself and playing the fool," the vet continued to holler, not listening to anyone. "I'm an old-timer and I'm telling you. The doctors pick up on shit like that right out of the box. They'll fuck you up good in training and you'll stop pissing altogether."

After his fourth shot, my Seryozha was drawn into the conversation.

"Let's go have a smoke." He elbowed me in the side.

When we came out in the hall I could tell just how fucked up he was.

"You need a break," I told him.

"I'm fine," he replied, and he spat on the floor.

"Nauseated?"

"I'm fine. Give me a cigarette."

We lit up and stood there in silence for a few seconds.

"You know why I took you with me to Marina's yesterday?" he began at last.

Of course I do, I thought. You wanted to show off.

"Usually they follow me," he said.

"You lost me," I interrupted him. "You mean you're working for the CIA?"

"Papa doesn't leave me without a tail. But when you're there, no one hangs around anymore. You're probably enough. I noticed it the very first day."

Yeah? I thought. Then why did he drag me to the apartment? He could have left me in the car...

"I don't want him to find out about Marina."

"Why?" I asked.

"I'd never see her again then."

"They'd kill her?" I chuckled.

"No," he replied seriously. "But they'd stash her so far away, you'd never fucking find her."

"Where's that?"

"Anywhere. Siberia, Europe, America."

"She probably wouldn't mind going to the States." I chuckled again.

"More than likely," he said. "But that's why I took you with me."

"What's got your papa's shorts in such a twist?"

"He wants me to marry this Italian girl."

"Is she rich?"

"Her father's a famous politician..."

At that moment the apartment door opened, and the drunken former military man appeared on the threshold.

"Guys!" he howled. "Here's where you are! We've been looking everywhere for you."

"We're coming," I replied quickly. "We needed to talk."

"Great, fellows! Just tell me where you have the rest of the beer stashed."

I gave him the keys and explained where our Land Rover was parked.

"Just lock the door after."

"Sure," he said with a thick tongue, and he rolled downstairs.

"Her father also owns ore refineries and two soccer teams," my Sergei said.

"Which ones?"

"I don't know. Second tier, I think."

"Well, still." I shook my head respectfully. "You've won the Italian sweepstakes. Get married. Why the second thoughts?"

"I've never seen her."

"So what? Italian girls are to-die-for gorgeous."

"What about Marina?"

"To hell with her, with Marina! What are you, a fool or something?"

"You're the fool!"

He broke off, but I could see what it cost him to restrain himself.

"Go to hell!" he finally forced out, and he kicked the door. I'm glad it wasn't me he kicked.

I stayed in the hall alone.

A minute later the discharged guy was panting on the stairs. He was dragging all five packages and was absolutely happy.

"Awesome wheels you've got!" he yelled. "Listen, what's your name? I forgot."

"Mikhail," I responded.

"Ah! Well, good going, Mikhail! You'll make an excellent soldier."

He had evidently decided that I was the one being seen off to the army.

The door slammed behind him, and I was alone again. It was time to go back.

---

At the table, the draft-dodging discussion was still under way.

"Well, how far has it gone there?" I said in a low, conciliatory tone as I sat down next to Sergei.

"Where?" he asked.

"In Italy."

I could tell he didn't want to answer at first, but eventually he deigned to.

"My father gave her father a boat."

I couldn't believe my ears.

"A fishing boat?"

"Yeah, I think so," he replied. "The Italian's big into fishing. What business is it of yours?"

I didn't know what to tell him. Because of that boat, which the boss had chewed me out over two days ago, it now suddenly seemed to me that I too was mixed up in this whole story with the Italian engagement. It was no accident he'd chosen me specifically. That meant that all this nonsense about "making a man of the boy" was just a pretext. And I'd been hired to spy on him. Especially since they'd lifted the outside surveillance when I was with the kid. They probably hoped he'd start trusting me. And then I'd have to rat him out to his papa.

It was an interesting scheme. Actually, I still wasn't sure of anything. The Italian boat story could have been a simple coincidence. His papa might have just have mentioned it, by the way. The man slipped, it happens to everyone.

"What business is it of yours?" my kid repeated.

"Nothing, I just had a flash. Give me that bottle of port. It's time to do some research. And the vodka's already aired out."

At that moment the guy who'd been discharged started hollering louder than usual.

"Get off my back! None of you are going to dodge this! Listen up! This is going to be specific now. I'll break your arm and fuck-all. No army!"

One of the draftees sleeping at the table woke up and asked in a husky voice, "Who's getting off whose back?"

"Quiet!" the discharged guy snapped. "Who wants to stay a civilian for real?"

"I do," the one who woke up said right away.

His eyes were totally bleary.

"Toss back some more vodka," this guy ordered him. "Then it won't hurt."

"I'll throw up," the draftee warned.

"Toss it back, I'm telling you. Learn to obey your elders."

"Okay."

They poured him nearly a glassful, and he drank it down in incredible convulsions.

"Another?" one of the "assistants" asked.

The discharged guy leaned over his patient and, looking him in the eyes, declared:

"Good boy. That's the right dose. Take him to the toilet."

"But what are we going to do?" came the baffled question.

The discharged fellow looked at the questioner with a grin.

"We'll put his arm on the toilet and you'll jump on it."

"Me?"

"Chicken?" the vet said. "He's too chicken to help out a pal!"

"I'll jump," the other draftee offered.

"We're going to break yours too," the vet objected.

"First him," the volunteer replied. "I need to see how it comes out."

"That's logical." The vet snorted approvingly. "Drag the first one to the toilet." Judging from his face, by now the first one was having a hard time understanding what was happening to him. Everyone got up from the table. That left just me and Sergei in the room, and also the fourth draftee, who was sleeping on the couch. Obviously they'd plain forgotten about him.

We sat there listening to what was going on in the toilet. I was waiting to see how it all ended, but evidently things weren't going too well. We heard the sounds of confusion, muted cursing, and, from time to time, laughter. The soldier sleeping on the couch groaned and tumbled to the floor.

"And does Marina know?" I said.

"About what?"

"The Italian girl."

He looked at me in amazement.

"She doesn't know anything."

"What do you mean? In what sense?"

"She thinks I'm from Kaluga. That I'm studying at the teacher-training institute. My mama teaches in a technical school. My papa lives with his other family."

"Shut up!" I couldn't hide my astonishment.

"Yeah. So what?"

"So nothing." I smiled. "But what the fuck do you need that for?"

He was silent for a second.

"Well, I didn't want her to find out right away..." He got a little embarrassed.

"How much dough you had?" I finished for him.

"That's not the problem. I wanted her to have the right to choose. If she knew, she'd have a hard time shaking the thought..."

"That your bread is a hell of a lot cooler than you are yourself," I continued for him.

"Well, basically, something like that." He grinned.

"I get it," I said.

Now I really did get it. First of all, it was now clear why he had lied to her papa about the metro. Secondly, why he'd hidden from the bodyguards.

"Well, how's about it? Some more port?" I asked.

"If you don't mind, that's enough."

"Have you determined which writer is responsible for it?"

"We were talking about poets."

"Well, poet." I gestured with my hand. "Decided?"

"Yeah, I think so. It's probably—"

At that instant a wild scream exploded in the toilet.

It worked, I thought. Gotta call an ambulance.

---

The next moment they carried the writhing body into the room. It was emitting horrendous moans and choice curses. The body belonged to the guy who'd been discharged.

"He decided to jump himself," one of the "assistants" explained. "Valerka fell asleep right in the middle, and his arm fell off the toilet. But that was right when he jumped. He said he'd show us all how you're supposed to love the Homeland."

After an examination, during which the vet cursed royally, we reached the conclusion that he'd broken his leg. Every time we touched it, he let up a wild howl and called us terrible things.

"We should take off his pants," one of the "assistants" suggested.

"Go to hell!" the vet exclaimed. "What, I'm supposed to go to the hospital in my boxers?"

"Then they'll have to be cut off," someone else said. "What if there's an open fracture there?"

"Though it doesn't look like there's any blood," a third spoke up.

"What if it's not bleeding just from the shock? That happens. The vessels contract."

"Take them off, shithead, and fast!" The vet was scared. "What the fuck are you standing there for? I could crap out here with you morons!"

No one knew how to pull his pants off without disturbing his leg. After consulting, they decided to hold him up and gingerly pull them off. This required carrying the soldier sleeping on the floor out of the room. Then they took out all the chairs. Then the table. As they were carrying out the table, the bottles started falling off it. It wouldn't go through the doorway.

"We're missing by a hair," the draftee who'd volunteered to jump first said. "A couple of centimeters. Maybe we can take down the door?"

"I'll croak while you're doing that!" the discharged guy shouted from the couch in horror. "Call an ambulance!"

We left the table by the door and picked the vet up off the couch. Pulling his pants off in a horizontal position proved nearly impossible. Not only that, he kept kicking at our faces with his good foot, and pretty cleverly. Someone suggested turning him upside down. Despite the fact that down below he kept up his terrible cursing, clinking the bottles that had dropped to the floor, and grabbing us by the legs, things now started going better. Soon afterward he was lying on the couch in lilac boxers, swearing loudly. His leg had swollen up like a log, but there was no blood anywhere to be seen.

"Thank God it's closed," we decided, but just in case we poured vodka on the break. Someone said we should disinfect it.

"Well, so how am I supposed to lie here now?" the vet asked, unexpectedly quietly. "The couch is fucking soaking wet."

Half an hour later, an ambulance arrived and took him away. It was a good thing they had a stretcher with them.

---

When we went outside, it was nearly morning. The sun still hadn't come up behind the buildings, but the birds were bawling like crazy. It had rained during the night, and now black puddles gleamed on the asphalt. Sergei took a noisy inhale and smiled.

"I love it when it smells like that. Fresh. Moscow in the morning is a pure high!"

I took a deeper inhale too.

"You said it. Especially when no one's around."

He glanced at me and started laughing.

"You should see yourself!"

"You should talk," I snarled halfheartedly.

"Let's walk," he proposed. "It's not very far."

"That depends on the person. I still have to drag myself halfway across town."

"Oh, come on. You can spend the night at my place. We have two guest rooms that are empty."

"Okay, let's go. There's no one at my home anyway."

"I'll feed you."

"Let's go, let's go. Listen, what are we going to tell your mother?"

"She lives in another country."

"Got it."

"And has no plans to visit."

"I get it. No more questions."

The morning really was marvelous. The air felt so light, every once in a while I felt like I was about to take off. Actually, more than likely, it felt that way because of the insane night.

"I shouldn't smoke so much," I decided. "Or else I should switch to lights."

"Look," Sergei said. "The leaves are out on the trees."

"For sure," I responded. "They're busting out everywhere now. It's spring, damn it."

A streetcar came rolling around the corner, jingling.

"Look how early it is. Those streetcar workers ought to have a life too. Where is it going at this hour?"

"You know how I met Marina?" Sergei said.

"How?" I asked, even though I didn't want to.

"On a streetcar."

"Shut up!" I feigned amazement.

That's what you do sometimes, so you don't have to say anything but you still find out what happened next.

"It's true. I was running away from my bodyguards and I hopped on a streetcar. It was pulling away from the stop."

"Why is it you're constantly running away from them?"

He stumbled and looked at me.

"Were you being followed twenty-four hours a day when you were seventeen?"

I thought about that for a second and all of a sudden had a very clear picture of the horror.

"You're probably right. So what happened on the streetcar?"

"I didn't know how to pay my fare. There were these things on the windows, and I didn't understand what they were for."

"Wait up. You mean you didn't know what the punch was for?"

"No. How was I supposed to know? That was the first time in my life I'd gotten on a streetcar."

"You mean you never took a streetcar?"

I actually stopped.

"No," he said. "Never until that time."

"What about a trolleybus?"

"No. A few times on the metro when I was a kid and my buddies and me skipped class, and that's it. There was always a special driver in the house who drove me everywhere starting in kindergarten. That's what my father decided."

Not half bad how this little generation's growing up, I thought.

"Okay, okay, so what then?"

"An inspector came on."

"And it was Marina!"

"No. It was an unshaven old guy with bad breath."

"What about Marina?"

"She was standing behind me and slipped me her ticket. But he immediately fined her."

" 'Oh, the women in Russia's towns…' Why didn't she take her ticket back?"

"I didn't know how to pass it on."

"You got flustered." I grinned. "You got a girl in hot water."

"I paid her back later," Sergei said.

"You ran away from the guards again and brought her what you owed?"

"No." He shook his head. "After the streetcar incident, it got very hard to run away from them. It almost never worked. Just once, much later. I had them take me to Kuzminki, and I pretended to go to the Budapest."

"Whatever was your reason?"

"Doesn't matter. They don't need to know everything."

"And did this go on for long after that?"

"Two months."

"Got it…And then all of a sudden I turned up. Is that it?"

He looked me in the face and said nothing in reply.

Well, to hell with you! I thought, suddenly angry. I'd be looking for shelter too. He's used to his papa buying people for him.

At that point, we walked up to his house.

"Okay, let's make today a holiday," I said. "I'll pick you up tomorrow morning."

"But you wanted to stay over."

"You wanted that."

"But you said…"

"It doesn't matter what I said. Maybe you don't need to know everything either."

I turned on my heel and started back for my SUV. As I was approaching the intersection, I looked back. Sergei was still standing where I'd left him.

---

I had to go to sleep on an empty stomach. That's probably why I had such lousy dreams. At first, there was some ship on skates, then wild horses, then Pushkin for some reason, and after him a duel and shooting. Then I was taking a train to where I was born, but I was scared because I didn't know what station to get off at. I ended up surrounded by a sea of high grass that blocked out damn near everything, and I was running, gasping, down a narrow path, and the long stalks were lashing me in the face. Suddenly, someone's hand thrust out of that green grove and grabbed me by the throat. I wanted to cry out, but even just breathing was impossible. A dark face appeared in the grass. "Get ready," it said. "We've come for you." I don't want to! I thought in horror, but the face shook me like a rag. "Get ready! Time's up. Get ready!" a voice bellowed.

I shot up from the bed like a rocket.

"Get ready," the voice repeated. "Enough of your siestas! People are waiting."

Finally, I figured out it wasn't a dream and I wasn't alone in my room.

"Come on, get up, and make it quick," said the man, who was sitting on my bed and shaking me by the shoulder.

A second man was standing by my cupboard, and after opening the door, he started rummaging through my things.

"Get dressed," he said, tossing jeans, a T-shirt, a shirt, and something else on the bed.

"Come on, come on," the first chimed in. "Time's all up."

"Where are your shoes?" the one standing asked.

I said nothing in reply.

"Where are your sneakers? Gone deaf, have you?"

"Who are you?" I finally said.

"Brad Pitt," the other replied. "Where are your sneakers?"

"I don't wear sneakers."

"What do you wear?"

"Doc Martens."

"Fine. Where are your Doc Martens?" I could tell he was angry.

"They're in the bathroom."

"Why the fuck did you put them there?"

"I wanted to clean them."

"You can clean them in the next world. Come on, up and at 'em! Are we going to have to waste the whole day on you?"

I threw back the blanket and stood up.

"You mean you sleep without underpants?" the first one snorted.

"Hey—" He turned to the other one, who had gone out of the room. "He sleeps without underwear! Probably jacks off."

"Lay off him," came from the bathroom. "Let him sleep however he wants. Time's up!"

I dressed in silence and considered my visitors. First of all, I had no idea how they'd come in. I had a precise memory of locking the door and even latching the chain.

They must have broken in, I decided.

Both my visitors were dressed in strict dark suits. Their white shirts and ties were impeccable. They looked like twins.

That's all I need, men in black, I thought.

"Ready?" the main one said, coming into the room with my boots.

"Jackpot! Now let's get the hell out of here. We've already lost too much time as is!"

---

Downstairs, we got into a black BMW with tinted windows, and I decided to remember the route. At least they hadn't blindfolded me.

"Why didn't you clean the windshield?" the main one asked when we were barely under way. "I told you yesterday, and you don't listen for shit!"

"I did clean it," the other responded, shifting gears.

"When? Look at all the dirt! There's slush everywhere, and you don't clean it. Pretty soon we won't be able to see where we're going! When did you clean it?"

"I cleaned it," the other one repeated.

"I'm asking you, when did you clean it?"

"The day before yesterday."

"And when did I tell you to?"

"I don't know."

"I told you yesterday! How often do I have to repeat myself? I'm sick of you. You're impossible to work with!"

"Listen," the other one said, stopping at a light.

"Well?" the main one responded.

"I told you my hands hurt me in the spring."

"Why do they hurt you?"

"Even I don't know. Maybe it's the water. They probably add more chlorine to the water in spring. First my skin dries out, and then it cracks. I used my girl's hand cream, but it still doesn't help. It really hurts. It's even hard to touch the wheel."

"A soft rag isn't exactly a wheel."

"And window cleaner? Do you know how it stings these little cuts?"

"Go to the doctor."

"I did. He says there's nothing to be done. I have to wait for spring to end. Avitaminosis. Bad nutrition. Go figure! He says I have bad nutrition! Jerk. It's just the shitty water. Maybe I should wash in mineral water. I'll get five cases or so, and I won't wash from the tap at all."

"You'd better wash the windshield."

"And I'm telling you. My hands hurt. I'm sick of spring. Next year I'm going to take a vacation around now. Do you think they add chlorine to the water on Cyprus?"

"Come on, hurry up! They add arsenic. There's the ticket."

They both fell silent, and the one behind the wheel hunched over resentfully.

A minute later, the car stopped beside a big gray building.

It was my boss's office.

"You know the rest of the way," the main one said, opening the door on my side. "Come on, shake that booty. They've been waiting for you for half an hour."

---

The building was desolate inside. It was as if all the halls had been deserted. I walked across the light, laminated floor, and my steps echoed somewhere in remote rooms. Where's everyone gone? I thought. It's not even five. War, is it? The doors to some offices were open, but no one was there. Something must have happened while I was asleep, I decided.

I didn't see anyone in the boss's waiting room either. No secretary, no visitors, no janitors—no one.

"Vorobyov?" came from the office's open door. "Is that you?"

"Yes."

"Come in here. I've been waiting for you for a long time."

When I walked in, he looked up from his papers and leaned back in his chair wearily.

"Hello, Mikhail."

"Hello…" I began, but suddenly realized with horror that I couldn't remember his name and patronymic.

"Pavel Petrovich." He grinned.

"Yes, of course, Pavel Petrovich. Hello, Pavel Petrovich."

"Sit down over here. Actually…do you want a drink?"

I can't say that didn't surprise me at all.

"Well, you know…I just woke up…"

"I know." He smiled. "You don't drink in the morning?"

"It's not exactly morning."

"Nevertheless?" He looked at me questioningly.

"You don't have any juice?"

"Mineral water."

"Fine," I said.

He nodded at a leather couch by the wall and opened a small cupboard.

"I'll have a drink, though," he said, taking out a bottle of whisky. "Sure you don't want some?"

I shook my head.

"As you like. Genuine Scotch. I have a friend in Glasgow—he sells me top-notch. It's a little expensive, but I can indulge myself."

"Fine," I said in a husky voice.

"Excuse me, what?"

I coughed and repeated, "Fine, pour me a little."

"And the mineral water?" He smiled.

"Just a little," I said again.

After we had a drink, he pulled out his cigarettes and tossed them on the couch.

"Well, do you like it?" he asked.

"Ye-e-es," I said slowly.

"Basically, of course, you should drink whisky in Scotland. In a cozy pub with a fireplace, at a big wooden table."

I pictured the scene. My head had started roaring.

"Cool."

"What's cool?" he asked.

"I've already got a buzz on."

"What did I tell you? It's jet fuel, not whisky. You can fill any tank with it and win any race. Formula One, not whisky. Another?"

"Let's."

Now I was feeling much better. I hadn't expected the boss to be such a pleasant person.

"Well, how do you like it?" he asked again when I'd swallowed the second shot.

"Significantly better."

"Any buzz?"

"I've had one for a while."

He took a deeper drag on his cigarette and a dreamy smile appeared on his face.

"When we were students we used to say 'smashed.' "

"You can say that now too."

"What else?"

"What else?" I thought for a second. "You can say 'wasted.' "

"What else?"

"Hammered."

"What else?"

"Fucked up."

" 'Fucked up' is a little much." He frowned. " 'Smashed' is still better."

"Basically people say 'fucked up' when they're smoking hash."

"I see," he said slowly, and his face became pensive.

We both fell silent.

"One more?" he asked a minute later.

I held out my glass.

"Why isn't anyone at work?" I finally asked the question that had been bothering me from the very start. "It's not late."

Instead of answering, he looked at me in surprise, tossed back his whisky, and held his breath a little.

"Today is Sunday," he said, barely audibly on the exhale.

"Sunday?" I echoed.

"Well, yes. And yesterday was Saturday. There wasn't anyone here then either."

I realized I'd lost track of time, and this thought struck me as terribly funny. I could barely keep from bursting out laughing. Great! It's Sunday! The glass in my hand shook as if I had a major hangover.

"Drink up," he said. "You're about to spill it. What's so funny? Even your face is red."

"I didn't know what day of the week it was," I barely got out, choking with laughter.

"It happens. Once I forgot what month it was. Drink, or you'll spill all over my couch. You okay?"

"Yes, thanks," I said, swallowing the whisky and wiping my tears with the back of my hand. "That was funny."

"Where have you been going with Sergei all these days?" he asked suddenly.

I instantly was on my guard, realizing that the moment of truth had come.

"Nowhere special. You know…I introduced him to some people…There was one beautiful woman…We spent all last night with my friends…"

"How's he doing?"

"Sergei's great…I think he already knows what's what."

"How did he react?"

"Oh, just fine…He reacted fine. How else could he react? He's a normal kid."

"Does he have someone?"

I realized his papa was asking about Marina. Not about Marina specifically, but in principle. He'd found out about her somehow. I thought, I wonder how much he really knows? This could be a trap, after all. He might just be checking up on me. Could that be why he'd wheedled me into his drinking session?

"No, doesn't seem so," I said, deciding to fly blind. "I haven't noticed anything. We've only known each other three days."

"Fine, then, fine. All right," he said. "You wouldn't lie to me, would you?"

He looked at me so intently, I nearly turned away.

"You see, here's the problem," he continued after a brief silence. "In fact, all these family matters have me very worried."

He sighed deeply.

"Another cigarette?"

"Yes, thank you," I replied.

"You're still young and you aren't paying any special attention to this. But later is too late. Too late in the sense that you can't change anything. You can't change the past, after all. Do you understand? You can't."

"I understand," I said. "You can't change the past."

"You understand that now intellectually. But when you start understanding it with your heart, then it's all in the past already. Everything you'd like to change. It's this incomprehensible paradox. You can change anything in the world except what you yourself have already done. No money or connections can help. It's a total impasse. The way back is cut off."

"Yes," I said, at a loss for what else to say.

He fell silent and we sat like that for what seemed like a whole hour.

"About twenty-five years ago, when I was studying at the institute, something terrible happened to me. A minor thing, you'd think, but I just can't forget it. I live with it like an inconvenient neighbor. I'd like to be rid of it, but I just can't! It's nothing all that serious, actually…A family incident, you see."

He fell silent for a moment.

"My mama was living in Siberia then, and she was planning a trip to the south. In those days they paid the fare for people who worked for the railroad. For the employee and one family member. My mama took my little sister. She was in first grade then, and she got to go. She'd decided to bathe in the sun and have a little rest. They were changing trains in Moscow. They had two hours here between trains. We called each other and agreed to meet at the station. I promised to show them the city and tell them about what I was doing. At that point, we hadn't seen each other in two or three years. Basically, it was a good occasion. It was summer and warm…"

He fell silent again.

"I nearly missed them. Everyone had already exited the cars and the platform was nearly empty, and only later did I notice them. My mama was standing with her suitcase a little off to the side, holding my sister's hand. Natashka was eating ice cream, and my mama was looking from side to side in distress. She was afraid I wouldn't come, and alone in Moscow she was afraid. That first moment, I didn't even know how to approach her. It felt awkward."

He took a drag on his cigarette.

"It's odd how you can't find the right words for the people you love."

I quietly placed my glass on the end table.

"Basically, we transferred to the other station, strolled across the square, and sat in a café, but I still couldn't say what was in my heart. It was as if a lock had been hung on it. And she kept looking at me with such eyes, I thought I was going to die. The longer this torture lasted, the more I understood how powerless I was. I stammered like a fool, said all kinds of trivial things, and with each passing minute felt more keenly that this was it, I couldn't take it anymore. Before that, I couldn't even imagine how hard it might be to be with someone you loved so much. I don't know what came over me then. Basically, I couldn't wait for their train to leave. They announced boarding, and I left. I told a lie about an exam, and fled plain and simple."

He lit a second cigarette off the first. I sat in silence.

"Later, when I was already down in the metro, my heart suddenly felt like it was bursting. I thought, 'This is my mama!' and I was so ashamed I nearly howled for the whole station to hear. I hopped off the car and ran upstairs. The train was supposed to have left already. I ran alongside it and prayed they'd delay it. Their car was at the very end. When I tried to jump up, the conductor wasn't letting anyone else on. I squeezed past her and ran down the hall, peeking into each compartment. I found them somewhere in the middle. People were shoving their suitcases onto the upper shelves, Natashka was jumping up and down by the window, and my mama was sitting by the window and crying. No one was paying any attention to her tears. Someone is leaving—no surprise…"

He fell silent. I looked up and I thought I saw the answer in his eyes…I can't say for sure, of course, but that's what it seemed to me. Though I was probably wrong.

"In short, all these family affairs are nothing but misery," he spoke finally. "Now it's all being repeated with Sergei…I want so much…Basically, I don't want to lose him. I hope you can help me. You definitely wouldn't lie to me, right?"

He looked me straight in the eye again.

"Of course," I said. "Of course I wouldn't lie. What's the point?"

---

I had to take the metro home. Naturally, those goons in their BMW didn't wait for me. I rode in an empty car and looked straight ahead at the black window, where only my face loomed. Hair on end, white face, black holes instead of eyes. The shade of Hamlet's father. Moreover, it rocked when the car shook.

I was sitting there thinking about what had happened to me in the last few days. All these fathers, money, drinking bouts, and prostitutes were whirling before my eyes, and I just couldn't catch the key to it all in that chaos. Then I started thinking that I should pay back my relatives and friends, and then all of a sudden I would remember the crazy guy who'd been discharged, or that nice lady from the bench in the

Alexandrovsky Garden would suddenly surface, and right after her, Seryozha's papa and his goons. Why did he tell me all that?

I closed my eyes and shook my head, trying to shake off these troublesome thoughts, but they kept returning, climbing into my skull, interweaving, and always ending the same exact way. Each time, out of all this chaos, for absolutely no reason, Marina's face kept surfacing. It smiled at me with its eyes and winked slyly. There probably wasn't anything strange about that in principle. It's just that I could tell I liked it.

---

Nothing new happened over the next two weeks. We kept making the trip to Kuzminki and I kept lying to my boss about educational excursions to the capital's tenderloin districts. Each time we went to see Marina, her papa would run out for cigarettes, and I would play with Misha in the kitchen. True, there were moments when the child wasn't woken up by what was happening in the next room, and then I would waylay Marina on her way to the bathroom and smile and she would smile back. She would fix her hair in the dimness and smile. Apparently, she liked this little secret of ours. Then the kid would crawl out, her concerned papa would return with his cigarettes, and we would have tea and leave. Everything was simply marvelous.

Then, suddenly, the fairy tale was over.

---

It all started with what seemed like nothing, actually. A trifle, a total bagatelle. As usual, I went by for Sergei at ten in the morning, and as usual, he switched off his computer at my appearance.

"Do you ever go to bed? Or did you spend the whole night on your Internet?"

"I slept," he said.

"On which website?"

"It's true, I slept. I just logged on half an hour ago. I was chatting with this guy from the States."

"What does he say?"

"The weather's great, he says."

"Where's that?"

"In Florida."

"Swimming already, most likely?"

"Easy. It's summer there year-round."

"Here it's friggin' cold," I said, dropping into a huge leather armchair. "There was a frost last night. Even all the puddles froze. Spring is over."

"Fuck a duck!" my Seryozha swore.

"What's with you?"

"I promised to take Marina somewhere. With little Misha."

"We'll do it some other time," I said lazily in reply. "Big deal!"

"But I've already put it off a few times. Today I promised a hundred percent."

"Promise a fourth time. The main thing is you're not refusing. Say I don't have the time. Say it's my car. You're here from Kaluga!"

I started laughing, but he remained standing in the middle of the room with a scowl on his face.

"What's with you, Seryozha? Fuck it, fuck the cold! Let's go, if that's how it is. Where were they planning to go?"

"I can't go anyway."

"Why can't you?"

"My father just called. He says you should drop me by his office."

"That means we aren't going kitchy-cooing today. For long?"

"All day, he says. He wants me to sit in on his talks with the Italians. I'm sick of it already!"

He flung a tennis ball at the wall. I barely dodged it on the bounce back.

"Damn it!" he hollered as hard as he could.

I'd never seen him get so worked up before.

"I'm sick of him! What does he want from me?"

I sat in silence and looked at this teenager. *I should have his problems* flashed through my mind.

"Okay, I'll take her instead. I'll tell her you're sick and I happen to have a free day. Where are we going?"

He unexpectedly pulled himself together. He sat down in the chair across from me, pressed his hands between his knees, and a minute later was fully recovered.

He's learning from his papa, I commented to myself. The boy's going to go far. He'll make a fuss and then do what he's supposed to.

"You'll pick her up from the institute at twelve o'clock and then take her to Lytkarino. She rides horses there."

"Lytkarino? And where's that?"

"Past Lyubertsy. First turn to the right. I think the sign says Chkalovo."

"What a joke! How do you know that?"

"I know it! I took the bus with her. I managed to shake the guards. For a whole day. I never managed it again. From Kuzminki, you take the three-four-eight and then a jitney. Half an hour by bus, and twenty minutes by jitney."

"Wow," I said slowly. "I'm impressed! Seems we're already familiar with the life of the people. Go figure what love does to people. Pretty soon there'll really be no telling you from an ordinary person!"

"Cut it out." Sergei frowned. "Don't forget, at twelve her dance test is over."

He thought for a moment.

"What do you think? What should I wear for the talks?"

---

When I arrived at the drama institute, I got a little flustered. The dimly lit lobby was covered with posters and jammed with people. I was getting pushed, pulled, and bumped on all sides. I drifted downstream with the crowd and found myself somewhere in the basement. I soon figured out it was the snack bar. I got out of there, and on the stairs between the first and second floors, I found a schedule. There was no way I could figure it out myself. A kind young woman explained to me where the dance class was. That young woman in jeans had legs that made me lose it briefly. Upon closer examination, I realized that nearly everyone here had legs like that. I was beginning to like this place. It was kind of like girls gone wild. And there were homos out the wazoo.

The dance class was full of them too. They were walking along the walls gesturing with their arms and poking their butts out. A fair number were hanging around with a vengeance. Potbellied old guys with beards and jackets were shouting at each other and waving their arms. About twenty people were crowded by the entrance, where I squeezed through the dilapidated door. Half of them were holding video cameras. Actually, there was plenty worth shooting.

I'd probably come too early, and their test wasn't over yet. This looked to be the break. Over in the far corner, which was almost all mirrors, was where all the girls were hanging out. Some were standing with straight spines, others had spread their legs and sat right down on the floor, and still others had lifted their feet onto the barre and were bending over so far it took my breath away. Some were just standing in place, like horses, shifting back and forth on their feet. They were all wearing identical black leotards, slippers of some kind, and ribbons around their head. My, my, I thought. Sure glad I came.

One of the bearded guys rushed toward them and started explaining something. In the process, he got so carried away that he started pawing them one after another. At first you couldn't tell, but after a while it was standing straight up. The girls giggled but put up with it. This must have been some dance boss. And maybe they liked it. One way or another, he was for sure an experienced old goat.

"Now, everyone prepare!" one of the gays suddenly exclaimed. "We begin!"

An old woman in a man's suit popped up out of nowhere. Putting out her cigarette, she sat down at the piano. The girls fluttered up, and at that moment I saw Marina.

She was standing like a darling in the second row and looking at me with a furrowed brow. I smiled and raised my hand, but right then the music started.

I wonder how it is a person can be so unlike herself, I thought, watching her dance. Look, all you do is put on a leotard, pin up your hair, and it's a completely different Marina! So new, severe, and alien. Where did that come from? And most of all, how well she dances.

Suddenly I caught myself thinking that I didn't like this whole crowd of viewers being there. Shifting back and forth on my feet, I bumped into the fellow with the camera standing to my left, accidentally on purpose.

"Be careful!" he hissed.

"Please, excuse me. I didn't mean to."

"I'm filming!"

"Of course, of course," I whispered, and I stepped on his foot again.

While we were whispering back and forth, the old woman stopped playing. Everyone perked up. The bearded man rushed toward the girls again, and I took advantage of the confusion to find myself a spot on a bench along the wall. I had scarcely sat down, having decided to wait for it all to end, when Marina popped up out of the crush.

"Where's Sergei?" she asked, leaning toward me and furrowing her brow.

The warmth that wafted from her made me catch my breath. Drops of sweat glistened on her forehead.

"Where is he?"

"He's…sick," I said slowly, bowled over by her scent.

"Sick?"

She bit her lower lip and furrowed her brow.

"Don't get upset," I began, but she straightened up abruptly and vanished in the crowd.

"What the fuck do we need him for at all?" I finished saying into the void.

True, this was more a rhetorical question. Obviously, we both needed unlucky Seryozha.

In the car, she frowned for a while, thinking about something and tapping her boots on the floor. Finally, she gave her head a shake and looked at me.

"Did you at least like it?"

"I arrived late. I saw almost nothing."

"And what you did see?"

"What I did see I liked. Only there are an awful lot of gays."

"They're not all gay. Some just look that way."

"Yeah? What for?"

"Oh, I don't know. It's fashionable now. At our institute some of the boys put on an act on purpose."

"As pederasts?"

"Yes. Why are you surprised? It's fashionable now. Elton John is gay, George Michael is gay, Keanu Reeves is too. Ricky Martin. Everyone over there is gay now. That's why people think it's cool here too."

"No thanks," I said, turning the wheel as far as it would go.

There was so much black ice on the roads that the car kept swerving from side to side. It was good that at least I had four-wheel drive.

"So what really happened to him?" she asked.

"Who?" I didn't catch on right away.

"Sergei. Why didn't he come?"

"He…" I realized she'd taken me by surprise. "He…didn't feel well…This morning…I went by and he was lying there."

"And where does he live?"

"Where does he live? Well, how can I tell you…"

I actually had to slow down.

"You mean you don't know yourself?"

"No!"

She looked me in the face, glaring.

It's a good thing I had to watch the road.

"He's never once invited me to his place."

I heard obvious indignation in her voice.

"Oh, there's nothing interesting there," I muttered, shifting gears hard. "You know, he rents a small apartment with his mama…One room…no bath…no toilet even…"

"And no water?" she added angrily.

"Yeah, I think lots of times there's no water either…It gets turned off…"

"Well, well, poor little boy!"

She started laughing, throwing her head back, and I didn't know what to think. Apparently I got by this time. Or not?

Meanwhile, she'd stopped laughing. She ran her finger across the glass and suddenly said very seriously, "You wouldn't lie to me, would you, Misha?"

I nearly lost control. The car swung sideways, and I had to put on the gas to keep from hitting the high curb.

"Of course I wouldn't. Where's that coming from?"

She said nothing in reply. She just turned and looked out the window.

---

When we drove up to her building, she got out of the car without saying anything. She didn't even nod, as if I didn't exist. She just slammed the door and walked through her entryway. I even had doubts I was supposed to wait for her. Maybe she'd decided not to go anywhere.

Especially unexpected was the change that came over her after I sat in the car like a fool, not knowing whether to go home or to wait. She hadn't been gone twenty minutes, and that obviously isn't enough time for a normal person's mood to change that much. She was actually humming as she walked up to the car. She stopped alongside the SUV, squatted in front of little Misha, straightened his cap, whispered something, and burst into loud laughter. I heard Misha trying to outshout her, but her laughter was too ringing.

"Receive the hamster," she told me, gasping from laughter as she opened the back door.

"Hi, Mikhail!" I said.

"Hi," he muttered angrily as he climbed into the car.

"You need to be more polite to Uncle Misha," Marina told him.

"You first," the child snarled.

"What a horrible boy!"

She slammed the door and walked around the car. I saw little Misha in the mirror as he angrily crossed his arms over his chest and scowled. Marina's face at the institute had been exactly the same, I recalled.

"What's got you so hot and bothered, Mikhail?" I asked.

At that moment Marina tapped on my door.

"Open up, please."

I opened the door, and she took a step back and opened her jacket.

"Look, I had a spot here on my sweater. Is it very noticeable? I think I got it out."

She turned from side to side in front of me, wearing an absolutely snow-white sweater that clung to her body so tightly, I could barely keep from reaching out and touching the taut whiteness.

"Well? See anything?"

She kept twirling, raising her jacket higher and higher and revealing her ass all tightly encased in jeans. Before me was a butt of such beauty that I was speechless.

"Well, why don't you say something? Anything there? I can't see it myself."

Suddenly, I thought she might be playing with me. If so, this was a dangerous game.

"Misha, wake up!"

"No," I finally said. "Not a spot in sight."

"Excellent." She smiled. "That's great how well it washed out."

When she sat down next to me I smelled perfume, which she'd never used before. At least, she never smelled like that around Seryozha.

---

After winding around the outskirts of Lytkarino, we finally found the right road and seemed to be on the right track. It was another ten or fifteen minutes to the horses, according to Marina. She hadn't said a word the whole way practically, though from time to time she smiled enigmatically at something. Little Misha simply fell asleep in the backseat. He slumped into the corner against the window and was now snuffling loudly. Soon after, we came to a very steep incline. I braked.

"Why did you stop?" Marina asked, roused from her daydreaming.

"I won't make it. The road's started to freeze. It's solid ice. Is there some way around?"

"I don't think so. Just straight. There's nothing but trees around here."

"That I can see for myself. All right, we'll give it a try."

I pulled back, then picked up speed and made it halfway up the hill. Then we glided back down.

"Just like skating!" I cursed.

"Let's try it again."

I tried once more, but again no luck.

"We'll have to go back," I said.

During this, Misha woke up.

"Try telling him that." She grinned.

"Meaning?"

"He'll raise such a fuss, we'll push this car up the hill ourselves."

"This steep?"

"You can't even imagine."

"Misha," I said in a slow, ingratiating voice. "Do you want to go to McDonald's?"

"When are we going to ride the horses?" the child asked in a sleepy voice.

"Fine," I told Marina. "Then we'll go on foot. How much farther is it?"

"Pretty far, actually. Half an hour, maybe. Or more."

"On the other hand, it's through the woods. I've never been in the woods so early in the spring."

She looked at the child and shrugged hesitantly.

"All right, let's go. Only he'll get tired."

"He was the one who wanted to ride horses. Right, Mikhail?"

"Yes!" the child exclaimed and he bounced on the seat.

---

"Boy, it's cold," Marina said when we all got out of the SUV.

"If we walk fast we'll warm up."

"We can't walk fast. Misha's slow."

"I'll carry him if need be."

"Is that so? Do we like carrying children?"

What she said actually shook me up a little.

"Well...I don't know...I was just saying..."

"Okay, let's go"—she shrugged it off—"or else we'll freeze solid here."

In fact, I'd never been in the woods in spring before. Only in summer, for shashlik with friends. Now it was all different somehow.

"Smell that air?" Marina said, taking my arm and gazing into my face.

I didn't say anything. I was much more aware of smelling her pressed close to me.

"Look, the grass is already turning green over there."

"Aha," I said, matching my step to hers.

Meanwhile, Misha had run far ahead.

"I should have worn a hat," she said, shaking her head. "My ears are frozen."

Such a marvelous smell wafted from her hair that I didn't know whether my head was spinning from the fresh air or that.

Half an hour later we really were there. With a clear face and shining eyes, Marina led me to a one-story barrack that was probably a hundred meters long. Misha was already there and peeking out a window, looking rather mischievous.

"Come on. I'll introduce you."

Inside, there was a small room where two young women were sitting at a table. They said a friendly hello. Marina took a large package out of her bag.

"Here. What you ordered. There weren't any small ones left. I had to take two big ones."

"Thank you. Sit down here. We just brewed some coffee."

Those were the magic words. I had never heard anything nicer in my life. I hadn't worn gloves or a scarf for a couple of weeks, and after that stroll in the frosty woods only hot coffee could warm me up.

Thick steam rose over the enormous coffeepot in the middle of the table. The cup they handed me gave off such an aroma that my head started spinning again.

Hell, I must be coming down with meningitis, I thought. What would be the point of all this money then?

Marina, her cheeks red, was holding her cup next to her face and observing me over the brim.

Really, all this silliness suits her, I continued my thoughts. The little sweater, the freezing air, the tight jeans. Her cheeks burning from the cold. I could grab her and eat her up, like the wolf did Little Red Riding Hood: "Granny, Granny, what big eyes you have!" "The better to see you with, dear granddaughter." "And what damn big teeth you have!"

Today she was especially pretty. And she obviously knew it. She was sitting there smiling and giving me sly looks.

"How about it, Mikhail." She finally turned to me. "Shall we go ride the horses? Or don't you know how?"

Her voice held an obvious challenge.

"Of course he doesn't," one of our hosts replied. "How is he, a city boy, supposed to know how to ride?"

"Some city boys ride well," the other chimed in.

"Why do you say that? As if I didn't..." I was surprised to hear my own voice.

"Then saddle up Ryzhik for him," Marina said gaily, getting up from the table. "I'll ride the white. And let the little guy ride in the yard in his cart."

"I want to go with you!" Misha exclaimed.

"If you're going to scream, we're going straight home! Do you understand?"

I noticed that she knew how to speak in a decisive tone.

Ten minutes later, I was alone with a brown giant that had obviously taken a dislike to me the moment they led him out of his warm stable.

It must be a cross with an elephant, I thought mournfully. Evil presentiments stirred in my mind.

Meanwhile, Marina had lightly mounted an attractive white horse, made several turns around me, and was shouting gaily, "Look how prettily she holds her head!"

I tore myself away from contemplating my brown monster.

To be honest, I liked the rider more. Actually, the horse wasn't half-bad either. As far as I could tell.

"Hey, what's wrong? Mount up," Marina shouted again. "He shouldn't stand in the cold too long. He has to move."

From what she said, I concluded that the key link in our duet was the horse. I was not the concern here.

I lifted my left foot slightly above my head, placed it in the stirrup, grabbed the saddle, and climbed onto that hulk. The horse took some anxious steps and turned around, probably to see what was climbing on him. Realizing it was just me, he turned his head hard and snapped his teeth right by my knee. The shithead bites, I thought woefully. Was he raised in a kennel or something?

"Up?" Marina said, riding toward me. "Well, let's go then. There are such pretty places here! It'll take your breath away."

I wanted to say it already had, but she'd turned her horse around and was dashing down the road and into the woods. I tugged on the reins, and my giant, in no hurry, started off after her. Judging from his pace, he meant to show me he was doing me a huge favor. From his high tower, he obviously scorned my manipulations with the reins. He was simply going where his girlfriend had gone. Who the fuck knows? Maybe they didn't have a thing going.

I was sitting right on top of my monster and looking around in search of Marina. There wasn't even the sound of hooves anywhere. She's galloped off! I thought. Racing like a house on fire.

All of a sudden, this Ryzhik switched to a trot. I was getting shaken like a sack of potatoes, so I grabbed the pommel in order not to fall off. After a minute of this beating, it occurred to me that I was going to hiccup for the rest of my life and bounce when I walked, and if on top of it all I fell right now from this height, I'd be left a cripple forever. *That damn Seryozha!* flashed through my mind. He should have come here and gone bouncing! Damn it, my ass hurt!

Because we had picked up speed, it got noticeably colder. I didn't have gloves. A wind came up, and in five minutes my hands, which were clinging to the saddle, turned red and doubled up like spider paws.

I'm sure as hell not going to unclench them now, I thought woefully. I had to go sign up for this bullshit! Damn aristocrat! I wonder where this beastie is running?

After I'd cursed all the horseback riders in the world, Marina appeared from behind the trees. Racing toward us like a whirlwind, she circled around behind me and a second later her laughing mouth popped up right behind my face. I could no longer turn my head. This horse of mine stopped immediately. This must have been just what he was waiting for, the beast.

"Well, where have you been?" she exclaimed. "I've already galloped around the lake!"

Steam was rising from her horse. She herself was talking, breathing hard. Her hair was flying in all directions. Her face was burning with happiness.

"How are you doing?" she asked, obviously catching something in my eyes.

Her horse clearly wasn't happy to be standing in one place.

"If you want, we can go back. It'll be dark soon. Stay!"

She shortened the reins on her dancing filly, which spun around and reared.

"Of course not," I said. "When am I going to get this chance again?"

"Then let's race!"

"Race?"

"At a gallop!"

"A gallop?"

I realized I should have agreed when she suggested we go back. Now it was too late. A tragic death lay ahead.

"When he shifts to a broad stride," she told me meanwhile, "you have to stand in your stirrups and under no circumstance sit down."

"Don't sit down," I repeated.

"Otherwise you'll break his back."

"His back." My voice sounded like an echo.

"You have to stand the whole time on half-bent knees, letting him move freely between your legs."

"Between my legs."

"It'll be as if you were hanging over him. But remember, it's a very high speed."

"How high?"

She thought for a second.

"Forty or fifty kilometers an hour."

*It's going to hurt* flashed through my mind.

"As soon as he shifts to a gallop," she continued, "start moving your pelvis."

"How?" I inquired.

"What do you mean, how?" She was suddenly embarrassed. "With your pelvis. I'm telling you—move your pelvis."

"Like this?" I rose and wagged my butt from side to side.

"No!" She got angry and showed me. "Like this!"

"What interesting movements," I said slowly.

At least I still had my sense of humor. Actually, she really had moved remarkably.

"Do you get it or not?"

"I get everything. But tell me…I read somewhere that women like horseback riding because…well…it's kind of like sex, right?"

"So what?"

"So is it true?"

She rode right up to me and smiled.

"Yes."

"So tell me…" I began.

"Catch me!"

She jerked her horse around and dashed off.

"Wait! What do I hold on to here?"

I was too late with that question. A volcano suddenly roared to life beneath me.

This monster took off after Marina in great leaps, and I flew up into the air like a balloon, waving my arms and trying to grab on to something. My instincts searched for the helm, but besides the small protuberance at the front of the saddle, all they found was emptiness. I was flying in every sense of the word. I was soaring over the earth like an eagle.

A humble eagle frightened to death, waving his arms, his mouth opened wide, making no sound.

Finally, I latched on to his mane. It felt like I'd grabbed someone by the hair. I actually felt embarrassed for a moment. However, I immediately recalled how this beast had dealt with me, and I burrowed into his mane like a tick. He obviously didn't like that much so he picked up the pace. The saddle started banging my raised butt. Hey! Damn it, you dog! I thought. He's banging me in the ass on purpose!

I wasn't giving in. The movements Marina had shown me were, in fact, useful. Very quickly I had nearly drawn even and had started to move my ass back and forth fairly decently. Though it definitely wasn't the least like sex. It would have been easier to fuck an operating bulldozer than to squirm over this beast at that clip.

I'm going to crash! I thought, trying to figure out where we were racing. Definitely, hell, I'm going to crash!

There could be no question of controlling this monster. He raced where he wanted. Today it was his party.

Evidently realizing he wasn't going to get rid of me that easily, he suddenly hugged the edge of the woods, which were flying by at a crazy speed over my left shoulder. A solid wall of trees hung overhead in a dark mass. The longest branches were starting to lash me in the face. "You bitch!" I cursed, spitting out last year's leaves. For a while, I could still turn aside from the big branches, but the horse was trickier.

I saw that huge bough at the same time he did. In principle, if I could have steered, everything would have been fine. But I was not in charge here. Noticeably picking up speed, he kept even harder to the trees, and I realized resistance was futile. The only choice I had left was to lean as hard as I could to the right and hope that beam didn't whack me in the head. After that there'd be nothing to collect. I imagined my brains hanging from the trees and in quiet horror simply closed my eyes. The horse guessed I didn't have long to live and laid it on even harder.

The blow came to my left side. It was like a whack from a rifle butt to the ribs, and I rocketed into the air.

*I'm flying!* flashed through my head like lightning. Look, Ma, no hands!

It took an awfully long time. I felt as though I'd been soaring for an eternity.

*That's it!* something squawked inside me, and I slammed into the ground.

---

Total silence all around. I opened my eyes and shook my head, but I still couldn't hear a thing. Not a hoofbeat, not a breath of wind, not a birdcall—nothing. Just dull thuds, my heart beating like a drum. I lay there perfectly still, eyes open, and before me, I saw roots, clods of frozen earth, last year's grass, and dead, dried-up twigs. All of a sudden, breathing became incredibly painful. I closed my eyes and swallowed my saliva. My heart was ringing in my ears. I felt nauseated. I started moaning and opened my eyes again. Ryzhik's legs appeared by my side. Then the white horse's legs ran up. Marina's feet hopped down. Then her face appeared. It was ghostly. Enormous black eyes and a face as white as snow. She opened her mouth and said something.

"I fell," I said, but I couldn't hear myself.

She said something else, but I could only hear my heart beating.

She started shouting, and I tried to take a deeper breath. The legs of Ryzhik and the white horse moved closer to each other. There's what they wanted, I thought. We should have let them be together.

Marina leaned over me and kept shouting something. I saw her tensed neck. Sweat was beading up at her temples.

And suddenly I could hear her.

"Breathe! Breathe!" she kept repeating. "Try to breathe! Can you hear me?"

"I can hear you," I replied. "Why are you yelling? I can hear you perfectly well."

She went still for a second and then dropped to the ground next to me, spent. She lay down and was quiet. She seemed to be crying.

I took a deep breath and felt a pain in my side.

Marina propped herself up on one elbow.

"You're so beautiful," I whispered. "I've been wanting to tell you that all day."

"Don't talk nonsense. You should lie there quietly."

"You know I lied to you about Sergei."

"I know. Stay there and don't get up. It could be dangerous."

"How do you know?"

"Stay there, I'm telling you. I know, that's all. Stay there and don't jerk."

I wanted to ask her something else, but suddenly I forgot what. My ears started ringing and bright spots twirled before my eyes, and I guess I passed out.

---

When I opened my eyes, Marina was on her knees, leaning over me, trying to keep her hair from falling into her face. I had no idea how much time had passed, or what had happened here while I was lying unconscious. The very first thing I saw was her white sweater. Right in front of my face.

I couldn't stop myself. It's not my fault that she leaned over so conveniently. Embracing her, I fell on her lips, something she obviously hadn't been expecting. I could feel a shudder run through her whole body, but she didn't try to push me away.

For a moment she fell still, and then I could feel her respond. I thought that I'd done well cooking up this whole thing.

"Is this what you were figuring on when you fainted?" she said, tearing herself away from me and gasping just a little. "I ought to try to go flying like that myself."

I winced from the pain.

"Lie there and don't move. What if you broke your spine?"

I propped myself up on my right elbow.

"To hell with that Ryzhik of yours! Shoot him. Or send him to the glue factory."

"Wait, don't get up! I'd better bring someone."

"To hell with them all! And their horses!"

"Don't get up, I'm telling you! What are you doing?"

I leaned on a tree and slowly stood up straight.

"Misha!"

"Scared for me?" I smiled and immediately winced from the sharp pain.

"Where does it hurt?" she asked quickly.

"Right here—" I pointed to my left side.

"And your back and neck?"

I twisted my head around.

"Seems okay. It's just my forehead here…"

"You've got a bruise there and a knot."

"A big one?"

"Not bad."

I sighed softly, checking whether it hurt, and then slowly slid down the tree to the ground.

"You fool," Marina said. "It's true, getting up could have been very dangerous."

"No more dangerous than flying off your Ryzhik."

"You mean he threw you?"

"No, I leaped off him myself. By the way, tell me, do they eat horses or not?"

"I don't know…I don't."

"I think I will now. I wonder whether you can get horse meat anywhere in Moscow?"

"Cut it out." She smiled and leaned toward me again. "Don't be mad. You survived, after all, thank God."

Once again she tucked that unruly lock behind her ear and, kneeling in front of me, kissed me herself.

"Oho!" I said when it was all over. "What might that be for?"

"It's the prize for the race winner."

"Like fuck I won."

"That depends. You don't always need to come in first… Can you walk on your own? Or should I put you on one of them? If you want, you can ride mine."

"I'd rather crawl on all fours!"

"You aren't going to ride horses anymore?" She grinned.

"If I get the sudden urge to kill myself, I'd rather jump from a nine-story building. First of all, it's faster. And secondly, it's surer."

"I heard of one guy falling from the twelfth floor and just breaking his leg."

"Maybe someone kissed him afterward too."

"You mean you jumped from the horse especially for that?"

"No, not especially. But it worked out pretty great."

"All right, time to go, or it'll be dark soon," she said. "Lean on me. We'll hobble back somehow."

The two horses followed behind us, side by side, all the way back. When we would stop to rest, they would put their heads on each other's backs and look at us with their brown eyes. I saw the trees and sky, Marina's face, and my busted mug reflected in their pupils. They liked looking at us. When we kissed, they snorted approvingly and tossed their manes.

---

A bright light in my face woke me. I opened my eyes and was nearly blinded. Streaming lights were sparkling, cascading, and blinding me so that tears welled up in my eyes. Squinting as much as I could and covering my eyes with my hand, I made out the sun reflected in a large mirror. Its rays were falling on a cut in the mirror, which made it burn with all the colors of the rainbow, scattering beams of orange, purple, blue, and green around the room.

I looked at all this delight stupidly for a while, until I figured out that I didn't have a mirror like that at home. I had a small one, but it was in the bathroom. I shaved in front of it.

Plain as day, the room wasn't mine either. I turned my head and saw Marina under my blanket. Actually, it wasn't my blanket either. It was someone else's place altogether. I'd woken up at a stranger's.

Well, well, I thought. I managed to get into this bed. What am I going to tell little Sergei now? And his papa? Fuck a duck, that's what I get for improvising…She sure is beautiful, though!

Marina was lying there with her left arm behind her head and the sunbeams trembling on her breasts and face. It's odd, but they didn't bother her sleep at all. She must have been used to them. The windows didn't even have blinds.

I had no idea what time it was. Probably very early. The sun had barely risen. In the light, the room looked completely different. It seemed to glow from the sun's morning rays. The walls were tinted a soft plum. Even the carpet was pale yellow.

Lying in this bed next to Marina, examining her room, which I had never entered before, I felt very odd. As if the world around had stepped away from its place and was taking quiet steps toward another. Not that it had to be very far away, but different in principle.

And he can't spend the night here, I gloated. His papa won't let him. He'd yell at him and sit him in the corner.

"I like the sun," Marina suddenly spoke.

I started and turned toward her. Hell if I knew how long she'd been looking at me like that. I hadn't heard her wake up.

"What?"

"I love the sun," she repeated. "I wait for the spring every year especially so it can wake me up in the mornings. And today you were lying in my place."

"I was nearly blinded."

"I always lie on that side. Every morning is like a holiday."

"When there's sun?"

"Yes. Only in the last few years it hasn't happened all that often. When I was a child it was nearly every day. I even had that feeling in winter. Now somehow it's much less."

"And I was nearly blinded today."

"Don't be in such a rush to open your eyes."

"How's that?" I asked.

"First you turn your face toward the light so it seeps inside your head. You lie there and wait for your eyelids to become transparent. Then you open them to narrow slits."

She showed me how.

"Then you squint again as hard as you can so sparks fly, and after that…"

"You open your eyes," I finished for her.

"No, you crawl under the blanket." Marina burst out laughing.

We were silent for a little while.

"How oddly it all worked out with you and me," I said.

The smile vanished from her face.

"Really?" She shrugged. "I think it's okay. You were the one who was always giving me the eye."

"Me? When did I give you the eye?"

"In the hall. Every time you came with your Seryozha."

"He's not mine."

"Then why are you always tagging along with him? Are you his nanny or something?"

I was silent.

"Nothing to say? Oh, all right…Let's get up. My father will be back soon. His night of love has come to an end too. Get up! Why are you lying there like a king?"

I was already about to get up when I suddenly saw my boxers on the rug. I don't know why, but I felt shy. It wasn't that I hadn't ever walked around naked in front of a woman before…I had…and more than once…But just then it felt weird. Like, I get up with a bare ass and go for my boxers…I screeched to a halt.

"Well, are you getting up or not?" she said, and she poked her fist right into my side.

Damn, that hurt.

I said, "Why are you hitting me so hard? Don't you know that branch whacked me there yesterday?"

"Sorry," she replied. "I didn't mean to. It's just that time's a-wastin'. I have to get to school. You probably have a job too. You do work somewhere, don't you? Or do you spend all your time hanging around with your Seryozha?"

"He's not mine."

"So I heard. So, where do you work, if it's not a secret?"

"It is a secret."

"You idiot. Naked men don't have secrets from naked women. Are you getting up? Misha's going to wake up soon."

"Yeah, yeah," I say. "I'm getting up. Right away…only…"

Meanwhile I'm lying there like a fool.

"Only what?"

"I'll lie here a little longer."

"Listen, you really are sick. I'm telling you, you have to get up. My father will be here soon."

"I shouldn't…oof…get up abruptly…I have to lie here just a little first."

"Why?"

"The doctor said so."

"Yeah?" She looked me straight in the eyes. "What doctor?"

"What doctor?…Well…that…"

"What doctor?"

"The throat specialist."

"Ear and throat specialist?"

Funny little imps were hopping in her eyes.

"Mmm. That one."

"Or the neck and throat specialist?"

I realized she was having me on.

"Nose and throat specialist," I said.

"Are you being shy in front of me or something?" She smiled.

"Of course not. Why should I be shy? I'm not a little boy. I just feel like lying here a little longer."

And right then the doorbell rang.

"We are so screwed," Marina said. "Papa's here. Now you and I are really going to catch it."

"Maybe I can hide under the blanket? And then when he goes to his room I'll sneak out."

"Stop it."

She threw back the blanket and, not shy in the least, walked all the way across the room for her robe. The same one she used to come out in when Seryozha and I visited. I watched her back as if I were bewitched. As she went, she picked my boxers up off the floor and threw them at me without turning around.

"You took your shoes off at the front door. Your clodhoppers are in full view. You think he's that dumb? Get dressed! We'll have to explain everything."

I sat down on the bed.

"And you know," she said, turning to face me, still naked, "as far as everything working out strangely for you and me goes, it's nothing strange. The main thing is to take it easy."

She threw on her robe and quickly did the buttons.

"Got it? There then."

"You don't think I'll take it easy?" I said thoughtfully, but the door had already closed behind her.

I heard her walk to the front door and then I heard the lock click. Someone started talking. Probably her father. I wondered what she was going to tell him. I quickly got dressed, all the while trying to hear what they were talking about. I listened hard and moved as quietly as I could. All for naught. I couldn't hear a damn thing. I had no idea what to do now.

After dashing noiselessly around the room, I finally perched on the edge of the unmade bed and started waiting. No, I could have gone out, of course. Like, Hi there, Ilya Semyonich, I just screwed your daughter. Somehow the words didn't roll off my tongue. I didn't give a rat's ass about the guy, I wasn't going to christen my kids with him, but still it didn't feel quite right. Hell if I knew, he might start yelling and throwing punches.

So I sat on the bed. Everything got very quiet in the apartment.

Maybe I shouldn't have gone horseback riding yesterday, I thought. We could have driven around town, taken the kid to McDonald's…And nothing would have happened…And my side wouldn't hurt so much.

I felt my ribs gingerly.

Shit, what if I broke something? And on top of that I'm going to have to lie to Seryozha. What if Ilya Semyonich decides to squeal on me? I'd lose my job, damn it. The money I was getting for this cushy gig! What an idiot…I had to take it one step further…Of all the girls around, no, I had to climb into bed with this one, damn it! Why are they so quiet out there? Is everyone dead or something?

I quietly rose from the bed and tiptoed toward the door. No sound came from the other side. Could they be signing? Like mutes? Wiggling their fingers in front of each other, damn it, while I'm here trying like hell to eavesdrop? If only Misha would wake up or something!

I pressed my ear to the door, but I still couldn't hear anything. On the other hand, I did see what kinds of books she read. There was a bookshelf by the door. All about the theater. Stanislavski. Nemirovich. Someone named Tolvstonogov. What a name! Fat Legs! I also saw photographs hidden behind the books. She probably tucked them away from Seryozha. He was in this room fairly often. They weren't mine, but it was okay to look. I was a bystander, I had no reason to be embarrassed.

Marina was everywhere in the photographs. There were some other girls and some guys too. I think there was one I recognized, that goat from the institute who was always circling around the girls during the exam. I also recognized one girl with a long braid. Yesterday she'd been standing in the same row with Marina. To her left, I think. Nothing else interesting.

I started listening to what was happening on the other side of the door again. Utter silence all through the apartment. Maybe they left? The thought flitted through my mind. Maybe Marina decided to take him out of the apartment so I could sneak away after them. This thought seemed so convincing to me that I decided to crack the door open and peek out of the room.

There was no one in the hall. Maybe they were sitting in the kitchen.

I turned my head both ways, trying to peek around the corner, where the light was falling from, but at the same time trying not to let the next door out of my sight. Who knew? What if they suddenly came out of there and I'm standing with my neck craned in the middle of their apartment like a fascist spy? Their own little Stirlitz. Like a house spirit. You don't have poltergeists at your house? What about Stirlitz? He's marvelous and almost tame. He likes to be petted, but he's kind of spoiled. You can often find him in the bed of young women. He answers to "kitty kitty," "here, take a little money," and the Russian name "Misha."

There was still total silence in the apartment. I decided to go back to the room just in case. I was still holding Marina's photographs.

What an interesting face she has sometimes, I thought, dropping my gaze to one of the photos. Here she has those big eyes, like yesterday. When she leaped from her horse. She must have thought I'd smashed myself up completely. She got a good scare.

And then I remembered that there in the woods, lying on the ground amid the horses' shifting legs, amid all that frozen junk, awful pain, fear, and palpitation, for some unknown reason I'd let slip about Seryozha. In the sense that I'd lied about him. But the main thing wasn't even that I'd slipped up. Who knew what I was thinking—maybe that this was the end, maybe I was thinking I just had ten minutes to live—but no, this wasn't about me. This was about Marina. What had she said there?

"I know," she'd said.

What the fuck, I thought. I mean, what's "I know" supposed to mean? What does she know? And how?

This thought struck me so hard that I actually had to lean up against the door. Not in the sense that I wanted to barricade myself in, hide so that no one could come in, but in the sense that yesterday a horse had thrown me and I might have broken my ribs and now these kinds of things were occurring to me. Who the hell knew what was happening with Marina in the kitchen (or wherever she was)?

I thought: How could she know? Who told her? Maybe she meant she knew about him getting sick yesterday. Or rather, the opposite, not getting sick, and I tipped her off by saying he'd started feeling bad all of a sudden. Could that be what she'd meant? Or had she guessed that all his talk about his proletarian origins was just a line? Did she really know about his papa? What did she ask me there about my job? She'd compared me to someone…I just couldn't remember who…

I got the strange general feeling that I had not ended up here entirely by accident. Exactly the same feeling as after the conversation about the Italian fishing boat. As if something were happening around me that had nothing to do with me, but here it was happening and what I was actually doing remained a puzzle.

"Take it easy."

I think that's what she'd said. An interesting approach to love in general. But what about Seryozha then?

At that moment, the door to the room opened abruptly and smacked me in the back. I hissed from the pain.

"Sorry," Marina said, taking the photographs away from me. "I didn't think you'd be standing so close."

I silently watched her hide them behind her books again.

"Let's have breakfast." She turned around. "Or your omelet's going to get cold. Do you drink your tea with sugar or without?"

I simply didn't know what to say to that.

---

After my conversation with Ilya Semyonich, I had to go see Seryozha. There are days like that. They start out lousy and only get worse. Progress knows no bounds. At both ends, moreover. All this affected Ilya Semyonich himself too, by the way. I never imagined something like this could happen. I may have read it in old books or seen it on TV, but I'd always thought it was just from literature from the school curriculum. Golovlyov, the hypocrite, is a "blot on humanity." Isn't that what they taught us? Or was that some other trickster? Plyushkin? Basically, they were all part of the same crew. And their captain was Ilya Semyonich. Flag officer and helmsman. He bent my ear full on.

And here I was going straight from him to see Seryozha. What was I supposed to do? I was taking his money. I had to report about the horseback riding. Great riding. But my side still hurt. It even hurt to shift gears. Maybe I should see a doctor after all.

"What happened to your face?" Seryozha said, turning off his computer. "Actually, it doesn't matter. Come with me. My father's probably still home."

It's good he didn't ask about Marina. Hell if I know what I might have said. I was in a lousy mood. I hadn't even come up with a story.

"What happened to your face?" Pavel Petrovich asked as soon as we walked into his study.

"He fell off a horse," Seryozha said. Sharp kid, damn it. A regular Sherlock Holmes. What does that make me? Not Dr. Watson, in any case.

"A horse? Do you need to see a doctor?"

"He doesn't need to see any doctor. We've come to talk with you."

I wondered what he meant by "we."

"Fine, I'm listening."

Pavel Petrovich tensed slightly. He had evidently also been struck by Seryozha's "we."

"How much are you paying Mikhail to spy on me?" A dumb show. Literally. We're standing looking at each other. *Silence of the Lambs*, the sequel.

"Two thousand dollars." Pavel Petrovich finally came back to life. "But who said he was supposed to...spy?"

"I did."

Seryozha's voice cracked a little. He was still a teenager. Sexual maturation and all that. Puberty.

"Sergei, I think you're being a little melodramatic."

"Stop saying those idiotic words of yours! You're always saying things that are totally out of place. Don't talk like that now!"

At this, I realized that my Sergei was getting worked up. Or already was by the time I'd arrived. Maybe something happened to them yesterday? At that meeting of theirs?

In short, thank God he still didn't know what I'd been up to.

"I'm speaking perfectly normally. But if you don't like my tone, you can do the talking. I'm listening."

At this, this Seryozha turned to me.

"Tell him you're leaving."

Silence of the baby elephants. Lambs wouldn't cover it.

"What?"

"Tell him you're quitting."

"I'm quitting?"

"Sergei, listen," Pavel Petrovich tried to cut in.

"Don't interrupt!"

He was nearly shouting now. This adolescent.

"Tell him!"

We were silent again. We were looking at each other. Now it was the silence of the elephants. Large, real, and dusty elephants. Embarrassment. I did still have a conscience. Marina next to me under the same blanket. Bummer.

"Tell him!"

"Fine." My voice was a little husky, so I had to cough. "Pavel Petrovich, I'm quitting."

Pavel Petrovich sighed like a hippopotamus and sat down. I would have liked to sit down somewhere too, but there weren't any chairs handy. Actually, now it didn't matter. What was the point of taking a seat?

"Excellent," this Seryozha said in a joyous voice. "And now that you're free, I want to hire you."

Now was when I could have used a chair.

"He was paying you two thousand. I'll pay you two and a half. Do you agree?"

I turned to Pavel Petrovich. Which of them was ultimately in charge here?

"Wait a minute, Sergei," he said. "What is this circus? How are you going to pay him?"

"In dollars. Mama left me a hundred thousand. You haven't spent it, have you? She trusted you."

"She asked me to put it away for your education…"

"That's what we're doing. Mikhail is a magnificent teacher. A pedagogue with a capital *P*."

"Listen, Seryozha…"

"Enough!" Suddenly he started shouting for real. "Enough, Papa! I can't stand this any longer! I can't! Do you understand? I'm tired! I'm tired of everything you're doing!"

Pavel Petrovich looked him in the face silently. Only his eyes had dimmed.

"There are six billion people living on this planet," Seryozha continued in an odd, gushing voice. "Six billion people who have nothing to do with me. Five billion nine hundred ninety-nine thousand give or take a few! And then there's you. My one and only father. I don't have anyone else. Mama doesn't even write from Switzerland. She may have died there a long time ago. Or had new children. But I have you. I have a father. And I want to love my father. Understand? I have that right. I want to love my father! Why do you keep making that so hard!"

"But listen, Seryozha...I too want—"

"You don't want anything! You just don't understand what the word *son* means. You keep hiring people to watch me! Do you really hate me that much? Of all these six billion people, you chose me to take such a dislike to? One and only me?"

"Wait, Sergei—"

"Oh, stop it! Even now you're not hearing me!"

"I hear you. I hear you very well."

"Yeah?"

He suddenly stopped. Like a sleigh that finally slid to the bottom of an enormous hill.

"Then let Mikhail go. Let him work for me."

Pavel Petrovich looked in my direction.

"Maybe we should ask him."

Seryozha turned toward me. His eyes were glittering.

Now they were both waiting for what I would say.

"This is kind of...I don't know..."

Caught!

"Do you agree?" Seryozha couldn't take his eyes off me.

"Well, basically...yeah. Why not?"

He nodded and looked at his father, who was laying out some papers on his desk.

Now it was his turn to say something. An important moment.

Plain as day. They probably didn't talk like this often.

"Maybe you should go see a doctor, Mikhail. What do you think? There's nothing seriously wrong?"

"Well, how'd you like that?" Seryozha asked me when we went back to his room.

"Cool," I replied. "Only you should warn me. I had no idea what you'd cooked up."

"I don't mean that. I mean Marina. She wasn't mad, was she?"

"Marina?"

"Well, yes, Marina. Who else? You went to see her yesterday?"

I needed a little time. He'd caught me unawares again.

It wasn't easy keeping up with this adolescent.

"Well, sure, basically, yeah...We went horseback riding."

"Excellent. She wasn't mad?"

"About what?"

"Hey, are you slow? About me. About me not going. What's the matter with you? Did you have an okay night's sleep?"

"Me? Sure, fine...What of it?"

"Nothing. You're just acting kind of strange. Did you hit your head or something?"

"Well, yes. I thought I was going to get smashed to pieces."

"All right. How's Marina there?"

"She's not mad. Only a little at the beginning...But then I explained."

"And how did she act?"

"Fine. She seemed to calm down."

"Did she ask about me?"

"What?"

"What do you mean 'what'? Why I didn't go, how I was."

"Well, no, I don't think..."

"She didn't ask? So what did she say?"

"She didn't say anything like that...She showed me how to ride a horse."

"Yeah?"

He frowned a little.

"What was she wearing?"

"Wearing? This white sweater...and jeans and a jacket."

"Cool. Did you see how she rides?"

"Yes."

"I like watching her ride."

"Understandably."

"She has that face...you know...like Audrey Hepburn."

"Who?"

"There's this actress. An American. She died a long time ago."

"Ah. I didn't know."

"Doesn't matter. So tell me, why weren't you home last night?"

I didn't like his segues. People shouldn't change the topic so abruptly.

"Home? But I was...I was."

"Don't lie. I called you eight times. No one picked up the phone."

"I...I...went to the emergency room."

"So late? The last time I called was at two in the morning."

"They're open twenty-four hours."

"Is that right?"

*How would I know?* flashed through my mind.

"Of course," I said out loud. "Call any hospital. They'll tell you."

"I did."

"And?"

"They're open until ten."

"Which hospital did you call? How do you know which ER I went to?...Wait up...Why the hell did you call the hospital at all?"

Seryozha didn't answer right away.

"You know, sometimes I feel so awful. It's like a presentiment...Like someone's going to die...Yesterday, for some reason, I got scared all of a sudden. I couldn't even sit at my computer. I called you and called you, but no one answered. The telephone nearly rang off the wall. And most of all, I couldn't get through to Marina. That Ilya Semyonich was there...Like a spy..."

He looked me straight in the eye.

"You aren't lying to me, are you? Nothing happened yesterday, did it?"

I looked at him devotedly. I only blinked twice.

"I'm not lying to you. Nothing happened yesterday. Although it's true..."

"What?"

A wave of fear ran over his face. A real wave. He'd really been scared yesterday.

"Marina knows everything."

"How?"

He was shattered. He definitely had not been expecting this.

"What does she know?"

"Everything."

"Everything in general?"

"Absolutely."

"Stop it. How could she—"

And at this I told him everything I felt was necessary.

First, about Marina. Then, about Ilya Semyonich. I told him how they both knew who he in fact was. And how they knew who his papa was. Or rather, about his money. So that it made no sense to playact about the poor relation from Kaluga anymore. They were just pretending when he blew smoke about their one-room apartment, his papa with another family, and his mama from the trade school.

"But how?"

"You tripped up somewhere. You make a shitty Stirlitz. You miscalculated. Remember the sign of failure he had in Switzerland? A pot of flowers on the windowsill? You can put one out. Mueller's got you under surveillance."

Naturally he didn't hear the full truth from me. The whole truth would have thrown him for a loop.

Because it had thrown me for one.

This young man didn't need to know that Ilya Semyonich had a hunt on for him, and that Marina was playing the role of lure in that hunt, and that I was supposed to drive the game toward her, and that papa Ilya was assembling an entire dossier on eligible bachelors, and that unlucky Seryozha had been number one in that dossier for a very long time—his was a well-known name in Moscow. Papa Ilya wanted grandchildren from Seryozha. He wanted Mendelssohn's march and Pavel Petrovich standing next to the bride.

"How's about we each have another, matchmaker?"

But I didn't want to lose my job. Ilya Semyonich understood that, but decided I was going to help him. And I knew I would. If I didn't want anyone to know where I spent the night.

"What am I supposed to do now?"

Seryozha's voice was suddenly distraught, as if he'd guessed Ilya Semyonich's true plans.

"Now don't you be afraid. It's all going to be like before. Get ready. We'll go to Kuzminki. They're expecting you."

# Summer: Sergei

### June 1, 1998
Children's Defense Day. My father said we're going to Italy soon. To get married. I'll take final exams early. My wife's name is Paola. It's an Italian name. My wife's name will be Paola. Not Marina. My father couldn't care less about Children's Defense Day. He's tough. What he says, goes. And I'm his son. But I'm not that tough. Or so he thinks.

We'll see about that.

### June 4, 1998
I'm not going. Tomorrow I'll tell him I'm not. Let *him* get married. Mama told him he could a long time ago.

### June 5, 1998
I'll tell him tomorrow.

### June 7, 1998
I'll tell him tomorrow.

### June 8, 1998
Vorobyov says I can take Marina along. He's a swine, but it's a good idea. He'll tell my father that she's his girlfriend. I'm paying for him now anyway. The three of us can go to Italy

on Mama's money. There's plenty. Let Papa kiss his Paola. Her last name's Panucci. Panucci—shitty goochy.

### June 11, 1998

I got a letter from Mama. The first in three years. I guess she doesn't like to write. She asked me to show it to my father. No way I would. She's weird. She says I'm a moron. And I'm doing moronic things. Maybe I am. But sometimes I find it entertaining. She also says that if I don't want to get married I shouldn't.

### June 12, 1998

Tomorrow we're flying to Florence. Vorobyov and Marina will take the train.

*The Marriage of Figaro.* I hate opera.

What idiot reserves tickets for the thirteenth?

### June 12, 1998 (late night)

I'm reading my old diary. Was that really me? Wilde said you should definitely take something interesting with you to read when you travel.

Which is why he took his own diaries.

Here's mine (am I any worse?):

### March 14, 1995 (16:05 Moscow time)

Today I woke up because they were playing the piano on the other side of the wall. An old lady lives there who gives lessons. They were playing like crap, but I liked it. I've decided to learn. I'll start tomorrow. I'm not going to take tennis lessons anymore.

### March 15, 1995

I'm not going to take swimming lessons either. I'm sick of it. The only reason guys go is to look at the girls. There's a special hole to the women's shower room.

I went to see the old lady about the piano. She agreed. Payment in advance, she said. She used to be the director of a music school. Then they either fired her or she left herself. She doesn't know how to play rock and roll. Her apartment smells like shit. Lots of books.

We'll see.

### March 17, 1995

I'm so sick of everyone. Nothing but morons at school. My teachers and classmates both. Pea brains. Thracian tribes. The stormy dawn of imbecility. Semyonov's trying to be my friend. Maybe I should ask to be transferred to a regular school?

### March 18, 1995

My father won't give me any money for the music lady. He says I never see anything through. Miserable skinflint. He says my tennis trainer cost him a fortune. But what if I'm the next Richter? The old lady needs to buy her groats. Skinflint. But he says it's a matter of principle. First I need to get my head straight.

If only I had a head to straighten.

Have you done anything about yours? I wanted to ask him. But I didn't. Must have been too scared.

### March 19, 1995

They kept me up all night again. Fighting. First in their bedroom, then in the dining room. Mama was shouting like a crazy woman. Maybe they think I'm deaf?

## March 20, 1995

The old lady gave me this ancient black-and-white film. She said I should watch it. She refuses to teach me if I can't pay.

School is a total nightmare.

"Let there be light," the electrician said, and he rubbed an egg with phosphorus. The eggs were from a chicken, naturally. They lay there quietly in the corner and glowed in the gloom of our system of enlightenment.

My teachers should be driven out with a stick. Let them work in their gardens.

I'm sick of them.

## March 23, 1995

I wonder how much a good submachine gun costs. It could come in handy at our school. I hate the girls. Stupid fools. They let their hair loose and sit there. What kind of idiot do you have to be to fall in love with them? Hell knows what they're imagining.

A submachine gun could come in handy at home too. They screamed all night again. You mean they have trouble hearing each other?

## March 24, 1995

My tennis trainer came to my school. He said I didn't have to come, of course, but he wasn't returning any of the money. Punk. I asked him whether he would teach me to play piano.

You take the submachine gun and shoot him in the forehead. A single shot.

## March 25, 1995

Anton Strelnikov said he was in love with the new history teacher.

He should eat rat poison instead. She's just as stupid as all the others.

You switch the submachine gun to fire rounds and start showering them all. Greetings from Papa Carlos.

## March 25 (evening)

What a joke! Semyonov came over again. He tried to talk me into going outside. He suggested a smoke, but I refused. I said I was taking tennis lessons. He started asking me where and when. I told him he didn't have enough money for that. Then he dropped his cigarette, but I went and picked it up. He came up to me very close and kissed me on the cheek. I didn't know what I was supposed to do. I stood there a second and then slapped his ugly face. He fell down and started crying. I told him I'd kill him, I have a submachine gun. I don't know why I said that. I just did, that's all. I was sick of him. Then he told me not to move my seat away from him in school. I should keep sitting at the same desk. And he would give me money for that. I asked him how much, and he said fifty. He'd gotten fifty bucks from somewhere. And I said, Show me. He really did have fifty bucks. I took it and slapped his ugly face again. He started bleeding and he said I was going to sit with him anyway. I smacked him one more time.

## March 26, 1995

The old lady took Semyonov's money and said her name was Oktyabrina Mikhailovna. Quite a name. Her apartment smells like cat shit. How can she stand it? She asked whether I'd watched her film.

I don't even remember where I stuck the tape. God forbid Mama threw it somewhere. Yesterday she was smashing lots of things against the wall. Maybe she should buy a submachine gun.

### March 28, 1995
I'm sick of everyone. I'm sick of this diary too. Why don't you go fuck yourself, diary? Huh?

### March 30, 1995
I found Oktyabrina Mikhailovna's tape. It was under the chair in my room. Seems intact. Am I really going to have to watch it?

### April 1, 1995
I told my parents I was being expelled. They forgot about not talking to each other for almost a week and immediately started shouting between themselves. Then, when they calmed down, my papa asked why. I said for homosexuality. He turned around and smacked me in the ear. As hard as he could. He was probably angry at Mama. She started shouting again, and I said, April Fools, today's April first, ha ha ha.

### April 2, 1995
I took Oktyabrina Mikhailovna's cats outside. It's hard for her herself. They race in different directions like crazies. They meow and call to the girl cats. I thought they only did that in March. Five crazy cats on leashes—and me. The neighborhood kids in the courtyard snorted like horses.

My ear still hurts.

Oktyabrina Mikhailovna asked me about the film again. It was probably shot during the silent era. I'm going to have to watch it. I feel bad misleading her.

## April 3, 1995 (almost night)

The kids in the courtyard helped me catch the cats. I got tangled up in the leashes, fell, and they ran in all directions. One climbed a tree. Two were sitting in the garage, screeching. The rest were racing around the courtyard. The kids asked me whose cats they were and then they helped catch them. They said Oktyabrina Mikhailovna was a great old lady. She used to offer to give them money so they wouldn't hunt stray cats. And then she just gave them money. Even after they stopped hunting. For ice cream or anything they wanted. When she was still going downstairs. But she hadn't gone out in a long time now. The boys asked how she was doing, and I said everything was fine. Only the apartment smelled kind of bad. And then they told me I could play basketball with them if I wanted.

This evening my father came into my room. He sat without talking. Then he asked me about my classes. He and Mama aren't talking again.

Maybe he wanted to apologize?

## April 4, 1995

Now that's great! Words cannot describe. I finally watched the tape. It's called *Roman Holiday*. I have to make myself a copy.

## April 5, 1995

Oktyabrina Mikhailovna says the actress's name is Audrey Hepburn. She was famous forty years ago. I don't get why she stopped being famous. I've never seen any…I don't even know what to call them, women?…like that before. No, there are no women like that. Women are what we have studying in our class.

Audrey Hepburn is a pretty name. She's completely different. Not like the ones in our class. I don't know what's the matter.

## April 6, 1995

I watched *Holiday* again. Incredible. Where did she come from? There aren't any like that.

Today I played basketball with the kids in the courtyard. Tall Andrei pushed me, and I fell into a big puddle. He came over, apologized, and helped me up. Then he said he hadn't wanted to beat me up two years ago, when all the kids got together to catch me near the entryway. They'd wanted to bust up my bicycle. My father'd brought it from the Arab Emirates. Andrei said he hadn't wanted to beat me up. It's just everyone decided and he fell in. I told him I didn't remember that.

They split my eyebrow that time. My eyebrow, and on my elbow two scars.

Tomorrow we're going to go play some guys from another courtyard. I'm already friends with all of ours.

My father came in. He said what happened on April first was my fault. I shouldn't have made such an idiotic joke. I told him, Yeah, sure.

## April 7, 1995

Mama says she's tired of me and my black-and-white film. She doesn't remember Audrey Hepburn. She said, What, you think I'm that old? I watched *Roman Holiday* for the seventh time. Papa said he saw one other film with Audrey, *Breakfast at Tiffany's*. Then he looked at me and added that I shouldn't fill my head with nonsense.

But I am. I watch her. Sometimes I stop the tape and just look at her.

Where did she come from? Why haven't there been any more like her in the last forty years?

Audrey.

## April 9, 1995

Oktyabrina Mikhailovna showed me "Moon River." From *Breakfast at Tiffany's*. She doesn't have the tape. When she was singing, she stopped a few times. And turned toward the window. I looked that way too. There wasn't anything there, out the window. Then she said they were the same age. She and Audrey. I nearly fell off my chair. 1929. She shouldn't have said that. She also said that Audrey Hepburn died two years ago in Switzerland. At sixty-three.

That's silly. She couldn't be sixty-three. No one can be that old.

But Oktyabrina Mikhailovna said, That means my time has come too. It's all over. There won't be anything more.

Then we sat in silence, and I didn't know how to leave.

## April 12, 1995

I told Oktyabrina Mikhailovna about Semyonov. Not about how I came up with the money for her, of course, but just in general. About Semyonov in principle. She gave me a book by Oscar Wilde. About some portrait. I'll read it tomorrow.

My birthday's in two weeks. I think I'll invite the guys from the courtyard. I wonder what Papa will say.

He came in tonight. I was already asleep. He came in and turned on the light.

Then he said, Don't pretend. I know you're not asleep.

I looked at the clock; it was 3:20. I could barely open my eyes. And he says, There, you see? And I thought, What's so interesting that I'm supposed to see?

He sat down at my computer and started drinking his whisky. Straight from the bottle. We sat there like that for about ten minutes, probably. He at the computer, me on my bed. I thought maybe I should put on pants. And he's asking, Who do I want to stay with if he and Mama are going to live separately? I say, No one, I want to sleep. And he says, You might have had a completely different mama. Her name could be Natasha. And I say, My mama's name is Lena. And he says, She's a slut. And I tell him, My mama's name is Lena. He looks at me and says, Did you do your homework for tomorrow?

## April 15, 1995

Yesterday, the whole gang of us went to fight with the next courtyard. They lost to us in basketball and won't give us our money. The deal was for twenty bucks. Our guys spent five days trying to collect our twenty. They shook down kids all over the neighborhood, the ones who have cash. They used to shake me down. Basically, tall Andrei said we had to punish them. They broke off half my tooth. Now I'll have to get it put back in. Everyone looked at my mouth and clapped me on the shoulder. Andrei said, Congratulations, it's your battle christening.

School is the same as ever. Total crap. Anton Strelnikov has fallen in love with another teacher. Algebra this time. Jerk. He's never even heard of Audrey Hepburn. At first I was going to give him the film, but then I changed my mind. Let him trail after his old ladies.

## April 16, 1995

Semyonov came to school covered in bruises. My upper lip hasn't healed yet either. It swelled up like a gigantic plum. We look pretty good at the same desk. Anton says Semyonov's papa did it to him. I have a good idea what for. But Anton says he's always beaten him. Since back in kindergarten. They went to the same kindergarten. He says Semyonov's papa beat him right in front of the teachers. The police even came. But he bought them off. He passed out cash to the cops and dragged little Semyonov to his car by the collar. Where he let him have it again, Anton says. And Semyonov squealed like a piglet from there. We were six then, Anton said. We were standing around the car trying to see inside. The windows were high. We could only hear him squealing and we wanted a look. And the teachers had all gone. Semyonov's papa gave them some money that time too. And it was cold. Almost New Year's. What were they supposed to do outside? Oh yeah, the next day they gave out presents, a holiday party, Father Frost.

## April 17, 1995

No one is yelling at home anymore. They aren't talking to each other at all. Even through me. Twice Mama didn't spend the night at home. Papa watched television and then sang. He shut himself up in the bathroom and sang these strange songs. At two in the morning. I wonder what the neighbors thought.

Oktyabrina Mikhailovna says that children have problems with their parents because children come along too late to catch their parents at a good age. Before they've become what they are now. Therein lies the drama. That's what Oktyabrina Mikhailovna says. Before, they used to be okay.

She says she remembers when my papa first came to our building.

He was so skinny and cheerful. You could tell right away he was from the provinces.

It turns out Mama already had a boyfriend then, almost a fiancé. Oktyabrina Mikhailovna doesn't remember his name.

Today, I walked the streets and looked to see how many women resembled Audrey Hepburn.

Zero.

My feet got soaked, and I lost my keys. Too bad about the key chain. If you whistle, it whistles back. I whistled in the courtyard a little, but it was no use. I must have dropped it somewhere else.

### April 18, 1995

Oktyabrina Mikhailovna remembered how my papa (only then he wasn't a papa yet, just no-one-knew-who) came to see Mama on her birthday, wearing a clown suit. He walked right down the street in it, and then he did magic tricks. In the entryway and courtyard. All the neighbors came out of their apartments. She says it was an awful lot of fun. Everyone was laughing and clapping.

I finished the Oscar Wilde book. Cool. Maybe I should invite Semyonov to my birthday party.

I went to whistle on the next street. My lip barely hurts, but the broken tooth makes it hard to whistle right. The key chain didn't turn up. But those jerks we fought last week did.

I barely got away.

## April 19, 1995

Today, a policeman came. Turns out tall Andrei broke one of those jerks' collarbone. Now his parents are suing. I saw Andrei pick up a broken pipe then, but I didn't tell the policeman anything. I wasn't even there, I say. And he looks at my busted-up face and says, You weren't? I say, No.

In the courtyard they told me I was an okay guy.

Not a rat.

Yesterday, I dreamed my father has dragged me to his car. And he's beating me as hard as he can, and I can't wiggle away from him. I just cover my head. My hands are too small—I can't protect myself from him. He's so big, and my coat is getting in the way. It has a collar. And it's hard to raise my arms in it. I'd forgotten about it, and now all of a sudden there it is in my dream. My grandmother gave it to me when I was five. And Anton Strelnikov is looking through the car window. But for some reason he's big. And he's kissing the algebra teacher.

Then I dreamed of Audrey.

## April 20, 1995

I can play "Moon River" on the piano. With one finger. Oktyabrina Mikhailovna laughs at me and says I don't need the other nine. Everything's clear as far as I go anyway.

We'll see.

Papa said a friend from circus school lent him the clown suit. He says he didn't have any money for a proper present then.

He says, What presents? I didn't have any money at all. I had to play the fool. I nearly died of embarrassment. How did you find out?

I say, From Oktyabrina Mikhailovna. And he says, Where did you find the money for her? I say, It's a company secret.

Mama didn't spend the night at home again.

### April 21, 1995

Semyonov said he knew Audrey's real name. And I told him I thought Audrey was her real name. And he says, The hell it is. Her name was Edda Kathleen van Heemstra Hepburn-Ruston. And I tell him, Write it down. He did. I say, How do you know that? He says, When I was a kid I liked memorizing silly names. The first Mongolian cosmonaut was Jügderdemidiin Gürragchaa. I say, You're lying. What about the second? He says, There wasn't a second. You can check it out. But the first's name was Gürragchaa. Look on the Internet yourself. They have Audrey Hepburn and damn well everything there. I say, For instance? He says, Well, she's the daughter of a Dutch baroness and an English banker. She was in movies in Hollywood in the fifties. And before that, in England. I say, Why did you look her up?

He doesn't answer me. I ask him again. Then he points to my notebook. Written four times there on a single page: Audrey Hepburn.

### April 24, 1995

I told Oktyabrina Mikhailovna about Semyonov again. She said the whole problem is that we all have to die in the end. That's the main thing. We're going to die. And if I understand that, then it doesn't matter whether your friend is or isn't gay. You just have to pity him. Regardless. And yourself. And your parents. Everyone, basically. All the rest doesn't matter. It will sort itself out. The main thing is you're still alive. She talks and watches me and then asks,

Do you understand? I say, Yes. Only Semyonov isn't exactly my friend. And she says, That doesn't matter either. You're both going to die. I think, Thanks, of course. But in some ways she's right. She says, Touch your knee. I did. She says, What do you feel? I say, My knee. She says, There's a bone there. Inside you is your skeleton. A real skeleton, understand? Like in your idiotic movies. Like in the cemetery. It's yours. It's your own personal skeleton. One day it will be bared. No one can change that. You have to pity each other while it's inside you. Do you understand? I ask, What's not to understand? Your skeleton's inside you, so everything's fine. She smiles and says, Good for you. I'm not afraid to die in general. It's like coming home. Like when you were a child. When you were a child, did you like taking trips? I say, To see my grandmother. She lives in a village. She says, Well there, that means it's like going to visit your grandmother. You mustn't be afraid. I say, I'm not. She says, Dying isn't frightening.

## May 2, 1995

Tall Andrei was arrested. Not over the collarbone. There's evidently going to be a separate sentence for that. It was all because of Semyonov. At my birthday party, Semyonov kept telling all kinds of stupid stories about black rappers and hip-hop. And the guys from the courtyard listened to him with open mouths. Afterward Papa even asked me, What, is he from some music group? I explained to him about the Internet. But the guys aren't up on the Internet. Only in the most general way. They didn't know that Semyonov asked me in advance who was going to be at my birthday party. In the kitchen, tall Andrei told me, He's a cool guy. What, did he, like, come from America? I say, He just reads a lot. He's curious. In short, he and Andrei left together and evidently got drunk somewhere. I don't know all that happened with them there, but by morning Semyonov's papa's SUV had burned up in his garage. Plus two cars owned by some deputy. He was hiding them there from an audit. They rake you over the coals in the Duma now for having extra wheels. Semyonov's papa beat him with a chair leg. He broke a few of his ribs and his left wrist. Semyonov must have tried to protect himself with that arm. But his papa bought off the police. Only Andrei got arrested. The guys in the courtyard are all bummed. They've stopped playing basketball. They don't talk to me anymore.

## May 11, 1995

Mama came. She said, Can we talk? I said we could. She says, You've been kind of strange lately. Is everything all right with you? I say, I'm the one who's strange? She says, Don't be rude. And look at me. Then we don't say anything for a good five minutes. Then she says, I may be going away very soon. I say, Ah. She says, Maybe tomorrow. Again I say, Ah. She says, I can't take you with me. You do understand, don't you? I say, I do. And she says, What are you getting at? And I say, I'm not getting at anything, I just said, I do. I said it and looked at her myself. And she's looking at me. And then she starts crying. I say, Where are you going? She says, Switzerland. I say, Audrey Hepburn lived there. She says, Is that from your movie? I say, Yes. She looks at me and says, She's pretty. I'm silent. And she says, Do you have a girlfriend? I say, And when is your plane? She says, Well, all right. Then we don't say anything for another five minutes. In the end, she says, Will you think of me? I say, Probably.

I can't complain about my memory yet. Then she stood up and left. She wasn't crying anymore.

## May 14, 1995
Oktyabrina Mikhailovna died. Last night. I'm not going to write anymore.

## Summer: Pavel Petrovich

Hello, dear!

Were you surprised when you got this letter? I can imagine you picking it up. I hope you didn't frown at least.

How are you doing? I hope everything's all right. I feel rather foolish in front of a piece of paper, but you aren't going to dictate a letter like this to your secretary for her to fax.

Great, I've nearly forgotten how to write. Excuse my disgusting handwriting.

How are you doing? Wait, I already asked you that. I guess you're getting married again. Don't be mad at me for bothering you during your honeymoon. Especially since you seem to be having them fairly often lately. Once you get to twelve, you can talk about an entire year of honeymoons. You always liked sweets. A year—just think!

No, of course, I was bad, and you were the epitome of nobility. I got money crazy, but you left Seryozha everything you had and rushed off on the wings of love to your poor Swiss artist. He must have drawn the Alps for you. A cliff a day. When you live in such beauty, you don't need money anymore, naturally. I understand that. Especially since even in Sergei's eyes you appeared in a much more advantageous light than disgusting, greedy me.

But, you know, I'm the one who has to raise him.

Listen, it's so silly that we haven't once exchanged letters in all these three years.

I feel no hatred toward you. I don't care if you don't believe me.

It's the truth.

Now you're drawn to scientists. He's a physicist, right? A poor Swiss physicist? Or a chemist? Poor, naturally. He does his chemistry in a small bohemian apartment in some attic in Zurich, and, of course, he's a genius. Isn't that so? You see how well I understand you. Love performs miracles.

You start understanding even the people you don't hate anymore.

Only I pay my people well for information, my dear. Your genius's poverty isn't worth a hill of beans. Not an Alp. Forgive the pun. What's his name? Schwarzenpupper? Or Morgenhrukker? It doesn't matter. The main thing is that several people with that same name are on the boards of directors of the largest Swiss banks. Or didn't you know? Or did you think he just had the same name? Lovely random namesakes with family castles all over Europe. This time your rebellion against the rich seems to have played a nasty joke on you. Or did you actually think he took you to restaurants wearing the same jeans because he had nothing else?

You know, yesterday, completely by accident, I opened the book you left behind during your hasty flight (or rather, retreat?) three years ago. It's Pascal. All your bearded, poorly dressed friends' favorite philosopher. In it you underlined thought number 103 in red pencil: "It is natural for the mind to believe, and for the will to love, so that, for want of true objects, they must attach themselves to something false."

You must have had me in mind, right?

Your Pavel

P.S. Because the pencil's red and not the usual, I'm going to risk making a small request of you. Seryozha needs this, not me. We're going to Italy in two weeks to finalize his engagement. The wedding, naturally, won't be anytime soon. Not until they're both twenty-one. However, we have been planning to finalize this all summer. His future father-in-law's name is Signor Panucci. He's a relative of the chairman of the board of one of the banks where your genius's "namesake" gets around. Talk to him about Seryozha. He's your son too, after all. Let your genius help set him up. We need this marriage. Ultimately, I'm not going to last forever. Someone is going to have to take care of our son. He himself doesn't seem to give a damn about anything. Help me. You're a smart girl. Kisses.
I hope that's still all right.

# Summer: Ilya Semyonich

"Hello! Hello! Is this Nikolai Nikolaevich? Hello! It's me, Ilya Semyonich. I'm calling from the market near the Budapest department store. In Kuzminki. Hi, Nikolai Nikolaevich… You have to forgive me for talking to you on your answering machine, but I just can't get a hold of you over the phone. So…Nikolai Nikolaevich, actually, here's what I'm calling about…Oh, wait, did I start talking right? They said after the third beep. I think I didn't wait for it. How many beeps was it? Fine, I'll start over…Hello, Nikolai Nikolaevich…Or should I call back?…Okay, one more time…Hello, Nikolai Nikolaevich. This is Ilya Semyonich calling from the market near the Budapest department store.

"I wanted, actually, to talk to you about the deadline for my debt payment. Look…That is, you absolutely should not worry about the money. I'll have it. First of all, my store is running in excellent order. It's just right now a few problems have popped up, but I'll pay you back. Down to the last kopek. There's nothing for you to worry about. And there's no need for you to send your boys. Secondly, I did already tell you that my circumstances should be changing very soon. For the better. For the very best, Nikolai Nikolaevich. Do you hear me? The very best. My daughter's going to get married very soon. My Marina. I told you. Remember? You know who to. Well, as soon as we celebrate the wedding, I'll pay back my debts to you. The deals you and I are going to do together! You'll be thrilled. You do remember who my future son-in-law's father is, right? So there you have it. Such opportunities there, Nikolai Nikolaevich—it takes your breath away…I just have to hold on a little longer. A tiny bit longer. Maybe by fall. Or winter. Marina's planning to go to Italy with her fiancé now. You can check, if you want. Through your own channels. They're prominent people. So…Italy for a vacation…To have a good time…Maybe you can wait a little bit, eh, Nikolai Nikolaevich? I'll pay you back more. Much more. We can reconsider the original interest. After the wedding, after all of it, the money I owe you will be nothing. A joke, not money. Such deals you and I are going to cook up together! So… Well, all the best. Thank you for your attention…"

## Summer: Elena Sergeyevna

Hello, my dear Seryozha!

Yesterday I received a letter from your father and after that I couldn't sleep all night. I was thinking about you and remembering you when you were very little. At dawn I even shed a few tears. You must be all grown up by now.

I don't want to write back to your father. Don't tell him I wrote you. If he sees the letter, just tell him some lie. By the way, have you learned to lie? You didn't use to be able to at all. I could tell immediately. You were so awkward and funny when you tried to hide anything from me. I always knew everything about you. But up until a certain age. Because then you changed. Children grow up, Seryozha. And that's simply horrible.

I remember my fear and distress when I realized you were becoming a different person. Still the same sweet Seryozha—the same eyes, the same pudgy hands. But it was as if someone else were already there behind that. My son. I loved you so much. In the very beginning I adored carrying you around. I carried you until you were four. My mama said, Let him down, you'll break something. But I liked it. You know, such an amazing sensation. You looked like the babes in the paintings by the Italian masters. Angelic creatures called *putti*. I always wanted to pick them up. You would pant and clamber as hard as you could. Then you would drift off with my hair clutched in your little fist. You had incredibly soft skin. I could hold your hand in mine for hours while you slept. And stroke it. I loved stroking you.

But then everything changed. Everything got much more complicated. I couldn't just pick you up and rock you to sleep. You had a life apart from me. Without me. Against me, even. You got shoulders. You were constantly shrugging them. Do you remember when you picked up that habit? Shrugging your shoulders? As if you were closing the door to your cellar. Really, it was as if you'd moved somewhere else. You stopped coming into my bedroom at night. Did you really not wake up anymore? I will never believe that. That means you were lying there and afraid, but you stubbornly wouldn't come to see me. Stubbornly.

When did you stop listening to me?

Dear Seryozha, I loved you so much, but you kept pulling further away from me. Maybe I should have had a second child. My mama kept asking me about that, but your father didn't want it. He said we had to raise at least one person decently, we weren't rabbits, after all, made to be procreating on the forest's edge. And I thought, What's so bad about that? Being a white rabbit on the forest's edge among the flowers. Loving each other and listening to the bees buzzing. You always liked catching grasshoppers. You would squat in the grass with your clumsy little bottom and breathe, loudly and patiently, holding out your hand. But your father said we weren't rabbits.

I would probably have gone on having babies. I just liked looking at you.

Then you became more and more like him. That's something I hadn't expected. I became upset because I thought you were yourself: I was one story. Your father another. And you an entirely different third. But that turned out not to be the case. I always thought that God had simply entrusted you to us for a while because you needed help. A funny little stranger with a potbelly who dropped in on my life for a few years. Possibly the happiest years. Later, I thought, you would be free. Of me and your father. Of any obligations to resemble either one of us. I thought you would look like yourself. Only yourself and no one else.

But you started to look like him.

With time, this became more and more noticeable. Evidently your father liked this, and that was why he didn't want more children. He was probably afraid there wouldn't be that resemblance. Sometimes I get the feeling that he treats you the way a photographer does a successful shot—he was lucky with the light and sitter, and the film developed excellently. Why go to the trouble of doing it all over again?

Then your endless enthusiasms began that never led anywhere. Your father encouraged them, but apparently even he eventually grew irritated. He was afraid nothing serious would ever come of you. That's what he wanted, seriousness. He didn't just want to have a son. A son was never enough. You had to excel. Which meant you had to become someone like him. A fine delusion of grandeur. Even the stupidest, most unsuccessful, and most untalented men crave that. It's a secondary sexual characteristic. On top of the Adam's apple and hairy covering on the face. Men want not just sons. They need a big mirror. And no one had better prevent them from gazing into it endlessly.

What did you have? Gymnastics, karate, swimming, tennis, and I think even music. That's not even the complete list. Why did you study piano? You don't have an ear. I tried to explain that to you, but you shrugged. Sometimes you did things that made absolutely no sense at all. You downloaded pictures off the Internet and sorted them by topic. Automobiles, landscapes, caricatures. You would sit at your computer for hours doing that nonsense. I once asked you why, and you said it might come in handy. Or suddenly you started making sure there was an identical number of objects on the table. I could never understand why you were counting the forks, notebooks, and erasers, or why you had to remove something if the result didn't coincide with certain numbers of yours. I didn't understand you. Even now, this seems like utter nonsense to me. Maybe I should have read those books on adolescent psychology. I wonder whether they write there about actions performed without any apparent purpose.

Then that clothing. You wouldn't listen to me when I suggested discussing your wardrobe. You wore those impossible pocket-shaped caps. It was awful. I was embarrassed to go outside with you. And those torn jeans. You were always hunched over like a camel.

Then even just talking to you became pure agony for me. You stopped answering questions. You would mumble unintelligibly. You'd interject. You wouldn't look me in the eye. And I needed your help so much. You would shut yourself in your room and watch some black-and-white film over and over. I didn't understand how you could watch a movie more than once. It's deathly boredom. Especially since the film was already fifty years old.

I probably should have had a second child after all. And a third. And then some more. You know, all my life I wanted a little girl.

Your father writes he wants to marry you off somewhere in Italy. Don't listen to him if you don't feel like it. Listen to your heart.

I love you very much.

Your Mama

## Summer: Sergei

### June 13, 1998 (2 in the morning)
Twelve hours to go until the plane to Italy. I should sleep. But I'm sitting and reading how all this ever happened. Here's my old diary again:

### February 2, 1998
Well then, and I said I wasn't going to write. Three years have passed. Quickly. I didn't even notice.

Today I ran away from my guard. I've wanted to for a long time but it didn't work out until now. I'm sick and tired of them. They just keep coming. Why does my father need that? Is he afraid I'll get kidnapped? That might even be better. For all of us. We could stop pretending we're kin. Father and son. We barely say hello. Who needs this? He hates me. He thinks Mama left us because of me. She ran out of options.

When I was running away from my guards, I hopped on a streetcar. And the inspector caught me. Where's your ticket? he says. And I say, Nowhere. And he says, I've got you now. I'm thinking, To hell with you, and then I feel someone behind me putting something in my hand. I looked and there was a ticket. It said "Single." I didn't understand what "Single" meant, but the inspector went away. He didn't care anymore. I turned around to see who gave me the ticket, and there was this girl. With a familiar face. I looked closely—she looked like Audrey Hepburn. I think, What the fuck. I searched for three years. And suddenly here, on a streetcar. And the inspector says to her, Where's your ticket? I wanted to give her her ticket back, but she told me with her eyes I shouldn't. She took out the money and paid the fine. Two stops later, she and I got off, and I returned the ticket. She says, What, you mean this is your first time riding the streetcar? And I say, Well, yes. She says, Why? And I say, I'm from Kaluga. We don't have streetcars there. I don't even know why I said that. I lied for some reason. I felt awkward talking about my father's driver. And she says, Well, good-bye. I say, Wait up, I have to pay you back. You paid that fine because of me. She stands there looking at me. Her eyes are like Audrey Hepburn's. She's waiting for me to pay her back. And I tell her, Except I don't have any money with me. She starts laughing and says, Then why did you bring it up? I say, I'll pay you back later. Where can I find you? She wrote down her phone number for me. Later, I looked on the computer; it must be somewhere in Kuzminki. Audrey Hepburn lives in Kuzminki. Funny.

I wonder what her real name is.

## February 3, 1998

My father said he'd hire me a new tutor. He's sick of me. Someone's going to call him from school. Jerks. Take a fragmentation grenade and toss it in the teacher's lounge. It's not my fault if someone doesn't hide.

My father says I'm supposed to go to Oxford in a year, but, like, I'm a total moron. Maybe I should tell him to fuck himself and that Oxford of his? I'm going to join the Red Army. I'll ask for a hot-spot assignment, and they can kill me there. A grenade launcher to the head. Or the heart. To the glory of Russian arms. Damn, I'm so sick of everyone.

And the tutor? What a waste. I already know all those tricks of his. The last one was obviously hired just to inform on me. He didn't teach me a fucking thing. That's all I needed, a Moscow State lecturer. Married. I got sick of his talk about his wife. I didn't tell him about my pornographic magazines.

But pretty soon I realized he was informing. My father slipped up a few times. And then I fed that jerk some nonsense. And Papa reacted to it. Homosexuality, he says, it's the dead-end behavior of depraved people. And I say, Well, I don't know. And then he says, I'll box your ears. Politeness gone in a flash. And I say, you already did that once. Remember, three years ago? When you and Mama were still fighting? He looks at me and says nothing. I say, Ever since, I can barely hear with that ear. Even you right now I can barely hear. Wait up, I'll turn my other side toward you. What did you say about dead-end behavior?

After that, the Moscow State lecturer popped like a cork. I bought a couple of condoms and put them in his briefcase and told his wife over the phone to look there. Like, it's not clear where it is your husband goes after his lectures at the university. He didn't show his face here anymore. She must have found him something to do at home. The hairless goat.

## February 4, 1998

Audrey Hepburn's name is Marina. I called her today. Took down her address. It's right next to the Budapest department store. I have to figure out how to get her money back to her. I'm going to have to slip away from my guard again. I don't want my father to find out about her. Not for anything.

Marina's a pretty name too.

## February 5, 1998

I ran into Semyonov today. He's going to a different school now. He says tall Andrei's going to be released soon. He went to visit him recently. I wonder what they talked about? He also says they're probably going to put his father away. The prosecutor found something at his place. They instituted criminal proceedings. Ties with criminals, something like that. Basically, Semyonov's very happy. He says that while his dear papa is in the slammer he's going to throw all his money down the drain. I say, He'll kill you afterward. He laughs and says, First he has to catch me. I understood him to mean he'd decided to get the hell abroad somewhere. In principle, if he knows where his father's money is, he won't have it bad there. Enough for fifteen years or so, probably. He says, How about you? Anything from your mother? I say, No, everything's fine. He says, Well, I'll stop by sometime. I say, Whatever. Stop by if you want. And then I say, Do you know what I spent your fifty bucks on back then? He says, What fifty bucks?

## February 6, 1998

My father brought me a new tutor. He says, This is Alexander Sergeyevich. I say, Pushkin? And the tutor says, That's what everyone says. And he laughs. I think, Great. Another jerk. What's so funny about that? My father says, Well, why don't you two get acquainted? And I say, We already are. I've read nearly all of Pushkin. And he says, Sergei, get a hold of yourself. I say, I can't. It's not my fault I read so much. He says, Forgive me, Alexander Sergeyevich, my son is out of sorts today. But Pushkin says, No problem. He and I will find a common language quickly enough. I think, Fine. Give it a try.

## February 7, 1998

I can't get away to Kuzminki. My father ordered the guards not to take their eyes off me. Has he guessed? I have to think of something. He can't find out about Marina.

## February 8, 1998

I talked to Marina on the phone again. She's studying at the drama institute, first year. She's going to be an actress. Like Audrey Hepburn.

## February 9, 1998

The business with the condoms won't work. Pushkin doesn't have a wife. Must be a homosexual. You can tell right off the way his eyes shine.

## February 10, 1998

I told my father that Pushkin had come on to me. He says, Listen, I'm tired of this. I say, I know. He says, What do you mean, you know? I say, I know that you're tired of this. He says, Stop it. I say, No, I really do know that. He looks at me and says nothing. So do I. Then he says, Go study. I say, Will you get rid of Pushkin? He says, No, go study. I say, He's a homosexual. And he says, Go study.

I have to think of something else.

## February 11, 1998

Today I told my father's driver I needed to go to Kuzminki. He says, What about Pavel Petrovich? I say, He doesn't need to. I do. And he says, I understand, but we have to tell him. I say, I'll tell him later. Tonight. He says, All right, then let's go. But where? I say, To the Budapest department store. I need to buy one thing there. They don't have it anywhere else. Just at that department store. He says, And what thing is it? I say, A fuckamagidget. He says, Ah. As if he really knew what that was. But he doesn't ask. Like he's so educated. I love people like that.

By the Budapest, I told him to wait and went to see Marina. There are lots of people at the outdoor market there. He didn't notice me walk past the store. There was some guy sitting around at Marina's. He said he was her father. I asked, Where's Marina? And he says, There are too many of you coming around here for me to report to each of you. I said, I brought her money. He says, Where? I say, Here. And he says, That's not enough. I say, It's what I owe. I brought her what I owe for the streetcar fine Marina had to pay because of me. And he says, I don't get it, but it doesn't matter, give the money over. I say, My name's Seryozha. Will you tell Marina? And he says, About the money? I say, No. About me coming over. And he says, Whatever you like. I say, Can I leave my phone number? She can call me later. He says, I won't give you my pen. Guys like you have walked off with it ten times by now. I say, Maybe you have a pencil? He says, No. And he waits for me to leave. And I say, Wait up, I'll go ask the neighbors. He says, I don't have time to wait. And he closes the door. I borrow a pen from the neighbors and ring his bell again. He opens and says, Still here? I say, Here's my phone number. Just give it to her, please. And he says, Go on, go on, don't worry.

## February 12, 1998
Marina hasn't called.

## February 13, 1998

Today, the English teacher told me to bring her journal from the teacher's lounge. She's got holes in her head. She forgets things. I left her office and went to the first floor. There was no one in the teacher's lounge. Or in the principal's office. I took the journal and went to the toilets. What was the point of hurrying back? That's where we always hang out during class. I was about to go in when I heard Anton Strelnikov's voice. He doesn't go to English at all. And I hear Anton say, That's why his father is always hiring him tutors. I think, Is this about me? I didn't go in. And Anton says, They may shut him up in a psych hospital altogether. The teach said he has cockroaches in his head. I'm standing next to the toilets thinking, What the fuck. And Anton says, He's definitely off his rocker. Ever since his mama left them. He's gone around the bend. She slept with every guy in Russia. Then she hustled abroad to sleep around some more. Yesterday, my mother and her friend were in the kitchen and they would not give it a rest. They went to the institute together, or something like that. Basically, they've known her for a long time. Go figure! And that's why Seryozha goes around so strange. Basically, his papa's about to pack him off to the doctors.

I stood by the toilets for a while and then left. I took the journal back to the teacher's lounge. At home, my father says, Why so early? I say, And you? He says, I'm on lunch break. I say, So am I.

## February 14, 1998

Marina called. She said it was the second time she'd called. She asks, Who was it who picked up? A man's voice. I think and say, No one. It's no one. Just the apartment owner. My mama and I are renting two rooms from him. It's expensive, but what can you do? We're making ends meet. She says, Was my papa rude to you? I say, No, it's all fine. Can I see you? She says, Come over. I say, Do you know Audrey Hepburn? She says, I adore her. Why? I say, No reason. I'll come soon.

## February 15, 1998

I'm sick of Pushkin. He decided to teach me algebra for real. He says, Today we're going to study integrals. I say, That's what my last tutor said too. He says, What tutor? I say, The one before you. He says, Fine. Don't change the subject. I say, That's what my last tutor said too. He says, What? I say, He said, "Don't change the subject," too. Pushkin looks at me and says, Maybe we can start studying? And I say, That's what my last tutor said too. All the time. And then he says, Why are you constantly bringing him up? You're keeping me from explaining integrals. And I say, It's just that I liked him a lot. He was a good person. And he liked explaining too. Pushkin says, Why "was"? I say, Problems came up. He says, What kind of problems? I say, You don't need to know about that. And he says, No, please. And then I tell him, This last tutor happened to see a certain person go into my father's study. That's all I say. Pushkin is looking at me and waiting for the continuation. But I'm silent. And then he says, So what happened? And I say, Nothing. He wasn't supposed to see that person. Pushkin says, Why? I say, Don't you know the prosecutor's office is keeping an eye on my father? He says, In what sense? I say, Connections with organized crime. Don't you watch television? They were talking about it on NTV yesterday. He says, No. I say, You should. The last tutor was careless too. The man he saw didn't want anyone seeing him at my father's. Too high a position. Pushkin says, And so? What ended up happening? I say, I ended up without a tutor. And he used to explain everything to me so well. Pushkin says, That's silly. I say, Silly? You must be a brave person. I respect brave people. Actually, excuse me for interrupting you. I think you'd started saying something about integral calculus?

## February 16, 1998

Today my father came back from his office a little earlier than usual and said, Come see me in my study. Usually, he and I talk just anywhere. Wherever it comes over him. Not necessarily in his study. I say, What's up? He says, Why aren't you going to school? You thought I didn't know? I say, I didn't think anything. It's just school is shit. He says, Do you know how much it costs? It's the best school in Moscow. I say, I couldn't care less how much it costs. And he says, I don't like your tone of voice. And I think, So it begins. He says, You have to graduate. This is your last year. And I say, I'd rather study with Pushkin. Then he says, And what is this nonsense you concocted for him about your last tutor? What do criminals have to do with this? And I say, It's Pushkin who's curious. He was asking questions about you. Who comes to see you. Who talks about what. Could he be tax police? Or FSB? He looks at me and says nothing. Then he says, Still, you're acting strangely. And I say, I know. Do you want to take me to see a psychiatrist? To a psych hospital? They say the food's good there. He says, Where did you come up with that? I say, You were the one who said I was strange. And he says, That's not what I meant. It's just you're acting strangely somehow. You don't go anywhere. You don't have any friends. For some reason you went to Kuzminki. I say, I needed to buy something. And I don't go outside because my watermelon gets cold. He says, What? I say, My watermelon. He says, I got that. Only I don't understand what a watermelon is. I say, It's a knit cap. It's round like a watermelon. Everyone's wearing them these days. It's considered cool. But it makes you cold. It's still winter after all. You can call it a condom too. I like "watermelon" better. It's zanier. He looked at me and says, All right, study with the tutor for now. I'll have a talk with your school.

## February 18, 1998

I was at Marina's again. I finally caught her in. Her father's name is Ilya Semyonich. He was home again today. I guess he doesn't work anywhere. Now for some reason he acted differently. Not like the first time. He said, Sorry if I was rude to you last time. He's so polite all of a sudden. I'm sick right now, he says, that's why I run off at the mouth sometimes. But we're always glad to see you. Come over anytime. And I think, That's odd, what's up with him? Marina says, Let's go to my room. And this is my younger brother. His name is Mikhail. I say, Hello, Mikhail. How old are you? And he says, Hello yourself. I'm already five. I say, You're all grown up. And he left. A funny little bear cub. In her room, Marina said, He likes you. I say, Yeah? How do you know? She says, He never tells anyone his age when they first meet. I say, Cool. Then we sat in silence and I looked at her room. She says, Well, how've you been? I say, Why did you give me your ticket that time on the streetcar? She's silent for a moment and says, You had that look. I say, What kind? She says, That...lost look. As if you were lost. Like when you're a kid. You know, like with little kids. I say, Yeah? And I look at her face. She says, Why are you looking at me like that? I say, Remember I asked you about Audrey Hepburn? She smiles.

I say, She's beautiful. I've never seen anyone that beautiful in real life. Then she picked up the guitar from another chair and started playing "Moon River" from *Breakfast at Tiffany's*. And started to sing. And I looked at her and thought, Too bad Oktyabrina Mikhailovna died.

## February 22, 1998

Today I ran into Anton Strelnikov in the courtyard. I don't know what he was doing here. Maybe he was looking for someone. Or chasing teachers again. He likes to follow them. One lives in the next courtyard. She teaches history in the parallel class. He says, Why aren't you going to school? I say, What's it to you? I don't ask you why you go. He says, Everyone does. I say, I don't. I'm not like everyone else. I'm strange. He says, Ah. I say, Don't fucking "ah" me here. He says, I don't understand. I say, Get the hell out, punk. He says, Seryozha, have you lost your mind or something? I say, It's your mother who sleeps with everyone. He falls silent and looks at me. Then he says, What? I say, She sleeps around. She sleeps with everyone.

## February 23, 1998

This morning Pushkin asked me, Where'd you get the bruise? I say, Today is Defender of the Fatherland Day. He says, And so? I say, Congratulations. He says, Thank you. But why the bruise? I say, It's a family tradition. My father likes ancient rituals. He thinks a real man should take pain easily. So on February 23, he always punches me. Pushkin says, What do you mean, punches you? I say, Oh, don't worry. It doesn't hurt at all. We just have this ritual. My grandfather beat him too. And my great-grandfather. My father often reminisces about the two of them getting together and pummeling him from time to time. Pushkin says, Why? I say, So he'd get used to it. Life is full of surprises.

## February 24, 1998
Today I couldn't visit Marina. I called her twice. And she called me once.

My father came in. He stood in the middle of my room for a long time and said nothing. Then he says, Who's that? I say, Audrey Hepburn. You saw her. He says, The same face in all those pictures? I say, Exactly. He says, Where did you get so many? I say, On the Internet. This isn't even all of them. I just don't have anywhere else to hang the rest. He says, Can I sit here? I say, Wait, I'll clear the photographs away. He sits in silence for a moment. So do I. Then he says, Listen, you're going to have to take your exams soon. I say, What of it? He says, You won't pass without Pushkin. I say, I won't? He says, Maybe you'll go to school after all? I say, Let's make a deal. You get rid of Pushkin, and I'll study for the exams myself. He says, You'll fail. I say, Bet on it? He says, I don't much like him either. I say, So it's a deal. Then he says, What do you have going on in Kuzminki? I don't answer. And he says, You've gone there several times. I say, Four. He says, There, you see? I say, Can we talk about that some other time? He says, Are you sure? And I say to him again, Can we?

## April 3, 1998
I haven't written for more than a month. Everything was fine. Now the surprises have started up again. My father hired a new tutor. He just can't let it go. Only this isn't a tutor exactly. It's some goof. His name is Mikhail. Last name Vorobyov. Young. No patronymic even. Maybe twenty-five or twenty-eight. I've never had a tutor like this before. And no

textbooks or studies. My father's come up with a new system of education.

Today this Mikhail took me to see some woman. He said my father told him to. Took me to Alexandrovsky Park and left me there to sit on a bench. Then she picked me up. I nearly froze waiting for her there. She says, What's your name? I tell her. Then I say, What about you? She smiles and says, Natalia Alexandrovna. I say, Pretty name. As pretty as you. She says, Oh my, where did you learn things like that? I say, What things? She says, How to treat women. I say, I saw it in the movies. Then we went to her place and she tells me, Take it off. I took off my jacket and sat down on a chair. She says, Take it all off. I say, Why? What are you, a doctor? She says, No, you're kind of strange. I say, Everyone says that about me. Even my father. He wants to send me to a psych hospital. But I can't take my clothes off. She says, Why? I say, Because I'm cold. And I'm embarrassed too. You're standing right here. You aren't planning on going anywhere. She says, But how are we going to make love? I say, We're not. She says, All right, let's start all over again. Are you making fun of me on purpose? I say, I'm not making fun of you. Where's your bathroom? She says, Do you feel sick? I say, I get nauseated when I'm nervous. She says, Go quick. God forbid you throw up on my rug. I went out and then came back. And she says, Then why did you come with me? I say, My father wants me to. She says, What an interesting father you have. Who is he? And I told her. I told her everything. I don't know why it happened like that. I'd never told anyone before, but I told her. About my mama, about Oktyabrina Mikhailovna, about Audrey Hepburn, and about my father. I even told her about Strelnikov and Marina. Basically, I told her everything. I don't know why it happened like that. She smoked cigarettes and cried. Then she says, Poor little boy. I feel so sorry for you. And I tell her, I apologize for telling you all that. But I didn't know how I was supposed to explain to you why I came here. She says, That's okay, it's all fine. Only you have to tell your girl everything. Don't mislead her. Stop saying you're from Kaluga. Tell her everything you told me. Otherwise it'll be bad. You shouldn't lie when it comes to thinks like that. Tell her. I say, I don't know. She says, Tell her. Or you'll regret it later. I say, All right. Then she took me back to Alexandrovsky Garden. Back to that bench. And when Mikhail came, she gave him a hundred dollars. And then I thought, If Papa wants me to be a man, I should justify his expectations. I tell Mikhail, Let's pick up a prostitute. I could tell he was surprised. Then we put some girl on Tverskaya into the car and went to Mikhail's place. Along the way she yakked a lot. Must have been nervous. Her first time too, probably. When we got there, Mikhail stayed in the car. He has a one-room apartment. And I told the girl to drink tea. She says, We're not going to fuck? I say, No. Only don't tell him anything. She says, What about the money? I say, Here, take it. She says, You're kind of strange. I say, We need to sit here for ten minutes or so. Then she left and I stayed there alone. I started feeling bad again. I'd never felt that bad before.

## April 4, 1998

My father gave Vorobyov the car, it turns out. So this isn't his car. That means I can ride with him now where I want. I don't have to ask my father's driver anymore. And my father won't find out. The main thing is to make sure Vorobyov doesn't blab. But I don't think he cares. He's only interested in the money. I wonder how much my father is paying him. Actually, I don't give a damn. What's important is that there's a car now. We'll visit Marina. Always.

Has my luck really turned? Just so he doesn't get fired.

## June 13, 1998 (nearly morning already)

That's where my old diary ended. There wasn't any more room in the notebook.

And there wasn't any time to write. I barely got prepared for exams. Especially since I had to take them without attending lectures.

My father's impatient to fly to Italy as is. Time to go to bed. Though it's obviously getting light outside. We're off to get married tomorrow. To my Italian Paola. Or rather, today now. True, my father says this is just a preliminary introduction. We have to wait until I'm twenty-one. Let her wait if he likes her so much.

When we're in Rome, I have to ask someone to show me where *Roman Holiday* was shot. Absolutely.

I wonder what Marina's dreaming right now?

## June 14, 1998

It's hot here. After Moscow, it's a real oven. Nothing but soccer everywhere. In all the windows, pictures of players on the Italian team. The World Cup's soon. Maybe I'll ask my father to let us go to France. Nothing's very far here.

Yesterday we paid them a visit. To get acquainted. Right away, as soon as we arrived from the airport. I said, Why so soon? And he says, That's the custom here. Courtesy. I think, What courtesy if I'm still nauseated after the airplane? But I didn't say it out loud. What's the point? He's so wound up over this, like hell you're going to stop him. He brought a stack of albums along from Moscow. Here's everything that's left from your mama, he says. She loved Italian painting. The Renaissance. Now it will finally come in handy. At least you get some use out of her. She hasn't written to you, has she? I sent her a letter a little while ago. But she didn't answer. She hasn't written to you? I say, No, she hasn't. He says, Are you sure? I say, A hundred percent. He says, So, take these and you can look through them in your free time. I say, You look through them. He says, I don't like your tone of voice. I say, Why should I give a damn about your Renaissance? He pauses and then says, Well, you can show off your erudition somewhere. I say, Who to? He looks at me and says, Listen, I'm sick and tired of you. Come on, get ready.

So he and I went.

But the AC broke in the car.

I say, We should at least have taken a shower at the hotel after the plane. In this heat, you and I stink something awful. Two sweaty Russians. He says, Stop talking nonsense. I'm plenty nervous without you. And his interpreter Dima adds, Three. My father says, What? And Dima says, Three sweaty Russians, Pavel Petrovich. There are three of us after all. He looks at Dima and at me and then says, Dima, you should open the window. As it is, there's really nothing to breathe.

This Dima has been living here in Italy for over two years. He's the permanent representative of my father's firm. Or something like that. Basically, he takes care of things.

When we finally arrive, they take a long time to open the gates. I say, I think we should have waited at the hotel. What kind of idiot is going to run around town in this heat? I look at my father and he too has started to get embarrassed. Not at all like he is in Moscow. No flash. He's just standing at these Italian iron gates embarrassed. He's not used to standing at other people's gates. Especially when they take so long to open them.

Eventually a little girl shows up. When she emerges from the trees I think, Why have they hired such an ugly servant? She must scare all their guests. As ugly as nuclear war. She walks up and asks us something and then pulls on the handle. The gates open. Dima starts talking to her, and my father and I walk toward the house. A minute later he catches up to us. He's out of breath. He says, Signor Panucci isn't here yet. He hasn't arrived. My father says, That's too bad. But I don't say anything. I'm silent. I've already said all I had to say. Back at the hotel. Dima adds, But we can wait for him. We can socialize with his daughter for now. I think, Here comes the interesting part. Where is my intended? My father says, Well then, let's go into the house. And this freak is already standing on the porch, smiling at us. I think, Fate has dealt her a nasty hand. It's good she landed in a wealthy house. No one here sees her. Just millionaire dolts. And damn if you can surprise them with anything.

We follow her into a large room and she brings us something to drink.

Then she calls Dima over. I pick up a bottle of Heineken and a glass. But my father says, Wait a minute until she goes away. Or else she'll tell her bosses that their future son-in-law swills beer. And where did you learn that anyway? I say, Vorobyov taught me. He said it was your idea.

At that moment, the freak returns. Dima's with her. They're carrying some kind of special little table.

We sit down around it. My father pours me some Pepsi. I think, Thank you. But Dima and the freak are talking about something in Italian. My father finally gets sick of this and intervenes in their conversation. And where is Signorina

Paola? he says. Is she coming down to join us or not? I think, Damn, what a cool papa. He knows "Signorina Paola." But Dima looks at him oddly and then says, But here she is, Pavel Petrovich. This is Signor Panucci's daughter. Signorina Paola.

My father chokes on his lemonade and then looks at me.

Evidently he finally felt sorry for me. But I don't care anymore.

### June 15, 1998

I don't give a damn about his pity. He can choke on it. I'm sitting in the hotel.

I'm not going anywhere. Outside, the sidewalks are melting in the heat. I don't understand anything on television. It's all in Italian.

Marina arrives tomorrow.

### June 16, 1998

They haven't arrived yet.

### June 17, 1998

I went to the station again to meet the train from Vienna. Dima whined the whole way that the traffic jams were killing him. He has a bad gallbladder. And pancreas. He must have repeated that a hundred times. But I can't go without him. I can't even read the train schedule properly. I tell him he can get out of the car while we're standing in traffic. He says, Thanks a lot. He's angry.

They still haven't fixed the AC.

I stood on the platform for half an hour after all the passengers had left. Dima says, Everyone's gone already. There's no one else. I say, Ask the conductors. And he says, Ask them what?

### June 18, 1998

My father says, You're wrong to refuse to go see the Panuccis. Yesterday we had a great time with them. Paola asked about you. I say, Isn't this enough already?

And he says, Why are you so wound up over your Vorobyov? I say, I'm not.

Meanwhile, I wasn't telling the truth.

And my father says, Listen, I didn't know what she looked like, really. But when you get used to her, she's basically okay. I say, Basically? He says, She sings well.

Dima says he's not going with me today. He has a doctor's visit scheduled. That's how he put it, "scheduled." He likes words like that.

### June 19, 1998

They haven't arrived. I don't know what's going on. Could their train have derailed?

### June 20, 1998

I'm sick of this hotel. I'm sick of Italy too. I told my father I wouldn't go to the Panuccis' until Vorobyov showed up. He says, Listen, this is getting indecent. And I say to him, Yeah?

### June 21, 1998

My father says, You mean you're going to go to the station every day? I say, A train comes from Vienna every day. So what? He says, So nothing. It's just Dima is complaining. Maybe you'll let him not go today?

### June 22, 1998

I don't need Dima anymore. I know everything at that station myself without him. Today I was nearly late for the

Vienna train. Traffic jam. If they don't come tomorrow, I'll lose my mind.

### June 23, 1998
The porters treat me to lemonade. Standing on the platform is too hot. They're always saying something and laughing. I can't understand them without Dima. They probably remember me by now. One keeps waving his arms and kissing the air. The others laugh. I hate Italian.

### June 24, 1998
My father says it looks like the whole thing's going to go bust because of me. I say it isn't because of me. Then he says that beauty isn't the most important thing. Beauty's only skin deep. And I say, What beauty? He says, Listen, maybe you'll go after all? It's awkward. After all, we've been hanging around here for ten days already. I say, How many? He says, Ten days. I say, What the fuck. Where did they get hung up? And he says, Who?

### June 25, 1998
After all the passengers from the Vienna train left today, the porters laughed at me again. One pretended to be a woman, and the other that he was accosting her. I guess they realized why I was coming here. Pretty soon they're going to start laying bets on whether I'll wait for her or not.

    Let them laugh.

    I'll wait.

### June 26, 1998
This morning I went to the foyer and there was Marina. And next to her was Vorobyov.

I walk up to them and say, Hi. They say, Oh, hi. What are you doing up so early? I say, I wanted to go to the station. They say, Yeah? What for? I say, To meet you. The Vienna train's arriving soon. And they say, We didn't come from Vienna. We were there a long time ago. I say, Yeah? Where did you come from? They say, Venice. You know how pretty it is there? They decided to stop by Venice on the way. I say, I can imagine. They say, Too bad you didn't come with us. We should have all taken the train. It's very comfortable. You can lay over in any town you want. I say, I've been waiting here for you for ten days. Marina looks at me and says, You're not mad at us, are you? And I think, Ten days. Ten trains from Vienna. I wonder how many thousands of people arrived on them?

You know how pretty it is there? In Venice?

## June 26, 1998 (evening)

My father says, We're putting Mikhail and his girlfriend in the same room. I say, What? And he says, It's very simple. You were the one who said they were getting married soon. I say, I said that? And he says, Or Mikhail. Now I don't remember who said it. One of you. So what? Does it matter? I say, Well, no, I guess not. It doesn't matter. Only they're not married yet. And he says, Oh, stop it. Who cares in this day and age? Mikhail will only be grateful. Wait and see. It's always important to give a little nudge in these affairs. I say, Nudge who? He looks at me and smiles. Then he says, Not "who" but "what." I say, Nudge what? He says, Circumstances. And basically, this Marina is a very attractive young woman. Tell Mikhail he has good taste. She reminds me of someone. Do you know who? I say, No, I don't. He says, Well, all right. But you still tell him what I said about his taste.

# THE LYING YEAR

Then I went to see Marina and told her about my father's idea. She just shrugged. I say to her, But how's that going to work? She says, It'll be fine. She says, I'll survive. I say, And what about me? She shrugs again. I've seen the room, she says. It has a bed and also a couch. It's like he's in another room. I say, Is it a two-room suite or something? And she says, Well, not quite. There's this kind of anteroom. And I say, Is Vorobyov going to be sleeping in the anteroom? She looks at me and says, Do you want me to? I say, No. And then for a long time we didn't say anything.

## June 27, 1998

Today I had to go to the Panuccis'. My father says, You did promise.

We sat in their living room looking at the walls. Dima talked to them nonstop. Utter boredom. Before this, my father said, Well, if you don't want to, naturally, don't marry her. But there's still a lot of time. Right now you can just get acquainted. You never know what will happen in three years.

And then I'm sitting in their living room and thinking, Really, you never know?

Vorobyov says that it was Marina who suggested they go to Venice. She said they needed to give me a little time. I say, What for? Vorobyov says, I don't know. Ask her. I say, So what did you do there? He says, Oh, nothing. I say, What do you mean, nothing? He says, We fed the pigeons. I say, What else? He says, Took a boat ride. I say, What kind of boat? He says, A little one. It goes all over the lagoon. You can take it to the Lido. I say, So what's there, on the Lido? He says, Well, restaurants. Tourists. All kinds of stuff. I say, So what else did you do there? He says, Nothing else, basically. We sat on the Piazza San Marco. I say, What piazza? He says, San Marco.

Everyone sits there. All kinds of cafés, lots of pigeons. Little tables right on the street. I say, Cool. He looks at me and says, Yeah, it was pretty good. Too bad you didn't take the train with us. I say, Too bad. And he says, No, it's true.

### June 30, 1998

My father stopped by Vorobyov and Marina's room and says to me, You're sitting here again? I say, What do you mean by "again"? He smiles and says, Well, when you're about to get married, you'll find out. I say, What will I find out? And he keeps smiling and saying, Your value to your friends. I say, In what sense? He says, Every sense. Especially how prepared they are to leave you alone with your intended. Isn't that so, Marina? She says, Oh no, Pavel Petrovich. Seryozha isn't bothering us at all. The three of us are all having such a good time like this together. And he says, Three is never fun. She looks at him and asks, And how is three? And he says, Three is usually very sad. But this is all sentimental talk. Then he turns to me. I came by to see you. This evening we have to go to the golf club. I say, I don't play. But it's as if he didn't hear me. What an interesting bed you have, he says. And he looked at the large carved headboard. Then he says, That's great having something so beautiful. I wonder what it is they've got carved here. It looks like a whole story here. Wait a minute, I'll bring an album right now. I have the same carving somewhere. Or very similar. While he went to his room, we sat and looked at each other. Then he brought a huge picture book. Gleeful that it came in handy after all. At least he didn't lug these bricks from Moscow for nothing. He brought Dima along too. He says, You know, the ancient Greeks hung images of beautiful gods on the walls in newlyweds' bedrooms. It was believed that if at the moment of conception the lovers were looking at beautiful faces, then their child would be beautiful. Do you believe in things like that, Marina? She says, Well, I don't know, Pavel Petrovich. It's kind of...But he says, You definitely should. After all, it's not for nothing that you've come with us. Look at what a magnificent bed you have. Only very beautiful children should be conceived in a bed like this. That's what he said: "conceived." I nearly threw up. But Marina was looking at him and smiling. So was Vorobyov. Even Dima started to grimace, sort of. My father says, Well there, exactly. I told you. Look. It's exactly the same carving in this book. What does it say here? We read, *The Life of Jacob*. I wonder who that is? But the carving is the same. Listen, could the hotels here really have such ancient furniture? What does it say here? Look, sixteenth century. How much might it be worth? But Dima says, It's not the real bed, Pavel Petrovich. Lots of these kinds of copies are made these days. It's stylish. They try to imitate old things. My father says, Really? Too bad. But it is still handsome. Imagine, Jacob's life on a headboard. I wonder who he was? Probably some religious figure. Dima says, I'm not up to speed, but if you like I can find out all about it by tonight. My father says, Yes, yes, you do that, please, look into it. Then he turns to Marina again, But your children should be handsome anyway. And then to Vorobyov, Go on, then, Mikhail. Get busy. In nine months we'll be christening a little Italian boy. Marina, what do you want more? A little boy or a little girl? She looks at him, then at me, and says, We haven't really decided yet, Pavel Petrovich. Then he says, A boy's better. Although they have their problems too. Are you coming or not, Seryozha? The car's been waiting quite a while. I say, Do you have a lot more picture books there? He says, Yes. What of it? I say, Nothing. I'd rather stay at the hotel. I'll look through your picture books.

## July 2, 1998 (Livorno)

This isn't Florence anymore. Which is why I'm writing on this crap paper.

I spent the night at the villa of the finance minister's son. Now I'm looking at the sea. I can see it right from my window. And hear it. I'm waiting for Marina to come. She went to look at the horses. With the son. He likes horses too.

Yesterday, my father said we were invited to a party at the finance minister's. I said I wasn't going. Then he said, You never go anywhere. I'm doing your work for you everywhere. And I said, This wasn't my idea. He said, Get ready, that's it. Enough yammering. Signor Panucci went to a lot of trouble to get this invitation for us. They're having a double celebration here today. Signor Cavalcanti is marking his appointment as minister, and his son is turning twenty-one. I said, Oh, an adult already. Maybe he should marry Paola? My father said, Stop talking nonsense. We'll be late. I said, What about Vorobyov and Marina? He said, Listen, why don't you give them a little time to be together? You're always sitting in their room. Have a conscience. I said, What's that? He said, Hurry it up. Everyone's already gathered there. I said, Paola too? He looked at me and then said, Hop to it. You've worn me out with your conversations.

It was dark by the time we arrived. Dima chattered on the whole way about this Cavalcanti. Then they went into the garden, and he started calculating loudly how much lighting the entire forest cost. I said, Then why doesn't he live in Rome if he's the finance minister? Dima said, Just wait. He has everything ahead of him. Do you know what a great success this is for a Florentine politician? Signor Cavalcanti was just an ordinary member of parliament from Tuscany. And now can you imagine how high he's flown? No, you can't? I said, I can imagine, but I basically don't care. He could be the pope. And Dima said, Don't say that. For Florentines, Signor Cavalcanti is practically a saint by now. Unfortunately, though, he can't become pope. I said, Yeah? Why is that? He said, First you have to be a cardinal. And I said, But you were the one who said he was a saint. At this, my father intervened and said, Sergei, enough fooling around. And stop drinking that filth.

When we'd drunk everything in the glass bowl, Dima said, It's time to go upstairs. There's going to be dancing now. I said, They're going to dance? These guys in dinner jackets are going to dance now? And he said, Well, not the way you're thinking. This isn't a nightclub, after all. They have a full orchestra. Different dances. I said, For instance? He said, Waltz. Tango. Do you know how? I said, No. Papa does. And my father said, Sergei, cut it out. I said, Cut what out? My papa's going to tango now. And he said, Stop making fun. I'm tired of it. I said, Yeah?

Upstairs, Dima said to me, Look, isn't that Marina? I said, Where? It can't be. And he said, Look, over there. Next to Signor Cavalcanti. I said, That's definitely Marina. What's she doing here? And Dima said, I wonder how she got in without an invitation. I looked at her, then at this Signor Cavalcanti, and I said, But why is he so young? What, do they have such young ministers in Italy? Dima said, That's the younger Signor Cavalcanti. It's his birthday. His father's standing over there. Near the column. See? I said, Yes. I wanted to spit on him. My father said, Sergei, I think you've had too much to drink. What did they mix to make that syrup? Dima said, Nothing special, Pavel Petrovich. Fruit juice and a little wine. It doesn't have to be strong. I said, It's like plain syrup. We should make it like that at home. I'm going over to Marina and talk. Dima said, You can't approach her right now. She's talking to the host's son. And we still haven't been introduced. I said, Well then, let's go and introduce ourselves. What's the problem? Dima said, You can't. Just wait.

But I went anyway.

But there were so many people. And they were all standing right in my way. Crowding. But I didn't take my eyes off Marina. I headed toward her like a navigator. I set my course. I heard someone shout something behind me. I think someone dropped a glass. You should drink at the table, Italian sirs. It's dangerous to drink standing. It's a good thing the dancing hadn't started at least. If they'd already started dancing around me I would for sure never have reached the other end of the room. I would have been surrounded. As it was, they were just standing and yakking. I walked quietly between them. Like an icebreaker. My guidepost was Marina's head. It disappeared from time to time, but I kept going. Russians do not give in.

I got there.

I said, Hi.

She said, Oh, we are so drunk.

I said, Cool dress. Where'd you get it?

I tried to speak distinctly. I pronounced all the sounds. But it was hard.

She said, Like it? I bought it especially for this party. I'd like to introduce you. This is Signor Cavalcanti. His name is Matteo. I said, How do you do. But I already know you. Dima's told me all about you. Or rather, about your papa. You have a hot-shit father. Almost as hot-shit as mine. Only even more so. How do you and he get along? Because I can't get along with mine. He's a very unmanageable papa.

Marina said, Wait, wait, Sergei. He doesn't understand Russian. Do you want me to translate into English? I said, What the fuck? Where do you get off? How did you get in here? Do you know I nearly died waiting for you to get here from Moscow? And you were with your Vorobyov in Venice. How did you get in here? What were you doing there?

At that moment, the music started right over my head. Blasted.

Just as Dima'd promised.

A waltz.

I raised my head to look, and the ceiling above me started to spin. The orchestra was sitting on a balcony. Somewhere on the second floor. Or third. I couldn't make it out. Someone grabbed my shoulder. If he hadn't, I would probably have fallen. Afterward, I looked around and Marina was gone. And so was that Cavalcanti. Everything was spinning. The whole room was spinning around me. I thought, How do they keep from falling? If I were them, I would definitely fall. They were spinning like windup toys. Flying all the way across the room. And the music was roaring right over my head.

And then I caught sight of Marina again.

She was spinning with that minister's son.

And I thought, I hope they croak, all those sons. Right on his birthday. In the middle of the room where everyone's spinning.

I realized I hated waltzes.

## July 2, 1998 (Livorno, after dinner)

Marina still isn't back. She's enjoying the horses. Dima says, Let's go to the sea. I say, It nauseates me.

If she doesn't show up in two hours, I'm going back to Florence. My father's called twice already. Asking whether or not to send a car. I tell him, What about Marina? He says, Is she still there? I say, No. She went to the stables. He says, Mikhail's not back yet either. He didn't spend the night at the hotel. Did you figure out how she got into the party yesterday?

After the waltz, there were a lot of other things. Dance after dance. I sat on a settee and thought, Did they have iron legs or something? Could you really dance nonstop? It's like they were stuck to each other. I could have taken a hand grenade and thrown it at the balcony where the orchestra was sitting. So they'd stop playing.

Or gone up and given them a shove.

Dima said, When the dancing is over, everyone's going to Livorno. To Signor Matteo's house. He has his own villa there. I said, What for? He said, To ride on his yacht. Signor Matteo is a magnificent yachtsman. I said, He's a magnificent freak. Dima said, Don't say that. He's the most eligible bachelor. All the young Italian women are on the hunt for him. A real prince. They say the ducal house in Monaco has started making inquiries about him. They have princesses there too. I said, He can go fuck himself. Dima looked at me and said nothing. I said, What are you looking at? You can go fuck yourself too.

Then everyone started getting into cars. There was a lot of jostling, and I lost sight of Marina. I only noticed them outside. She was getting into Matteo's sports car. I found my father and said I wanted to go to Livorno. He said, Fine. I'll send Dima with you. I say, Only in another car.

En route, I kept searching for that sports car. But I couldn't see anything in the fucking dark. First one car overtook us, then another. There were just lights shining. I told the driver, Faster. But he laughed. He didn't understand. And these Italian girls were falling all over me. Their perfume was nearly suffocating me. Stop the pushing, I told them. Are you total fools or something? You were just waltzing. I have to catch up to this sports car. And you're getting in my way. Understand? But they were trying to make out with me. Totally drunk. I said, Lay off, you fools. I have to get to Livorno. And they shouted, Livorno, Livorno. Bravo, Livorno. I said, What are you hollering about? Are we at the theater or something? Faster, driver. I'm going to vomit.

When we arrived, I saw that sports car right away. Next to the dock. No one was in the car.

I said, Where's Signor Matteo? Where's your boss? Everyone around me was laughing. They poured me champagne from different bottles. Spilling on my jacket. I thought, Where is that idiotic Dima? They were pulling me in different directions. Then there was a boom in the sky. The fireworks started. Everyone around me was shouting and pouring champagne on each other. I was shouting at them, Get off me. Where's your Matteo? They were kissing, laughing, pawing me. Then I looked, and Marina was standing on the yacht next to the dock. Standing and looking up. At the fireworks. And next to her was that Matteo.

## July 2, 1998 (Livorno, almost night already)

I'm getting out of here. I'm sick and tired of them. My father just called. I told him to send a car. He said, Vorobyov finally showed up at the hotel. I'm coming and I'll talk to him. I can't figure out how she got into the party yesterday.

They got back an hour and a half ago. I said, Well, how are the local horses? She said, Cool. I've never ridden horses like that before. Smarter than a person. I said, It's crazier riding a person. She said, What are you talking about? I said, Oh, nothing. Pay no attention. You could have introduced me to your

Matteo. Everyone here is crazy about him. She said, He's not mine. And I did introduce you to him yesterday. Right then, this very same Matteo walked up to us. She said something to him in English. He looked at me, smiled, and gestured to me to follow. We went to his study, and Marina said he wanted to give me a present. I said, Cool. He opened a cupboard and took out a gun. Just what I've been dreaming of. A small revolver with a very short barrel. Marina said, Like it?

I looked at him and thought, Finally.

## July 2, 1998 (Florence again, very late)

Vorobyov doesn't know when Marina met this Matteo. He hasn't heard anything about him at all. He says, Who is he, some soccer player? I say, What does soccer have to do with this? This is someone else completely. It's just she knows him from somewhere. When I saw her there, she was already talking to him. And he says, Talking? That's okay. Don't you know Marina? All she has to do is get in. Then she can talk to anyone she wants. The Prince of Wales, if she wants. True, I don't know whether there is one. I say, What does the Prince of Wales have to do with this? How did she get in? He says, The usual way. She bought herself a dress and walked in. She knocked a little sense into the guards' heads. At first they didn't want to let her in. I say, But how did she get there? And where did she spend the night? Why do you have a bruise on your face? Did you have a fight with someone? I don't understand anything at all. What's going on? And he looks at me and says, First, you have to calm down. Why are you shouting? He's speaking in this quiet voice while he's looking at me. And I'm looking at him. Neither of us says anything for maybe a minute. Then I say, Okay. How did she get in there finally? He says, You want to know? I'll tell you tomorrow. In the morning. I haven't slept for over twenty-four hours because of her. I'm sick and tired of you and Marina both.

## July 3, 1998

Vorobyov isn't up yet. Dima hasn't come either. Could he still be in Livorno? What about Marina?

My father says, What got you up so early? I say, What time is it? He says, Five in the morning. I say, They're making a lot of noise in the next room. And he says, They're Americans. The day before yesterday, they started celebrating their Independence Day. Like Russians, God help us. I say, You go to sleep. I'll sit here alone for a while. And he says, Listen, you've been kind of strange lately. What has you so nervous? If you don't want to get married, don't. No one's going to force you. I didn't know she was so, well, unattractive. I say, Yeah, yeah, I understand. And he says, Whoa. Is that them starting to fight first thing in the morning? Hear that? I say, Yes. And he says, They've been pulled apart already. The police came the night you left for Livorno. They didn't take anybody in. They like Americans. Or they're counting on their dollars. They leave a lot of them behind here on their holidays. How was it there? I say, Where? He says, In Livorno. I say, Fine. We watched a fireworks display. He says, Anything else? Did you ride on the yacht? I say, I didn't get there in time. They may have sailed some afterward without me. He says, What about Marina? I say, What? He says, How on earth did she get there? I say, I don't know. He says, She's turned out to be some resourceful young woman. The minister himself even asked me about her afterward. He wondered who his son was dancing with the whole time. Listen, how did she get there? Did you ask her? I say, No. I didn't. He says, How's that? I say, I couldn't care less about her. What does it matter how she got there?

## July 3, 1998 (10 in the morning)

Vorobyov says, What are you, a fool or something? I told you I haven't slept in forty-eight hours. I say, I've been waiting five hours for you to wake up. And he says, No, you really are a fool. Why the fuck did you wake me? Now I won't be able to get back to sleep. Who is that shouting? I say, It's the police, they've come to take the Americans away. From Room 202. And he says, Well, thank God. Those jerks are getting what they deserve. They should have gotten it even worse. All right, come in. Are we going to hang around here in the hallway or something? I say, Was that you fighting with them yesterday? He says, I wasn't fighting. I punched them in the face a couple of times so the freaks would know. I say, How did you get into their room? He says, I didn't get in. They're the ones who found me at this place outside town. I was trying to catch a ride home. Without money. And they took me for free. They found out I was in the same hotel with them. They've got lots of cash. They showed it to me. A whole suitcase. Not a real suitcase, but, you know, that kind of case for documents. But it's full. Stupid jerks. They fucking cleaned up in Las Vegas. The whole way they kept hollering, Viva Las Vegas, and now they've skipped out for Monte Carlo. Europe. They should spend a while in jail. Freaks. I say, Why didn't you have money? I gave you some. Back in Moscow. A whole five thousand. Didn't you have time to exchange it? He says, I did exchange it. Only it's already gone. I say, What do you mean gone? Five thousand dollars. I couldn't spend it that fast. He says, I couldn't either. But did you see the new dress on Marina? I say, The black one? He says,

Well, yeah? I say, What of it? A dress can't cost five thousand dollars. He says, That's what I thought too. I say, Damn. You mean she asked you for five grand? He says, She didn't ask. She just said I should pay. She said that without that dress she had no chance of getting into that stupid party. She said she had to go there. Come hell or high water.

I say, That means you took her there. He says, Well, yeah. I spent my last lire on a cab. I say, How did she find out the address? He says, Your Dima yammered on about that party to everyone for three days. She ended up asking him everything. I say, I get it. What happened afterward? He says, I told you. These Americans found me and took me back to the hotel. But on the way, I fought with them. I say, They brought you at night. Where were you before that? Where did you spend the night? He says, Nowhere. I dodged around that village there. I say, All night? He says, What do you want? I told you already I didn't have a kopek. And your Marina abandoned me. She just waved after she went through the gates. They wouldn't have let you in anyway, she says. You're wearing jeans. Everyone there's like in tuxedos. They're all insiders. So basically I hung around there all night. Amid the nighttime hills of Italy.

I look at him and say, She dropped you like a hot potato, Vorobyov. He says, Yeah? What about you?

## July 3

The end. There's not going to be anything more. Ever. Because my father came out in the hallway and said, Are you going to be hanging around here for long? And I say, Yeah. What time is it now? He says, Nine. Go on, you were going to watch soccer. I say, I was. He says, Well, go on. It's the middle of the second half. I say, Yeah? When did they start?

And he runs off. Because someone kicked a goal there. And I follow him. My feet hurt by then. But I leave the door to the room open. And miss her coming in anyway. I only hear her when they start arguing there. I didn't even know she could shout so loud. The whole hall could hear. I have to close the door to my father's room. Even though he has the television shouting like a maniac. And Vorobyov says to me, Damn it, you should knock. She's standing facing him and says, Go choke on your dress. He says, Fool. She grabs the hem and peels it off over her head. Because she's hot. Go to hell, she says, and she throws the dress at him. I'm standing looking at them. And she's standing between us. Not a stitch on her. Vorobyov says, You left the Italian your panties as a memento. What's his name? Hey, kid, what's the Italian's name? I say, Matteo. The finance minister's son. Vorobyov laughs and says, Cool. Now our Marina even has ministers. She doesn't need guys like you and me anymore. I say, I am so sick of you. He looks at me and says, Get rid of the gun. Where did you get it? I say, Marina's friend gave it to me. Like it? And he says, Get rid of it. Or I don't know what I'll do. I say, You don't? He says, Get rid of it. But I didn't. Cocking the trigger was easy because I'd been practicing all day. I tell them, Bye-bye, jerks. I'm sick and tired of you. And I point it at my ear. They fall silent and look. Then Vorobyov leaps and jerks the gun toward himself. But I'd already squeezed. My arm got pushed. And Marina's looking at him and saying nothing. And then she drops to the floor beside him.

    And right then I'd thought, This is the end. It's all over.

## Fall: Mikhail

After our return from Italy, Pavel Petrovich suggested I move in with them. He said he was very grateful and he wanted me to feel like a full-fledged member of the family. I told him I was just fine as I was, and then he gave me five grand.

The money came in very handy because that was when this idiotic crisis started. I took two thousand dollars to my mother in Kaliningrad, and when I got back to Moscow, I could sell the three thou I had left for a fantastic price. There were rumors going around that Moscow was about to be hit by famine. I'd only read about things like that as a child in books about the war, which is why it didn't particularly grab me.

I still had "my" Land Rover, and every day I drove to their house as if I were on duty. Sergei didn't turn off his computer when I showed up anymore. He shook my hand and then we sat in silence in his room, each doing his own thing. Or rather, he did his own thing and I watched over his shoulder.

I liked sitting like that. I didn't understand much about the whole Internet thing, especially when he went on English-language search engines, but the silence in his room, the soft armchair, and the muffled humming of the computer lulled me like when I was a kid. I would shut my eyes and see myself as a little boy on the sofa when it was growing dark outside and the snow was falling in thick flakes. I have a temperature and so I won't go to school tomorrow. Mama's covered me up with a blanket, turned on the television, and is sitting in our old armchair holding a ball of yarn and thin needles. I can touch her, and then she turns her head and smiles at me in response. "Careful," she says. "I'm counting stitches. Wait a little. I'll bring you something soon." She gets up and goes to the kitchen, and I hide my head under the blanket and smile in the darkness. Mama is knitting me a sweater.

Sometimes he would start explaining what things were for on the Internet, but I wasn't really listening, and eventually he would turn away, leaving me in peace.

We didn't talk about Marina anymore. There was a ban on that name. I don't know what happened with them while I was lying around that private clinic, but when they signed me out she wasn't in Italy anymore. One day I blurted something about her in Pavel Petrovich's presence. He didn't say anything, but he frowned so hard that I had to pretend I'd misspoken. If I can't I can't, I told myself. Especially since this worked out even more conveniently for me.

Basically, everything was going perfectly smoothly until one day, all of a sudden, she called.

"Hi," she said softly, and I immediately recognized her voice. "How are things?"

"Fine. How about you?"

"Things are fine with me."

"Uh-huh," I said, and we both fell silent.

"Do you think you could help me out?"

"I don't know. What do I have to do?"

"I want to move to the dacha."

"Yeah?"

"I need a car to move my things."

"It's not my car."
"I know. But you don't have to tell them anything."
"I really don't like that."
"What?"
"Not telling them."
"Why?"
"The last time it all ended badly."
"Lord, I just need to move my things."
"This isn't the Lord, it's just me."
"Still like to joke, do you?"
"What else is left?"
She was silent for a moment.
"Are you going to help me or not?"
"I don't know yet."
"When will you know?"
"Maybe a little later."
"Fine, I'll call you back tonight."
"Don't bother. I'll call you myself."

When she hung up, I thought her voice had sounded very tired. They were probably giving her lots of work at school.

When I got back from Sergei's that night, I called her and said I would.

---

If anyone were to ask me why I agreed, I would probably have said I didn't know why myself. All the problems in Italy, all that chaos, ultimately didn't misfire for anyone but me. Seryozha's bullet broke my left collarbone, and I still have a hard time making certain movements. There were times when it hurt so much I cried. And most of all, I knew full well who was the cause of it. This is even if I don't take the business with the dress for five thou too much to heart.

Nonetheless, I agreed.

Why?

True, I do have the tiniest of suspicions on this subject. The thing is that while I was lying around the Italian hospital, tenderhearted Dima brought me a pile of different books. "I don't want you to die of boredom here. As it is, you've suffered more than enough for all of us." I have to say he had exquisite taste. All the books were from the school curriculum. At first, out of habit, I used them to put me to sleep, but later, when I couldn't sleep another wink, I started leafing through them, since I had nothing better to do. Good thing I had one arm free of plaster. I lay on my back, my left arm pulled back in a Pioneer salute, and with my right thumbed the pages of Dima's books, groaning in pain from time to time.

And somewhere there in one of those books, Tolstoy I think it was, there was one guy I remember now. It wasn't that I was in the same situation, but he too agreed to a meeting without himself being quite clear why. Or rather, that's what he said. He explained his own unexpected compliancy to himself. But in fact, it was all quite clear. He simply wanted to see her, and that's why he said yes. So, if you interpret this as Tolstoy did, what happened to me was something like that too. I wanted to see Marina. Damn them all, all those classics. I got all mixed up and decided we'd see tomorrow. Everything's always clearer in the morning.

---

It was nice at the dacha. Before this it had drizzled for two weeks nonstop, but now the sun unexpectedly peeked out. Islands of blue sky peered through the fluffy pine tops. For late October it may have even been excessively blue. The occasional birches amid the green spruce glowed red and yellow.

I love fall more than anything in the world. When fall comes, I feel like telling everyone to go to hell and sitting in the grass with a yellow birch leaf between my teeth. In fall, I feel like I become myself. Not that it lasts long.

Marina was totally changed. She was noticeably haggard and thin. In her pale face, her eyes now seemed much bigger. Her skin was almost translucent. There were dark circles around her eyes. Her movements revealed a hidden caution and even a kind of shyness. At first I was surprised, but then I decided it wasn't my problem. Maybe she'd been sick or something.

Even though the tall log house was hidden in dense woods, I was able to drive right up to the porch. Little Misha hopped right out of the car and with a shout ran back somewhere.

"He wants to close the gates," Marina said.

"Cool," I replied.

"Do you smell that air? The leaves have started falling."

I opened the door and sucked in the air with pleasure.

"Like it?" she said.

For the next half hour we didn't exchange a word. I silently carried her things, trying not to disturb my left arm. Marina was busy with something in the kitchen. Misha first played with a big orange ball and then started gathering fallen leaves.

"Hey," she said in a troubled voice, suddenly appearing on the porch. "I totally forgot about your injury. You probably shouldn't lift anything heavy, right?"

"That's okay. I'm already done."

She looked at me for a long time, wiping her hands on her apron. Then she tucked a lock of hair that had fallen over her eyes behind her ear.

"I nearly died of fright then."

"I can imagine," I said.

"At first I thought he'd killed you."

"So did I."

"There was such a big spot on your shirt."

"Everything's fine now. I bought myself a new one."

"Everyone started shouting in the hallway and I'm standing there naked. You're lying in a pool of blood and Seryozha's there…with that gun in his hands."

"It was a horrible picture."

"Are you angry at me?"

"That's the wrong word." I smiled.

Once again she tucked that unruly lock behind her ear and looked to the side. I could see only her profile, but suddenly I realized she was trying to hide her tears from me.

"Forgive me," she said softly. "I never wanted that."

"It's all fine," I replied.

"Forgive me," she repeated.

At that moment, Misha ran up and tugged on her apron.

"Give me the matches."

"What for?" she said, trying not to look in my direction.

"Gimme! I want to be the yardman. Yardmen burn leaves."

"Let's go," I said. "I have a lighter."

"Only I'm going to light them myself!"

Ten minutes later, the entire lot was cloaked in acrid smoke. Misha had gathered a big pile of fallen leaves, but they were all damp, and the fire just wouldn't catch.

"Wait up, I'll bring a little gasoline," I said, wiping my tears.

He remained squatting by the smoking pile, poking a twig in it, coughing, and tossing pinecones into it from time to time.

"Where's Ilya Semyonich?" I asked Marina, who had once again looked out on the porch. "Why didn't he come with us?"

"He died," she said.

"What do you mean, he died?"

She announced this so calmly that at first I simply didn't believe her.

"The usual way. He was walking down the street, and he fell down and died. You thought I decided to live at the dacha in the winter just like that? For my own pleasure? It's a good thing he bought it a few years ago from this professor. He wanted Misha to breathe more fresh air in the summer."

"Why did he die?"

Her calmness seemed supernatural.

"He had a bad heart. A very bad heart. But he didn't trust the doctors."

"You mean he wasn't getting any treatment at all?"

"He said they were just prescribing him all that muck so they could squeeze more money out of him."

"Where's the gas?" Misha poked me in the side.

"Damn it!" I winced from the pain.

"Be more careful!" Marina shouted. "Get away from him."

"That's okay, it's all fine," I hissed. "It was just a little surprising."

"He promised gasoline."

"Sorry, little one, I completely forgot. You and I will pour it on right now. You hold this hose. No, not like that. Hold it at the other end. There you go, good boy. Well, now run and pour all that right on the pile."

"And it'll catch fire?" He raised his funny, spattered face to me.

"It has no choice."

"Misha, come here," Marina said. "I have to wash your face."

"Come here yourself!"

"Hey, hold your horses," I said. "Give it to me. I'd better pour it myself."

"I'll wash my face." He nodded readily.

"No, that's not the problem, you know."

"It's not?" He frowned cautiously.

"It's dangerous. You could burn yourself. Do you like going to doctors?"

"No. Papa died from them."

I looked at Marina. She sighed and shook her head.

"Just give it here. You still don't know how to make magic fire."

"Magic fire?" Interest gleamed in his eyes. "How's that?"

"Very simple. Want me to show you?"

He handed me the container readily.

"So you've decided to spend the entire winter at the dacha?" I asked Marina five minutes later as I walked up on the front steps.

She looked at where Misha was jumping around the tall flame.

"He won't burn himself?"

"He shouldn't."

"I don't know." She sighed. "What choice do I have? I have almost no money. When he died, these men came and took away almost everything. They said he owed them a whole lot. So I gave up the apartment too."

"He had some kind of business at the market near the Budapest?"

"I went by there after the funeral."

She was silent for a moment.

"And so?"

"There were these strange people there. I was supposed to get at least the goods. He was selling something there. There had to be something left, after all. They told me to go away. They said they'd take Misha if I showed my face even once more."

"They were that tough?"

"I don't know. They said they would. That scared me."

"Had you ever seen them before?"

She furrowed her brow.

"One of them, on the short side, stopped by our place once. He brought money or something…"

"Do you remember his name?"

"No. I just remembered him because of his tattoo. Here, on his right arm, he had a sports car."

"A car?"

I was surprised.

"Well, yes. Very pretty. A Ferrari."

"How do you know it was a Ferrari?"

All of a sudden, she fell silent.

"You mean you've started to tell cars apart?"

"Matteo taught me," she said after a brief pause.

Now it was my turn to be embarrassed.

"Yeah?" I said. "Well, all right. And this tattoo…It's kind of strange…A car…"

"There are lots of parlors in Moscow now," she rushed in, happy we'd changed the subject. "They can tattoo anything you want. Not only that, all the tattoos are in color and very high quality. In principle, they are real artists."

We were silent for a minute.

"So how are you for money?" I finally said.

"I've got enough for now. At the building management office, I wrote that Misha and I were going to visit family. A boss there took pity on me. He and my father used to drink together. So I didn't have to pay for the apartment. I shut off the phone. If it weren't for the drop in the ruble, I would have had enough for a long time. We were saving for a new apartment. There's enough firewood brought in for the whole winter."

"Is everything you have in rubles?"

"My father hated dollars. A patriot."

"You should have exchanged them."

"Who knew it would all turn out like this?"

"Monsters," I said.

When we came out on the porch, Misha was still running around the fire.

"How is Seryozha doing?" Marina asked in a quiet voice.

"Fine."

"Sitting at his computer?"

"For days on end."

We fell silent again, not knowing what else to say.

"Maybe you'll stay for tea?" she said finally.

"No thanks. Some other time."

"You'll come by again?"

"I don't know."

"Do. We're all alone now."

"I don't know. I'd have to lie to Sergei."

"What did you tell him today?"

"I said I was going to the dentist."

"You mean your teeth hurt?"

"No. I had to think up something."

"You don't like lying?"

"No," I said. "I'm sick of it."

When I was already in the car, I watched her in my rearview mirror. She was standing on the porch bundled up in a large man's jacket. A gust of wind suddenly ruffled her hair. She raised her hand to fix it. Misha finally abandoned his fire and ran up to her, hugging her around the knees. She was hugging him with one arm and waving to me with the other, as if she knew I was watching her in the mirror.

I have to do something about that tattooed guy, I told myself.

To judge from everything, she didn't have that much time left.

---

The market by the Budapest was especially crowded those days. People were in a hurry to get rid of their rubles, which were swiftly losing value by the day. It made no sense to save them now. Anyone who couldn't spend them today would buy much less for them tomorrow. Savings were melting away in pockets like gray, smelly ice pulled out of a refrigerator. Only the totally broke were staying home, and those whose cash was lying in foreign bank accounts. Neither one had any need to fuss. The former had lost everything they had long ago. The latter had pocketed everything the former had lost. Therefore, it was the third force that was lounging around the markets, having yet to determine which to join, the former or the latter. This indecision made people nervous. It made them sick, angry, and ugly.

"I hope that whore Yeltsin croaks, and the same goes for his Chubais!" a gray-haired woman was shouting for the whole market to hear.

Her hair was escaping from her kerchief, her face was beet red, and she was threatening someone upstairs with her dry little fist and spitting every once in a while. The buyers didn't pay any special attention to her, they just glanced sullenly in her direction. The two guys wearing riot-police uniforms tried not to notice her.

They were talking up the girls in brightly colored jackets who kept blowing huge bubbles, popping them, and laughing loudly.

"I hope they screw each other good in that Kremlin of theirs! Pederasts!" The old woman would not stop. "They ate up my whole pension! I can't buy bread! They cut my grandson's leg off in Chechnya! A free wheelchair—they won't even give him that! Damned country! Fucking Russia!"

She choked on her shouting and finally fell silent. I tried to dash to the other end of the market as fast as I could.

"Buy some sweatpants." A woman of about forty tugged at my sleeve.

She was standing right by the fence, having hung her goods on nails. Some of her rags were lying in front of her on newspapers spread on the ground.

"I don't need sweatpants. I don't do sports."

"Then buy them for your girlfriend. It's a good present. Italian, excellent quality."

"Well, if they're Italian…"

"Ninety rubles. I'm practically giving them away."

"How much would that be in dollars?"

"You want to pay me in dollars?" The interest in her eyes intensified noticeably.

"What's the rate today?"

"You can't keep up with it now. It's different every day. People say it could fall back to seven rubles."

"Seven rubles? Hardly. Not everyone in the White House has cleaned up yet."

She looked where the old woman was clamoring so loudly, still swearing.

"What they've led people to!"

"You said it," I agreed. "If I give you ten dollars, can you help me with something?"

"For God's sake!" She even threw up her hands. "Of course I will. What do you want?"

"I want to find out about someone…Did you know Ilya Semyonich? He traded here."

"But he died!"

"I know. I'm interested in the people running his store now."

The woman frowned for a second and stared into my face.

"Are you from the FSB?"

"No." I actually laughed. "Where's that coming from?"

"Lots of people are interested in Sasha Mercedes now."

"Who's Sasha Mercedes?"

"You're sure you're not from the FSB?"

"I can show you ID."

"To you it's a joke! But I have to earn my living. I can't lose this spot. They've already driven me all the way to the edge. Buyers almost never get this far. And who's going to feed my girls? They're probably not coming from the FSB with a subsidy!"

"I don't work for the FSB. I can swear on the Quran."

"What, are you a Muslim?" She gave me a suspicious stare again.

"Of course not. I'm just joking."

"A creep...So where's your ten dollars?"

"Here, take it."

She examined the bill in the light, spat on it, and rubbed it between two fingers.

"The ink's not running?" I said.

"Basically, he's a snake, of course." She sighed, putting the bill away in the pocket of her gray raincoat.

"Who?" I was a little taken aback.

"Sasha Mercedes. Who else? You were asking about him, right? While Ilya Semyonich was alive, he behaved okay. What choice did he have? He'd only been at the market a week shy of a year. It's when he made himself all comfortable. He does what he pleases. He drives people out of their legitimate spots. I had my own stall at the very center of the market for three years. And now I'm standing by the fence. I should be grateful they didn't drive me out of the gates. You can't make a space for yourself there either because of those old women. Selling all kinds of nonsense."

"You mean he was afraid of Ilya Semyonich?"

"Everyone was afraid of Ilya Semyonich. You have to know the connections he had! Because of that, everything at the market went by the book. You pay for your spot and you stand there as much as you want. Now Sasha makes people pay by the hour. It comes out nearly triple. And anyone who can't pay that much gets driven to the fence. And now the dollar has taken a leap like a bat out of hell. I don't have any money to pay for my apartment and my older daughter's school."

"So this Sasha's taken over Ilya Semyonich's store now, right?"

"He's taken over everything here now. And it's not Sasha, it's Sasha Mercedes."

"That's a strange name. Why do they call him that?"

"Maybe you'll take this little sweater too?" she said artificially loudly, making an idiotic face. "I'll let it go for half price. You won't find one like it anywhere else."

"A little sweater?" I repeated, puzzled.

At that moment a disheveled man with a drunkard's face emerged from somewhere behind me.

"Stop by and see Sasha today," he grunted, addressing the frightened woman. "They told you yesterday. Why didn't you come?"

"I had to meet my daughter from school," she replied softly.

"You'd better stop by today," he repeated persistently. "People are expecting you."

"Let me wait on this customer!"

"Wait on him, wait on him." His glance slid over me quickly. "Just don't take too long."

"I'm so sick of them!" She said this in a fit of anger when the disheveled man had disappeared. "They keep coming after me."

"What do they want?"

"What do you think? Money, naturally. I wish that Sasha would croak! Him and his cars."

"What, he likes cars?"

"And how. That's why they call him Sasha Mercedes. He's plastered his whole store with posters and sits there like a pimple, admiring his pretty cars."

"So tell me, he doesn't have a tattoo of a sports car right here on his arm, does he?"

"Where doesn't he have them! If he could, he'd probably tattoo a car on his ass! Miserable idiot!"

"No, no. I'm interested in a tattoo right here, on his right arm."

"Yes, he has a tattoo there," she waved her hand irritably. "I wish he'd croak! There's no living at the market because of those cars of his. They held a race here recently. He shut down business for everyone for a whole day."

"What race?" I wondered.

"What race? The usual. They laid out a track between the rows, appointed a judge, and started racing their cars. They even invited famous actors. There's this one, you know, real tall. He used to be very famous. He was always in war movies. The uniform really suits him. Churbakov, I think. He has a lover, a famous singer. Plump and juicy. You might have seen her on television. I think her name's Lyuba. Yes, that's it, Lyuba. Her singing's more like a screeching cat."

"How did they ever drive the cars between the stalls?"

"They didn't have real cars."

"What do you mean not real?"

"Of course they're not real. How could they drive real cars here? You're very funny. They had models. Didn't I say that?"

She looked at me, amazed.

"No," I replied.

"Of course. Models. These little tiny cars. About the size of this box here. But they go just like real ones. They even use gasoline. And they're very loud."

"So they held races here?"

"Did they ever! Then they partied all night long. One actor drank so much, they say, he danced naked on the stalls."

"In this cold?"

"What do they care? I'm telling you, they're idiots!"

She jerked her shoulders, chilled, and looked at me inquiringly.

"Maybe you'll buy that little sweater after all? It's true, I'll give it to you for cheap."

---

It was three days before I could get to Marina at the dacha. Sergei wouldn't let me take a step away from him, so eventually I had to lie that I had a relative coming to see me from Irkutsk. I asked for time off until the end of the week, claiming my "uncle once-removed's" vulgarity and the fact that he would get lost in Moscow without a guide. The cops on the streets were shaking down out-of-towners worse and worse every day.

Driving up to the gate, I parked the car at the fence. The gate wasn't locked. I pushed the small door and started down the barely noticeable path toward the house. Before I'd taken a few steps, I realized Marina had visitors today. I could hear the sounds of lively conversation and snatches of music. From time to time there was laughter. I froze in place, trying to figure out whether I wanted to see her in this kind of situation, and whether it wouldn't be better to slink off right now, but at that moment little Misha jumped out from behind a currant bush.

"Let's go!" he exclaimed. "Marina waited for you the whole day yesterday."

Now I couldn't disappear.

When we came out from behind the bushes, I saw that Marina's visitors had spread out right there among the trees. They'd brought the large table from the porch and set it next to the porch, between two birches. Obviously, the conversation was very important. They didn't even notice our arrival. Only a minute later did Marina glance in my direction.

Seeing me, she smiled and waved, inviting me to sit down. The others continued arguing about something, paying me no attention whatsoever. As soon as I sat down on a free chair, Misha clambered into my lap.

There was an almost-empty bottle of Kindzmarauli on the table, a few glasses, a plate of cheese, and a fruit basket. There were still some grapes left. The dark-blue berries were covered with a velvety film. I reached out and pinched off one grape. The juice was amazingly sweet.

The long-haired young man sitting to my left was talking. "If you had put the energy you've spent chasing after money your whole life into something else, eventually you might have turned the world upside down."

Kind of by chance I overheard what he was saying and I suddenly thought he was saying interesting things. In any case, I'd never considered the problem from that point of view before. Who knows, maybe it's true, and we would all have been geniuses a long time ago. If we hadn't homed in so specifically on money, like now, for instance. Although, on the other hand, tell that to Chernomyrdin. Pudge-o would probably get a good laugh out of that one. One way or another, I started paying attention to their conversation.

"Then there's Nietzsche," a second guy, who was actually the one Longhair had been talking to, replied. "A philosopher...the greatest, the most famous...a man of tremendous intellect, he says in his writings that it's okay to make counterfeits."

"Did you ever even read Nietzsche?" Longhair grinned.

"Well...Dashenka was telling me. And I'm in the kind of position now where I can make all the counterfeits I want...

The day after tomorrow I have to pay three hundred and ten rubles…I've already got a hundred and thirty…"

He stuck his hand into his coat pocket, and suddenly his face changed.

"The money's gone!" He exhaled barely audibly. "I've lost the money!"

Everyone looked at him in alarm. He started feverishly patting all his pockets. His face was white as a sheet. I even thought I saw tears glittering in his eyes.

"Where's the money?" he muttered. "Where did it go?"

Everyone sitting at the table froze in tense anticipation. Even I started to worry. Though it had nothing to do with me. I'd never seen this guy before in my life.

"Here it is!" he finally shouted joyfully. "In the lining. I actually started sweating."

Everyone heaved a sigh of relief and exchanged looks. Total silence reigned at the table for a minute. We could hear the birds chirping in the bushes. Longhair took his empty glass from the table and twirled it aimlessly in the air. All of a sudden, the sound of an electric guitar being tuned came from the house. That's odd, I thought. They brought an amp along?

"What's taking Leonid so long?" the girl sitting directly opposite me suddenly spoke up. "What's he doing in town?"

I guess not everyone's here yet, I thought.

"The deal must not be done yet," Longhair responded, setting his glass down next to the bottle.

I was glad he did that. Because it seemed to me in another second he was going to drop it. Lousy juggler. He could juggle his own glasses at home. I can't say I was thrilled with these visitors. They were kind of strange. They were saying silly things. I should have slipped away at the very beginning.

"The musicians shouldn't have come." The girl sitting opposite me sighed again. "And really, none of us should even have gotten started on this...Oh well, that's all right..."

She smiled sadly and started humming something. A yellow birch leaf fluttered smoothly to the table.

At that moment, Marina took a pack of cards out of her jacket pocket and turned to the guy who was still sitting counting his money.

"Pick a card, any card."

"Okay," he said.

"Now shuffle the deck. Very good. Give it to me. *Ein, zwei, drei*! Now look. It's in your side pocket."

He immediately took a card out of his pocket and looked at her in amazement.

"Eight of spades, that's absolutely right! Imagine!"

Marina turned to Longhair.

"Tell me quickly, which card is on top?"

"What?" he stammered. "Uh...queen of spades."

"Yes!" Marina said, and she turned to me.

"Well? Which card is on top?"

"Ace of clubs," I said without thinking.

"Yes!"

She slapped her palm and the deck disappeared, as if it had dissolved into thin air.

"What fine weather today!" Marina said, smiling blissfully and pinching several grapes off the bunch at once.

"Where did you learn to do card tricks?" I asked.

To my amazement, suddenly, everyone around me broke out in friendly laughter. What did I say that was so funny, I wonder?

"We were just pulling your leg before," Marina said, laughing. "Don't be mad. It was just so entertaining. It's Chekhov."

"What Chekhov?"

"*The Cherry Orchard*. The very beginning of act three. Remember when they're sitting there waiting for news from town about who bought the orchard?"

"Chekhov?"

"Well, yes. Anton Chekhov."

"Yeah, yeah, I remember," I said. "The very beginning of act three. Sure."

"Then Lopakhin arrives and says he bought it."

"Lopakhin," I repeated. "Why are you doing things like this at the dacha?"

"We have to prepare for our graduation performance. The kids like to rehearse here. The forest, the fresh air."

"I get it."

"Ira here is playing Lyubov Andreyevna."

"Very nice," I said.

"And our Ramil is Petya Trofimov." Marina nodded toward Longhair.

"Petya is playing Ramil," I clarified.

"No, Ramil is playing Petya."

"Ah! I see. So he's not Ramil, he's Petya."

"Well, yes. Only the other way around."

"So, wait up. You've lost me completely, I think. Who's Petya? Who's Ramil?"

"It's all going to be fine," the guy who'd been searching for his money said. "My name's Boris Borisovich Simeonov-Pishchik."

"Stop pulling his leg." Marina started laughing again. "This is Ira, this is Ramil, and this is Igor."

Right then, one more person appeared on the porch.

"And this is Lopakhin," I said.

"Exactly," Longhair said, amazed. "How did you know?"

"You were the one who said he was supposed to come."

"Iron logic," the other responded.

"Boys," Marina broke in. "Stop teasing him. This is my good friend. His name is Mikhail."

"Good evening, good friend," the man on the porch said in a thick bass.

"His name is Mikhail," Longhair responded like an echo.

"The cherry orchard's been sold," "Lopakhin" said in the same bass voice.

"And this is our Repa." Marina smiled. "He has the prettiest voice in our class."

"I can say, 'I fell and did a push-up' two times lower than General Lebed."

"Liar." Longhair gestured dismissively. "Repa's always telling lies."

The man on the porch coughed, leaned on the railing, and in an absolutely incredible voice said, "Anyone who isn't going to do push-ups—finish him off!"

"Cool," I said. "Even Lebed can't do that."

"See?" Repa chuckled. "Listen to what these people tell you. These aren't some lousy newspaper critics."

"We're almost out of wine." Marina sighed with regret.

"Repa drank it all up," Longhair said.

"Why is he picking on me? He started back on the train."

"I have two bottles of Bordeaux in my car," I interjected.

"Red or white?" Repa asked quickly.

"Red."

"Marina, you really do have a very good friend. Why didn't you ever tell us about him before?" Longhair said.

"In the bag on the backseat," I managed to shout after him. "There's also some meat and greens, and ice cream in the large thermos."

Before very long it was totally dark. Marina brought a candle from the house, but the light, barely detectable gusts of wind made the unsteady flame tremble, and our light kept going out. Repa brought a glass jar, inside of which the candle burned as evenly and steadily as in a room.

"Now we have a little lamp," he intoned in his thick bass. "Anyone who doesn't like it can take two extra details." In that light, the wine in the glasses looked almost black. We chatted, ate ice cream, laughed, and took turns running after Misha's ball, which he would throw as far into the darkness past the trees as he could.

Lifting a branch of a currant bush in search of the ball, I happened to glance in the direction of Marina sitting with her friends. The glowing sphere emitted just enough light for me to see their faces. Everything else disappeared in the impenetrable darkness. On the black backdrop, the circle of smiling faces glowed, and there was nothing but them in the whole world. I froze, forgetting all about Misha's ball, as if I'd discovered something very important. These faces turned to one another glowed like pure gold. They kept turning, approaching, nodding, as if they were completely independent, as if they required no support and they could hover like that freely in the darkness, smiling at each other, nodding, occasionally disappearing for a moment and then once again lighting up out of nowhere in this golden glow.

"Thank you for coming," Marina said when all her friends were already sitting in my car. "Misha was asking about you all day yesterday."

"Misha?" I said.

"He likes it when you come."

"What about you?"

"Me?" She paused for a second. "I do too."

"You're not afraid to stay here alone?"

"We'll get used to it soon."

She huddled, chilly, under her jacket.

"It's getting cold," I said.

"That's all right, we'll fire up the stove right away."

Someone in the car rapped on the window.

"Look," Marina said, and she started to laugh.

I turned around. Longhaired Ramil had pressed his face to the glass, and his lips had smushed out like a black guy's. He crossed his eyes and kissed the window a couple of times with those outturned lips.

"You idiots," Marina said, laughing.

"Love!" Ramil shouted out in a muffled voice. "Love!"

"Driver," Repa intoned from the darkness. "Let's go. Or we'll put you on trial."

"Idiots," Marina repeated.

"I have three hundred bucks here," I said.

"Don't. I can't take it."

"Why?"

"I can't borrow it from you."

"From me in particular?"

"I can't take it, Misha."

"Driver," Repa intoned again. "What unit are you assigned to?"

"Get going," Marina said. "They aren't going to let us talk anyway. I'll explain everything to you later somehow."

In the darkness, I could barely see her face.

"Are you sure?"

"Yes, I'm sure. But thanks a lot anyway."

She got up on tiptoe, and a light, fleeting kiss slipped across my cheek.

"You're a wonder," she whispered.

# THE LYING YEAR

The next day I went off to pay Sasha Mercedes a visit. On my front seat was a magazine with a photograph of Schumacher on the cover. The racer was standing on a podium with a beaming face, pouring champagne for his public from a gigantic bottle. Sasha should snap at a photograph like this like a pike at a good piece of bait. All I had to do was just neatly hook him and then watch the fish's scales sparkle in the air.

My old friend wasn't in her former spot. She probably hadn't been able to withstand the burden of Sasha's taxes after all. What can you do? We're all on our own. At least I was able to help her a little with those ten bucks. I hope they put her in good stead.

I took a stroll between the stalls and almost immediately ran into Ilya Semyonich's old store. I never had the slightest doubt. All the windows were plastered with posters, each one featuring some team's fireball. This Sasha was obviously wild about Formula 1. My little mag should work like a charm. If only Schumacher knew what his photograph could be good for.

As soon as I walked inside, an amazingly familiar face looked at me from behind the counter. I'd met this person somewhere, but where and under what circumstances I just couldn't recall that quickly.

"Listen, man," the face said. "I've seen you somewhere before."

"Same here," I replied.

"Your mug is really familiar."

"Meaning?"

"You didn't serve at Borzya, did you?"

"Where?"

"Chitinsk province."

"No. I definitely didn't serve there."

"Damn if I can remember!" he cursed. "It's spinning right there in my head! Maybe we were both in trauma surgery this summer? First City Hospital, eh?"

"No. I was in a different hospital. But in trauma surgery too."

"You're sure it wasn't First City?"

"A hundred percent."

"Damn! Where have I seen you? Maybe at Nikolai Nikolaevich's?"

"Of course not. I don't even know who Nikolai Nikolaevich is."

"Wait!" His face suddenly lit up. "Do you have a car?"

"Yes."

"Where is it?"

"In the parking lot by the market entrance."

"Let's go!"

He stood up behind the counter.

"Where?"

"To look at your car."

"What for?"

"Let's go, I'm telling you. We'll sort this out there. Hey, Kirya!" he shouted in the direction of the half-open back door. "Quit picking your nose and come here. Do a little work."

Skinhead Kirya appeared from the shed. He glowered at me and plopped down on the chair behind the counter. His leather jacket bulged suspiciously around the waist.

"You and I are going to clear this up right now," my "old friend" said. "Let's go take a look at your wheels…"

As soon as we were near the car he said, "I remember! A '92 Land Rover. The special safari model. Improved transmission. I think the upholstery above the driver's seat is a little beat up."

I was so surprised, I didn't know what to say. I still couldn't remember this guy.

"You are Mikhail, right?"

"Well, yeah...only..."

"We had a party for you six months ago when you were going into the army. That's when I broke my leg. So you managed to dodge after all?"

My head just started spinning. Suddenly I realized I was talking to the same discharged guy responsible for the mutilation debacle at the party to see off my friends in the spring.

"Did you dodge it?" he repeated, looking into my face.

"Well, no...you know...It wasn't me they were seeing off then."

"It wasn't?" He slapped the hood and guffawed. "At the time I actually thought, too bad about this kid. He's going to have to give up those wheels for two years. You're sure it wasn't for you?"

"No, it wasn't."

"Fuck a duck. I guess I got good and tanked that time. I had no fucking idea. Remember how I broke my leg?"

"Yes."

"Freaks! Though it was still too bad about those kids. Did you hear what happened to Petrovich?"

"No. I...I was away for a while."

"A little while ago, I stopped by to see his mama. She's sitting there sobbing. I say, 'What's up?' And she says to me, she says, 'The Chechens took Petrovich.' Petrovich was taken captive. Go figure, shit, a prisoner of the Caucasus."

"You mean he was serving in Chechnya?"

"Of course not, somewhere in Russia. But it's close to there, in the south. Go figure, the Chechens are getting pretty cheeky. Now Berezovsky's gone to buy him back. They said so on the TV news yesterday. There are a helluva lot of our guys there now. And those goats are just starting to scratch."

"But what about his mother?"

"What about his mother? She's sitting there crying. She's afraid they're going to cut off his balls. 'I'll never see my grandchildren,' she says. Go figure, Petrovich captive."

"Gee," I said. "Well, and how about you? Did your leg heal?"

"Yeah, seems okay now. It didn't mend right. They kept tightening and tightening the Ilizarov frame. And then another pin got infected. It's shit, basically."

"Boy, you had no luck."

"Depends on how you look at it."

"Meaning?"

"I got to know some good people there."

"Nikolai Nikolaevich?"

He looked at me suspiciously.

"What, you mean you know him?"

"No. You were the one who brought him up ten minutes ago."

"Ah! Well, yeah. When did I say that?"

"When you were trying to remember where you'd seen me."

"Yeah? What does Nikolai Nikolaevich have to do with that?"

"How the hell would I know? You asked whether maybe we'd met at Nikolai Nikolaevich's."

He shook his head thoughtfully.

"Hey, what a man! A real dude. That's who we should have for president. He could figure out all this crap. If it weren't for him, I'd be shoveling shit at a gas station right now."

"You used to work at a gas station?"

"Well, yeah. I was making okay money, of course, but not what I am here at the market. This is serious cash. No fuss, no muss, just serious cabbage. Greenbacks, and always like clockwork."

"So how'd you meet him?"

"We were in the same ward. I had the frame on my left leg, and he had one on his right. I diagnosed what was wrong with his car without leaving the hospital."

"How's that?"

"His Volvo'd been on the fritz for a whole month. He was complaining that his mechanics couldn't do a fucking thing. So I asked him a few questions and figured it all out just like that. I explained it to him, but he couldn't remember it either. Then I told his guys everything on his cell, what was what. They had it fixed the next day. After that, Nikolai Nikolaevich offered me a new job."

"Here at the market?"

"Uh-huh. 'That's enough horsing around,' he says. 'Those dickheads can go work for somebody else. A man should only work for himself,' he says."

"Ain't that the truth."

"So as soon as they let me out, I moved over here. And I told everyone at the gas station to go fuck themselves. You don't know how sick I was of them."

"Sasha!" someone shouted from the market gates.

He turned and waved in that direction.

"Coming! They can't do a fucking thing without me!... Well, that's it." He turned toward me again and held out his hand. "Or do you want me to hire you on?"

"I'll think about it."

He had a neat Ferrari tattooed on his arm.

"Like it?" he said, noticing my glance. "Classy needlework. I did it after the hospital. Well, so long! Stop by when you make up your mind."

I stood and watched him walk away until he turned around.

"Listen!" he shouted. "Why were you in the ER?"

"Oh, nothing"—I waved my hand in reply—"a thug's bullet."

When he disappeared behind the market gates, I threw the magazine with Schumacher's picture into a trash can.

---

Now I started visiting Marina at the dacha nearly every day. After the departure of my "Irkutsk relative," the building management "suddenly decided to replace all the pipes in my building," and naturally, that required my presence. After that, I had to take serious care of my wound, because in driving through Moscow, I'd found a "famous psychic" who could heal the effects of the most serious traumas with just one touch. Naturally, I couldn't pass up that chance. Therefore, Sergei had to do without my company for a few more days. After that, I would get away episodically on less convincing grounds, but one way or another I always had to tell some lie. Lying had become an inalienable part of my life once again. What other choice did I have? I couldn't say I was going to see Marina. Seryozha was hardly going to take that the right way. To say nothing of Pavel Petrovich.

It was nice at the dacha. At first I really didn't like the fact that Marina's classmates were always hanging around, but in time I got used to them, and when they didn't come I actually missed them. Usually it was Repa and long-haired

Ramil, whom I met on my second visit. Sometimes there were others, but those two came nearly every day. They had to rehearse their show, and these two were in all the same scenes as Marina. In time I guessed they were coming to the dacha because of her. Not in the sense that they had anything going on with her but that they understood her situation. It was hard for her to go to Moscow every day because of little Misha, and since Ilya Semyonich's death, money matters were less than ideal. I'd tried to slip her a few dollars a couple of times, but she was like a stone wall.

"We still have lots of potatoes," she said, smiling, and I shoved my money into my back pocket.

In short, I liked those two. They obviously had no intention of abandoning Marina in her time of need.

By all accounts, they liked me too. At least, they liked my SUV. If I might have had doubts as far as I went, I was absolutely confident of their feelings for my car.

"Some classy wheels you've got," Ramil would say as he sprawled out on the backseat.

"A fine machine," Repa would intone approvingly.

"What would we do without you?" Ramil said.

"You'd take the train," I smiled in reply.

"So what do you do basically?"

"Meaning?"

"Hey, lay off him," Repa intoned. "You should be happy the man is helping us out."

"I didn't mean anything, I was just wondering in principle."

"You can stick your principles you know where."

"You are a rude Repa. Unsympathetic."

"That's just my voice. In fact, I'm white and fluffy and I have a cute tail."

"It's all very simple." I laughed. "I don't have to work. I'm Chernomyrdin's illegitimate son."

"That means you and I are brothers," Ramil exclaimed. "Do you have a birthmark right here?"

In the evenings, when they were winding down rehearsals, we would drink tea on the porch. Marina would brew it with currant leaf, and we would gab for a long time, not getting up from the table until the sun had set behind the treetops. After sunset, the forest cooled off, and then there was nothing nicer in the world than holding a hot cup of tea. Nights were pretty chilly already, so before leaving every evening, we conscientiously stoked the stove.

"Otherwise when we come tomorrow," Ramil would say, "you'll be all huddled up here."

"I know how to make a fire too."

"I don't know, I don't know. In fact, this really calls for a professional. See how the flame is moving from this log to the others? See how it's spreading? You think that happened all by itself? No, my dear. Years of intensive training plus a gold medal first degree in young firefighter training courses."

"You are the most incredible windbag." Marina laughed. "Hurry up. Mikhail's been waiting for you for fifteen minutes."

"It's all good," I replied. "I'm in no hurry to get anywhere."

"I'm not a windbag," Ramil said. "I'm smart, talented, and charming."

In the beginning, their manner surprised me, but gradually I got used to it. Their very profession demanded that they stand out from others. What would have been considered boasting in a normal person, or even maybe insolence, among these actors passed as "charming." At times I found their jokes jarring, but I would look at Marina and she would signal to me with her eyes just to ignore it.

Soon after, the grass started being covered with frost in the mornings. It was still green, but when I would arrive a little earlier, a neat white film lay silver on it. Ramil called it radioactive sludge. We didn't even notice when the first snow fell. Generally in the fall, everything happens imperceptibly.

"That's a heap of snow," Repa said one day as he walked onto the porch, knocking his boots on the threshold. "Great. The first snowfall, and so much at once."

"The first? Have you turned stupid or something?" Ramil responded slowly, shutting the stove door and turning his red face around. "There was snow last week, and on the second too."

"What's today?"

"Hello! Today's the fourth."

"Of November?"

"He woke up! There's almost no time left till the premiere, and you're never going to memorize your part."

"Let's go horseback riding," Marina put in. "In the snow, you know, it's pretty."

"Let's go," Ramil exclaimed. "I'm sick of this Chekhov!"

"I don't know," Repa intoned. "I really do need to learn my part. Another ten pages...But oh well, I've got nothing against it."

They all looked at me.

"I'll give you a ride, of course," I said. "But...I'm never getting on a horse again."

"Why 'again'?" Ramil asked.

―――

When we got to the place I had rather conflicting memories of, the snow had covered virtually everything. And it was still falling.

"It's like a fairy tale," Marina said, catching the large, slow flakes in her hands.

"What did I tell you," Repa rumbled.

"You don't have to tell us anything," Ramil responded. "You should have stayed home and learned your lines."

"Listen, why is it I have so much trouble memorizing parts?" Repa sighed.

"Do you know the weird thing he did at the last show?" Ramil turned to me.

"All right already," Repa boomed. "Other people's ad libs have been worse."

"He came out in the middle of the stage and instead of saying, 'If anyone knows what the Russian heart is, I do,' he up and blurted, 'If anyone knows what the Russian fart is, I do.' Go figure! And there was a whole mess of reporters there. They were marking the master's anniversary that day. Everyone starts guffawing, but Repa just stands there and doesn't leave. His eyes are wide as saucers, and he's frozen in the one spot."

"I'm telling you, I didn't notice I'd slipped."

"And you can imagine the voice he said it in!" Ramil was still laughing. "He rolled it out through the whole hall in that bass voice…Everyone got gooseflesh."

"That's enough," Marina said, launching a snowball at Ramil. "Let's go to the horses before the snow melts."

The whole forest around the stables was sprinkled with snow. We were walking down a barely discernible path, through a shroud of swirling flakes dropping smoothly to our shoulders.

"And most of all, not a bit of wind," Ramil said, leaning over to scoop up a handful of snow. "I've loved eating it since I was a kid."

"You shouldn't eat snow," Misha, who was scurrying around us back and forth like a puppy dog, informed him.

"My mama told me that too." Ramil nodded. "But I ate it anyway. Want to try?"

"Yes," Misha said.

"Don't even think of it," Marina said. "I'll make you take pills."

"Blah." Misha made a face and fell backward in the snow.

"Okay, up you go, you're all wet and dirty as it is."

Their voices reached me as if through cotton wool. The snow muffled all sounds, filling the forest with silence. The stables, the trees, the figures of my companions—everything had plunged into this white, wordless mass that was slipping slowly, from the top down, as if the sky had decided to descend to earth and spread over it like an enormous, glowing blanket. I even thought I heard the snowflakes rustling as they dropped onto the pines, us, the roof of the long wooden house—everything.

"Don't lag behind," Marina shouted to me, turning around nearly at the stable door. "You don't have to ride if you don't want to. I can go alone."

"Hey, why alone?" Ramil replied.

"No, no, it's all right," I said. "My head just started spinning for some reason."

"It's the fresh air," he said authoritatively. "You need to go back to the car and breathe some exhaust. You'll feel better right away."

Actually, he shouldn't have tried to put a brave face on things. It quickly became clear that he had a complicated relationship with horses too. If I was able to stay on the last time for nearly half an hour, his troubles started the very first minute. The horse assigned him by the stable's crafty residents immediately refused to recognize his right to sit on its back. I understood perfectly. When some long-haired Tatar wants to sit on your neck, your head practically, a few doubts can't help but immediately arise. The animal spun in place, threw darting glances, wheezed, and basically did everything it could to express its disapproval. It was clear at first glance how little this whole plan suited him. Naive Ramil thought this would pass quickly and the horse would get used to him. But I knew what lay in store. I was familiar with the ways of the local beasts.

Nevertheless, the stubborn Tatar continued to hop around the stallion on his left leg, while trying at the same time to lift his right as high as possible. Occasionally, he would manage to lift it over his own head, but that lasted literally a fraction of a second, not enough to get him in the saddle. In any case, the horse did not find these attempts altogether convincing. After five minutes of this furious ballet, we were simply expiring from laughter, but Ramil would not give up. His face was red and his hair had fanned out in a wave, sometimes covering nearly the entire back of the now obviously frightened stallion. Who knows, it may actually have been a very young horse. Then I understood it doubly. Who wouldn't be scared in its place? You should have seen that Ramil's eyes. He was plain crazed. A little bit longer and he might well have bit the poor horsey. In any case, the snow kept clumping around the pair.

Looking at them, Repa said that he was probably just going to breathe the air and he wasn't in the mood for horseback riding today. Barely catching my breath from laughter, I told him he had made a wise decision. Marina called us all fools and quickly leaped onto her white horse. By this time, Ramil had made enough progress that he had started appearing above the battle-weary horse's croup. It had obviously let down its guard, and the frantic Tatar was almost there. In breaks between fits of wild laughter, Repa and I started cheering our comrade on in discordant voices. Soon after, we could no longer stand up, and we fell right in the snow, one after the other, doubled up with laughter. Then Misha joined our little pile-on. He was utterly happy.

Finally, by some miracle, Ramil managed to stay on. The horse froze for a moment, dumbfounded by its defeat. We held our breath, and Ramil looked down on us triumphantly with a look that gave me gooseflesh. Genghis Khan at the Battle of Poltava. At that moment, the horse obviously recovered and made an imperceptible sideways movement, as if it were planning to fall on its back. Ramil waved his arms awkwardly and started slipping to the left, hidden from our eyes behind the brown croup. The last thing we saw were his eyes. They were the eyes of an angry but very distraught person.

Eventually we decided not to leave our comrade up a creek, especially since he obviously had no intention of giving up. We got him back on his feet, brushed the snow off him, and promised we would hold the damn beast from both sides until Ramil got his wish and was on its back. While we were conducting all these negotiations, the horse was watching us carefully with its big, shining eyes, obviously guessing that we were readying another dirty trick for him. Sometimes I am amazed how intelligent different creatures can be. And I don't mean just horses.

Basically, we stole up to the stallion from either side and caught him by the reins coming from his mouth. Now he couldn't twist his head like before. True, he still had his rear end at his disposal. The branch office of its horse organism. And right then was when he decided to give us no quarter.

Or rather, not us, but once again, stubborn Ramil. No matter what side the Tatar tried to approach from, each time he came up against the horse's backside and a pair of legs so powerful that one kick from them could bump off a platoon of tough paratroopers, to say nothing of one subtle, long-haired actor.

Nevertheless, nature ultimately won out. The generations of nomads slumbering in the blood of this crazed Ramil rose from their slumber. His face was distorted by a horrible grimace. He ran about five meters away from the horse, scooped up a big handful of snow, stuck it under his jacket, and howled as if someone were knifing him. The horse went noticeably on its guard, but it was all over. Ramil bent low over the ground and ran toward it with strange, hopping steps. Never in my life had I seen anyone moving across the earth in this manner. One step shy of his goal, Ramil soared high into the air like a rocket. Actually, not a rocket so much as a comet because his hair looked like an ion tail, fanning out behind him like a black ribbon. I even had time to think that this could be a fresh idea for a Head & Shoulders commercial.

While Ramil was airborne, our poor horse was standing calmly, not expecting any kind of trick. However, the moment the Tatar was about to drop down on his back like a wild cat, it reared, easily tearing a startled Repa and me off the ground. I was pierced with a pain as if someone had shot me in the collarbone again. I'd never suspected that horses could be that powerful. Hanging in the air over the snowy field, we both let go of the infuriated animal. At the same time, naturally, we tried to jump back as far as we could. Its front hooves whistled over our heads like two lightning bolts.

In the next moment, the freed horse took a head-spinning leap, trying to rid itself of Ramil, who was clutching its mane.

There was no frightening the Tatar now, though. His blood was seething, leaving no room for normal human fear. He shouted something in a savage voice and struck the horse on the head. Eventually the horse started wheezing and jumped a low fence. Thrusting its back legs, it raced toward the distant forest. A minute later, Ramil's receding shout reached us. It reminded me personally of the farewell song of departing cranes. My heart actually sank from sadness.

"Let's hope he comes back," Repa said, gasping.

"We should call an ambulance," I said, rubbing my collarbone. "I wonder where there's a telephone in this stable."

---

Marina said there was no need to call anyone and that she'd simply go find Ramil on his runaway horse.

"True, I need someone to go with me. I could be searching for him for a long time alone. Who knows where he galloped off to."

Repa and I looked at each other. I read cold hatred for horses in his eyes. He obviously read the same in mine.

"I'll go out with you, of course," I said. "Only…on foot."

"On foot?"

"Well, yeah. I'll run alongside your horse…Listen, you think maybe the SUV can get through there somehow?"

"You were there this spring."

"Was I ever," I sighed.

When I recalled that excursion, my ribs actually seemed to start throbbing.

"You and I are going to look like two idiots," she said.

"That's vastly preferable to looking like one idiot and one corpse."

"And what am I supposed to do?" Repa boomed, shaking the snow from his pockets.

"Watch the little one," Marina said. "God forbid he should run away somewhere."

"I'm going to run away!" Misha exclaimed, curling into a snowy heap. "I'm going to run away to the forest too."

"Just you try," she threatened. "I'll call Podzadovsky immediately."

"Who's that?" I asked.

"Let's go. There's no time now. I'll explain later."

We found Ramil almost immediately. He was sitting under a fir, looking at us with sad eyes.

"Well, how was it?" I said.

He shook his head gloomily in reply.

"It should be shot."

"My, my. I said the very same thing this spring."

"What, you mean you already tried?"

"I tried riding, but pretty soon I may try shooting."

"Cut that out," Marina broke in. "Where did he gallop off to?"

"I'm not so bad, thanks, it's nothing," said Ramil, rising with a groan. "Meanwhile, I could easily have been smashed up."

"But you aren't worth a few thousand dollars."

"What, he's worth that much?"

"Where did he gallop off to?"

"Thataway." Ramil waved straight into the thicket.

"Good." Marina calmed down right away. "He can't get anywhere from there. Mikhail and I will go and lead him out, and you go back. Can you get there, or should I give you a ride?"

"Not for anything in the world."

"Right answer," I said. "This spring she asked me the same thing."

"Are you coming or not?" Marina hurried me along.

"Coming, coming! Let's show some concern for the injured."

"It's his own fault. He shouldn't have made the horse so nervous."

"I made it nervous?" Ramil's voice caught out of indignation.

"Let's go," she shouted, and she turned her mare toward the forest.

"Don't be angry," I told him. "Women and horses have a lot in common, in general."

"What were you and he talking about?" she asked when I came up closer to her.

"Nothing."

"Just don't lie to me, please."

"I had no intention of lying."

Soon after, she dismounted and led her horse by the bridle. I walked alongside, watching her out of the corner of my eye. The snow had nearly stopped falling.

"Lately you've been visiting us less often," she said unexpectedly.

I was so surprised I didn't even answer right away.

"And Misha misses you."

"Less often?" I finally said. "I come by nearly every day."

"Really?" She stopped for a minute and fixed something there on her horse. "Actually, it doesn't matter. Remember this spot?"

"Is this it specifically?"

"Yes."

"Well, what can I tell you…I remember the forest in principle, but as to this spot exactly…Everything here's different now…It's been six months…"

"Over there is where you fell." She pointed ahead and a little to the right.

"Where?"

"Over there, by that tree. See? Next to the big bush?"

And suddenly I really did recognize it.

"Exactly! Great, the very same tree. What a memory you've got!"

"And then we came back down that road."

"I remember," I said. "You were wearing a white sweater that day."

"I was?" She shrugged. "I don't remember."

We walked for a minute in silence, listening to the snow creak.

Then, suddenly, we both began simultaneously: "Remember…?" and burst out laughing.

"What were you going to ask?" she said.

"No, you first."

"Oh, I…It's nothing important…"

"No, no, go ahead. You started first."

"I was just going to…No! I can't like this."

"Finish up. First you say what you were going to ask, and then I will."

"Fine." She slapped her horse's flank and smiled. "I was planning to ask you about that kiss…"

"That kiss? What kiss? I don't seem to remember."

"Misha!" She scooped up a handful of snow from the ground and launched it at me. The snow flew apart in the air like a wide veil and slowly settled without flying even half a meter.

"What kiss, I'm telling you? The first or the second?"

She waved her hand at me, turned, and walked on. I had to pick up the pace to catch up. And that horse was constantly nudging us toward the trees. I nearly poked my eyes out before I caught up.

"What were you thinking about then?"

"Me? I was thinking about how to kiss you."

"Stop it."

"No, it's true. You were so classy in your white sweater."

"I had no such sweater! Where did you come up with that?"

"Nowhere. You were wearing it that day. You can believe me."

"Why is that?"

"Why is what?"

"Why should I believe you?"

"Because I remember everything."

"Everything?"

"Every minute."

"Impossible." She stopped and brushed the snow dust off my face.

"Why impossible? It's the truth. If you like you can test me."

She furrowed her brow intently.

"What did I have on my head?"

"Nothing. You didn't wear anything. There was a light frost that day, but you forgot to put on a hat. Everyone thought winter was over already."

"Is that right? I don't remember."

"You'd taken a test in dance, and I picked you up at the institute. Later, we talked about homosexuals."

She looked surprised.

"Then we stopped by for Misha and headed here. But the road had iced over a little, and it took us a pretty long time to walk it. That's why your ears froze."

"Fabulous," she said. "What a memory you've got."

"On the other hand, I didn't remember the spot where I fell."

"And then?"

"And then we drank hot coffee and it was good."

"And after that?"

"I had problems with Ryzhik."

"You even remember its name."

"There are things you don't forget. Try it. Tell Ramil what his stallion was called today and then check again in fifteen years."

"You think?"

"Even ten."

"Fine, and what happened afterward?"

"Then I fell and you kissed me."

"Wait a second." She started laughing and shook her finger at me. "You were the one who kissed me."

"Me?"

"Who else? You attacked me like an animal. I thought you'd decided to rape me."

"I don't rape girls in white sweaters."

"Are you positive it was a white sweater specifically?"

"A hundred percent. Never in my life had I seen a sweater look so sexy."

"There, you see?" She started laughing again. "You admit it yourself you were preoccupied."

"Maybe," I said. "But then you kissed me."

"Me?"

"Who else? You leaned over and kissed me."

"Well, that must have happened by accident somehow."

"By accident my ass. You know, you looked so serious."

"Serious how?"

Her look suddenly changed.

"Just like now," I said.

She started fixing something on her horse again.

"Look!" I pointed toward the snow-dusted bushes. "There's our horse."

It was calmly standing in one place, shifting from leg to leg and jingling its bridle.

"Now we've found it," I said.

She took a step toward me. I looked at her without stirring.

"You looked like this then too," she said, and her eyes were suddenly right next to mine. "Remember?"

"No," I managed to whisper.

"Liar."

She pressed up to my lips so hard, my head started spinning. Another second and we would have fallen.

---

The next few days Ramil had to laugh off our endless allusions to his adventure.

"When I saw you on that horse," Repa said, "I immediately thought, 'Wow, look how he's seated! He fits like a glove!' You don't happen to have any cavalrymen relatives, do you? There is definitely something about you."

"Okay, okay." Ramil shrugged. "Have your fun. It's your big day."

"His grandmother must have been a cavalryman," someone else chimed in.

"Yeah, yeah," Ramil agreed. "She served in Budyonny's army. As a horse. By the way, I didn't see you there with us in the forest. So you can relax."

"But I can picture it all so vividly. It's as if you were standing right in front of me. Could she have been a horseback rider in the circus?"

"I'll tell you a secret, boys. I'm a horseman by nature, in general."

This went on for rather a long time. They tortured him literally from morning to night. His only respite was during rehearsals.

During those hours, little Misha and I had absolutely nothing to do, so we usually sat somewhere in a corner. I didn't understand much about all this theater of theirs, but I had nothing else to do. So we waited calmly for rehearsal to be over so we could do something interesting. Actually, our actors weren't crazy about these "rehearsals" of theirs either. They argued a lot, sometimes angrily. They would call each other names that normal people might easily rearrange your face over. For some reason, though, they never took offense. First they would shout in shrill voices, they might throw whatever was at hand at someone, and then they would calmly drink tea on the porch and laugh at each other. I personally found it hard to accept these people's ways.

All one of them had to do was say, "Chekhov meant to say this," for someone else to respond, "Up yours!" "Why is that?" the first would ask, and immediately get an answer: "Because he wasn't an idiot like you!" They could argue that way for a very long time, but the argument almost always ended with the same conclusion, that Chekhov was a genius and that "he meant each and every word."

Honestly, I didn't always agree with them. Not that Chekhov didn't mean each and every word, but that he was this great genius. In fact, when they weren't arguing or discussing Bruce Willis and Demi Moore's divorce, I tried as hard as I could to follow what was going on in this play of theirs. I made a very honest try. So honest that I once even

# THE LYING YEAR

asked Repa for his script. But that didn't do anything. I took the script to see what it was like in Chekhov, but everything in the play was exactly like what they were doing. That is, there was nothing there.

They paced from corner to corner with bored faces and recited long monologues that almost always put little Misha to sleep. I noticed you could judge confidently what was good and what was bad based on his reaction. For instance, when someone brought a Mozart CD, Misha jumped around the boom box like a monkey. Beethoven was a big hit with him. Vivaldi made him sit quiet as a mouse. Elvis Presley turned him into a real devil. He would rock back and forth on his little legs, throw his head back, and make incredible movements. We would all gather around him and laugh for a good fifteen minutes. That was not to be missed.

But Chekhov's play as performed by my new friends was almost completely to be missed.

They kept pacing with bored faces, sitting in chairs, and looking at each other and up at the ceiling. Each time they looked at the ceiling there was a long pause, and then someone would always say, "Genius," and they would repeat that like windup toys: "Genius! Simply genius! Chekhov was a genius!" Evidently they liked it when they were able to be silent that way.

But then this Chekhov didn't have to write any words at all. They could have come out on stage, not said anything for a while, and gone their separate ways. Now that would have been genius.

The biggest scream started when it came around to Ramil's turn. He was playing a natural-born dolt. It took everything I had to keep from bursting out laughing when he would take to showing everyone about how "mankind is moving forward, perfecting its powers." Genius definitely had to have taken hold of Chekhov there for him to write a part like that. Meanwhile, all the other characters looked more and more bored, but they stared intently at his mouth. They had to know when he was going to stop. He pushed hard at them about people who "call themselves intelligentsia, speak familiarly to their servant, spout philosophy, and meanwhile, right in front of them all, the workers are eating terribly, sleeping without pillows, thirty or forty in a single room, and there are bedbugs, stench, damp, and moral turpitude everywhere." What got me most was his "workers sleeping without pillows." That was great. That hit the nail on the head.

Naturally, though, Misha and I always livened up as soon as our Marina came out. She had this bizarre part. Bizarre, but very funny. She always spoke with a German accent, kept doing tricks, and ate cucumbers nonstop. Even Chekhov probably had no idea why she kept eating cucumbers. He must have had her eat the first thing that came to mind. Maybe he was rinsing himself a cucumber right then. But somehow, it was zany.

What I liked best about her part was the place at the beginning of the second act where she talks about her parents. Each time she started that short monologue, I felt so sorry for her that I had a hard time looking in her direction. I had to turn away and tell myself it was only a play that had just turned a hundred years old. I have to admit that in this instance Chekhov hit a bull's-eye. As if he in fact knew everything about Marina.

She started out by recalling her childhood with a smile and how "her father and dear mama would go from market to market and put on shows, very good ones." But at the last moment, a shadow would cross her face, and she would lower her eyes and say that her "dear papa and dear mama" were now dead.

I can't say I was a great friend of Ilya Semyonich, but in those moments I felt her loneliness amazingly keenly. In that scene Marina didn't even have to act. The words Chekhov wrote then had so much of her in them that they came out perfectly naturally. They sounded as sad as a last sigh, and a chill ran down my spine each time.

Then she would drop her head even lower and say in a dull voice: "I wish I had someone to talk to, but there is no one...I have no one." One time she started crying at that point, and Misha slipped off my lap, ran toward her, tripped on the way, fell between the chairs, jumped up, and wrapped both arms around her legs, with the same tears as hers. They stood there like that, embracing, and weeping, and we didn't know what to do, so we sat with serious faces, trying not to look at each other.

Otherwise, though, she had a very funny part. Just as funny as Epikhodov's. He said sad things sometimes too, but more often he was just hilarious. He would call the guitar a mandolin, talk about the cockroaches in his kvass and the spiderwebs on his chest, sing songs, and carry on in general. I liked those two parts in the show. At least I understood them.

The postrehearsal discussions were a headache. Sometimes they would prevail upon me for my opinion. They were interested in a "fresh, impartial view." I kept making excuses, but sometimes they could be very persistent.

"Well, how do you like it?" one of them would ask.

Not always someone I liked.

"Quite topical," I would say. "Lifelike. Not enough sex, though. Basically, I don't get what they all want."

"Not enough? There isn't supposed to be any sex in this. This is a classic."

"That's what I'm saying. There's no sex."

"And so?"

"I don't know. It just doesn't grab me. What's the point of them getting together then? They aren't going to a job."

"What, you mean to say *The Cherry Orchard* is dated?"

"I mean to say I don't understand why they need all this."

"Wait, I'll explain it all to you right now…"

And that person would launch into long discourses on the deeply poetic nature of Russian plotless drama, the brilliance of the psychoanalysis, and things like that, and I would watch Marina, who was changing Misha's clothes because he'd been playing in the dust, crawling under the bed. I watched him lift his clumsy, pudgy little arms over his head and her turn him around and tickle his tummy, and him squeeze his elbows in, giggling, trying to get away from her. In those moments, I could easily have endured the most idiotic chatter. I just nodded and looked off into space.

"Yes, yes, of course," I said in a monotone.

---

Sometimes, though, Misha was simply unbearable.

"Eat, or I'll call Podzadovsky," Marina would say in an irritable tone of voice.

"I'm not going to eat this clay!" Misha would shout back. "Eat it yourself!"

"It's not clay, it's mashed potatoes"—and she did her honest best to control herself.

"Clay! Clay! I hate clay! I want sausage!"

"I'm going to box your ears!" she finally broke down. "I'm not even going to call Podzadovsky."

"There is no Podzadovsky!" Misha kept shouting. "There isn't! And there's no Father Frost! You're always lying! I want sausage! I'm sick of clay!"

"Now you be quiet!" she shouted and finally boxed his ears.

Misha ran from the table and hid somewhere in the attic, while Marina sat in the kitchen, wiping away her tears. I didn't really understood how you were supposed to deal with small children, but in this situation I sensed that even grown young women needed help. To be honest, I felt sorry for them both.

"Stop it, what's the point of crying now?"

"I'm a fool. A stupid fool. He's so little."

"It's not so terrible."

"He doesn't understand. And I hit him. I got angry, as if it were all his fault. Lord, I'm so ashamed."

"Everything's going to be fine."

"Last night he asked me, 'Are we going to be much longer without a papa?' "

"Stop torturing yourself. He's asking for it sometimes."

"He's little."

"That's true," I agreed. "But who's this Podzadovsky? You mentioned him back in the forest."

"Podzadovsky?" She wiped her tears for the last time. "That's something Papa dreamed up a long time ago. When I was little. If I was naughty, he always said he had this friend who came to see disobedient children and punish them instead of their parents. It wasn't until later that I realized Podzadovsky wasn't a name at all. It's from *pod zad*—on your butt. Get it? Mama was still alive then."

Finally, she smiled, but the sadness in her eyes remained.

"Nothing is working out for me. Since his death nothing seems to be going right. Money vanishes like the wind. Whether I'm thrifty or not. Pretty soon I won't have enough for bread. We really are sick of potatoes. What can I do? Maybe I should sell the dacha."

She sighed deeply and her face became somber.

"Like in your show," I said.

"What?" She looked at me uncomprehendingly.

"In Chekhov. They're thinking about selling the orchard there too."

"Ah," she said, and she dropped her head again. "That show comes at the wrong time too. I have no interest in a diploma now. Oh, why did he die?"

"Sure you won't borrow a couple of hundred from me?" I cautiously asked my daily question.

"Stop it," she said wearily, and she stood up to go find Misha. "What good does two hundred do? Thanks anyway, though. You're terribly sweet. Help me find him?"

I realized things couldn't go on like this forever. Prices were rising every day at lightning speed. There were demons on the loose in the government. In Moscow and Petersburg, politicians were being shot, one after another. Even Starovoitova was killed. The money bosses were giving their Western creditors the finger and refusing to repay their debts. The entire country had been declared bankrupt. In this situation, only a cretin could have any hopes. Russia was going down the tubes and taking us all with it. I had the feeling we had only a few months left. But the country as a fucking whole didn't get me too worked up. I worried about literally four people. Among these, two places were held by Marina and her brother. I had to worry about those two. Ultimately, I decided I couldn't put it off any longer. I finally had to do what I'd been thinking of doing for two weeks.

Sergei didn't even ask me why I needed the gun. I don't know why. Maybe because it was *that* gun. Or maybe he was just too shy. Probably not everyone can shoot someone in the collarbone and then start asking questions about the gun. After all, I didn't ask him how he smuggled the thing across the border or why his father hadn't confiscated it. I especially didn't ask him why the hell he had it on him at all. Did he keep it as a souvenir or something? Or in case I turned up nearby again? Under some unforeseen circumstances?

I could come up with different things along these lines, but now I had a gun in my pocket. That was a fact. A pretty classy piece, by the way. True, minus one cartridge in the drum. The Italian surgeon had cut that bullet out of my shoulder and plunked it into a steel basin. I probably should have asked him for the bullet itself so I could make some kind of cool talisman out of it. Maybe...I don't know....The snow that had fallen three days before had melted by now. When we were in the forest, it actually seemed as though real winter had come. It didn't anymore. My SUV reminded me more of a boat. The whole way to Kuzminki I never once came across a dry spot. Streams of melting slush flooded the entire roadway.

Downtown, I hopped out for ten minutes to go to Children's World Department Store and then drove straight to Kuzminki. Because of the mud, the trip took longer than usual. I tried to slow it down a little. I didn't want to speed through town like a total idiot. Especially since I had a gun with live cartridges in my pocket. Definitely the last thing I wanted right now was a run-in with traffic cops.

There were very few people at the market near the Budapest. Either because it was early morning or because everyone's money had run out. And there was no one at all in Sasha Mercedes's store. That shaven hulk Sasha'd had take over last time was standing behind the counter.

The ox is going to have a tough workday today, I thought. You can rely on that.

His jacket didn't bulge. That meant I was the only one packing. For now, at least.

"I want to see Sasha," I said—ingratiatingly, I thought.

"And who wants to see him?"

*I would love to shoot you in the brains* flashed through my mind. "Are you blind or something? Me. I'm an old friend. He and I were talking a week ago."

"He's busy."

"Who the hell are you to ask who I am?"

I squeezed the pistol grip in my pocket. Not that I was tempted, it was just that…I just did.

"Still, you tell him Mikhail's come. Who has the Land Rover. The '92."

The hulk glowered at me and then disappeared through the door into the shed.

A minute later a beaming Sasha appeared.

"Great!" he exclaimed. "And I'm thinking, who is that Kirya's haggling with? It's all good," he told the hulk. "He's one of us. You can go take over for me. I'm going to stand here a while."

"He doesn't like you," he said, laughing, when the hulk had disappeared behind the door. "Kirya is a very serious guy. My security service."

"What keeps you so busy?" I finally asked. "It's like a spy conspiracy. Planning a coup?"

"Fuck, what coup? We're counting bills. I haven't slept for more than a day. Do you know what kind of cash is coming in now because of the crisis? People have gone nuts. They're dragging in Russian rubles by the sack. Anyone who has any. They can't get rid of 'em fast enough. They're buying all kinds of junk. See, they've cleaned us out almost completely. And I have four spots in this one market alone. I have more on Ryazansky Prospekt. Were you able to unload your Russian bills?"

"I didn't have any."

"You kept everything in dollars?" He laughed again. "Smart guy! Why didn't you warn us?"

"Where would I have dollars from? I'm basically indigent. I don't work anywhere."

"By the way, about that job. Thinking of coming to work for me?"

"Oh, no, I'm here about something else."

"Yeah? What's that? Only make it quick. Kirya hates counting. He broke his math teacher's arm in high school."

"At school?"

"Where else? He was a very developed little boy. He used to bring a baseball bat to class."

"So how many like him have you got?"

"However many there are, they're all mine. Why do you care?"

"Oh, just asking. Here's what I came to see you about…"

At that moment, yet another shaved head appeared from behind the door.

"Hey, Sasha. Come quick."

"Just a sec," Sasha Mercedes said quickly.

For ten whole minutes, I was alone in the store. If my plans had included stealing anything, I could have walked off with the whole shop. But I'd come here about something else. So all I could do was stand and wait.

"Hey, buddy, sorry," Sasha said when he finally appeared from the shed. "They ran into a glitch. No way they could make it right without me. Money's a tough thing. It confuses people. Even good guys mix things up pretty good. Why did you say you came?"

"I need to show you something."

"Yeah? Well, come on, show me."

"No...See, this thing...it's far away."

"Far away? Then fuck it. Show me later."

"No, I really want you to see it now."

"What the hell do you have there? Can you talk normal?"

"You and I have to take a ride somewhere."

"Right now?"

"Well, yeah."

"No, bro. I can't right now. You can see, my guys are getting antsy. If I leave, they'll start shooting each other, and then my business is fucked. And I have to account to Nikolai Nikolaevich by six for a whole stack of bills. I told them not to take drugs, damn it!"

This was something I wasn't prepared for. I'd completely lost sight of the fact that this moron might be busy. I had no idea he might have that kind of responsibility.

Nonetheless, the fact was plain as day. He was refusing to go with me. My plan had fallen apart at the very start. I could quietly go away and forget my career as Robin Hood.

"Maybe we can go anyway? Eh?"

"No, bro, I can't. Any other day, all right? Who knew this crisis would turn out like this? I haven't made as much money the whole year as I have these last five days. Go figure. So, go on, make tracks."

He quickly shook my hand, and a minute later a sullen, shaven-headed Kirya was standing in front of me.

"Maybe you want to buy something?" he inquired with the irony of a bulldozer. "Except we're nearly all sold out."

---

No, that was a turn I hadn't anticipated. The whole idea was built on Sasha Mercedes going with me. I just couldn't imagine he might up and say, "I'm not going." It's not as though I could pull out my gun and force him. It was still too soon for the gun. In my plan it was supposed to appear much later. Here in the store, it would just spoil the whole picture.

All I could do was turn around and go in silence. I didn't see Kirya's smirk so much as I felt it. Never before had I ever felt anything with my back, by the way. Evidently, that freak was really smirking. It was like he was smearing lard between my shoulder blades.

I emerged from the store distraught. What could I do now? I couldn't come back in five minutes. I had to think of something. I stopped on the front steps and looked around. The entire market had turned into an enormous mud puddle. A horrible rotten smell was coming from the corner where the Chinks were selling fruit. The sleepy sellers were pottering around their wooden stalls under the awnings. Hanging over their heads were black jackets, pink underwear, straw hats, and Chinese toy guns. I had to do something. I had to lure him out of the store.

Casting one more glance around at the cheap Turkish panties, I got really worked up. If only this Sasha and all his morons could know how much I hated their market, their squalid lies, basically everything they did, they would probably up and shoot themselves. To be honest, I hadn't felt hatred like that for anyone in a long time. Now I couldn't care less what I was going to tell them. If necessary, the words would come of their own accord. The main thing was to be true to my feelings. In any case, that's what Marina's classmates said.

If it worked for Chekhov, that meant it ought to work for me.

"Listen, call Sasha for me again," I told a very surprised Kirya when I walked back into the store.

It was worth coming back just to look at his ugly face. In the first minute, before he could get all mad, he looked pretty crazy.

"He told you he was busy," Kirya grumbled at last.

"Come on, call him, or you're going to be pretty unhappy later."

I'd already realized you had to put a scare in these jerks. Moreover, you'd never do that with a club, but they feared their bosses more than fire. As do all Russians, probably. This one was in no way an exception.

"Come on, come on," I hurried him up. "Or I'll tell Sasha. He and I are buddies since kindergarten. He's going to knock some sense into you over me later."

"Well, what's with you?" my "buddy" said in a displeased voice as he appeared from the shed.

"Basically, I decided to do without the surprise."

"What surprise?" he said cautiously.

I could imagine what he was thinking about me.

"What are you talking about?" Sasha Mercedes said. "Are you all right?"

"I'm fine. I just wanted to surprise you. But I guess I'm going to have to tell you everything right here."

"Tell me what?"

Sasha Mercedes looked at Kirya, and it looked as though he were going to tell him to throw me out. I had no doubt that Kirya thought he would later remember this day as his luckiest all fall. Ripping one on for a whiner like me would probably be an incredible high for him. I realized I had to do this fast. My gaze fell on Sasha's tattoo. Not the best option, naturally. But it was worth a try.

"I'm here about that car…"

Sasha looked at his right wrist.

"A Ferrari?"

"Well, yeah. You do like sports cars."

"Yeah."

"Well, I had the idea that you probably wouldn't exactly hate getting a look at wheels like that."

"And you know where I can get a look at an F50?"

In his voice I distinctly heard a mixture of distrust, excitement, and sudden joy. This idiot was now one hundred percent mine.

"Not just a look."

"They'll let me go for a ride?"

I couldn't share his feelings, of course, because I myself don't get that much of a kick out of cars, but for a few seconds I suddenly felt ashamed. I had tricked him like a child. There may not have been anything bad about my trick, but I realized that in his case, this was love. Touching, genuine, childlike love.

"I don't know exactly. But I think you could reach an agreement."

"I could drive it myself?"

I felt so ashamed.

"Yes…You probably could. They're good guys there."

"Just a sec, wait up. I'll just grab my jacket."

"You're supposed to make your report today," Kirya grumbled disgruntledly. "Nikolai Nikolaevich doesn't like glitches."

"Yeah?" Sasha stopped for a moment.

Distress flashed through his eyes. Actually, I realized this was nothing but a child's distress.

"They're taking it out of Moscow today."

Even I didn't know I could be so heartless.

"Come with us," Sasha said to his ox.

Obviously, he was trying to find a compromise. He wanted to salve his conscience somehow.

"They'll get the wrong idea," I interjected.

Kirya absolutely did not figure into my plans.

"Okay, let's go." Sasha was beside himself with impatience.

Now he didn't give a damn about the simple decencies. Before me was a man who was no longer responsible for himself.

---

When we got in the car, I still couldn't quite believe I'd lured him to come with me. Holding my breath, I pulled the keys out of my pocket and froze for a second, as if I were afraid the sound of the engine would scare Sasha off after he'd decided so suddenly to trust me. Especially since it was an idiotic ruse.

"Well, what's with you?" he said impatiently. "Crank 'er up. Let's go. Is it far?"

"No, no," I mumbled. "It's pretty close."

"Imagine, I had this dream today," he went on. "It was like, I was sitting in a blue Porsche, and this classy chick was coming toward me on a motorcycle. A Harley, go figure!" His dream played right into my hand. Only here it was a Ferrari, not a Porsche.

"No, you go figure! A blue Porsche. Really, really bright, like in the movies. What color's this Ferrari?"

"What?" I said.

"What color is it?"

"It's...beige."

"Beige?" He was surprised. "That's odd. They don't usually paint them beige."

"Well...it must be an experimental model."

"You think? Maybe...Who knows what-all they come up with. Stop!" he shouted suddenly. "I get it!"

I slammed on the brakes I was so startled.

"What do you get?"

Beads of sweat appeared instantly on my forehead.

"I get it," he repeated. "Your wheels aren't the blue Porsche."

"Well, yeah," I began, stammering. "I told you it was a beige Ferrari."

"No, no." He waved his hand impatiently. "Your wheels are the chick on the motorcycle."

"What chick?" I forced out.

"From my dream. I was just telling you. Remember?"

"A chick?"

"Well, yeah. Only at first I thought your ride was my blue Porsche, and now I realize it's that classy chick. She was riding straight toward me. Get it? I was supposed to meet her. That's how it was in my dream. There, you see? Now she and I are going to meet. It all matches up. It's all coming together."

"In your dream?"

"What, you don't believe in dreams?"

"No, why..."

"Figure it out!" he hollered. "My real-life dream fits perfectly. She was such a classy chick. I nearly came. I even woke up from the tension. That ever happen to you?"

To be honest, I hadn't quite expected such an outburst of emotions. This guy who'd been formerly discharged had surprised me again. He was as carried away as if he'd been properly stoned since morning.

"I have strange dreams sometimes anyway," he continued, not waiting for a reply. "Once, go figure, in the army, I dreamed I was a chick for some reason. Meanwhile, inside I was still me. That is, a guy inside but a chick outside. I kept wanting to stop into a bathroom and take a look at my tits in a mirror. Go figure. A totally cool dream in the army! I told the guys about it later and they gave me a real hard time. They were green with envy. All they ever dreamed of was grub and getting discharged. I must have told them that dream ten times. And the one about Khazanov organizing his damn concerts in the depot. The guys liked it. But that isn't even all. The best prank I had in a dream was me going to Requisitions and buying twenty pairs of shoulder straps. A big fat pile of 'em. Then I sent them to myself. How about that! I wrote a letter too, saying, Change your shoulder straps more often so they don't stink or your comrades will make fun of you. Go figure! Or your comrades will make fun of you! It's, like, socks stinking, right? But this was fucking shoulder straps. A dream like that could make you crazy. You can tell we were consuming all kinds of nasty shit then. Vodka was nowhere to be found. Ever try sniffing glue?"

I shrugged noncommittally, pretending to be concentrating on the road.

The car really was swerving constantly.

"I like dreams like that," he started in again. "Sometimes they're pretty crazy. Like today. I dreamed of a chick on a motorcycle, and now we're going to look at a Ferrari...Which came from where?"

"Who?"

"Where are the wheels from?"

"The Ferrari? It...This hot-shit bozo ordered it...From Kaluga...Very hot shit. He wants to have his own Ferrari."

"Who doesn't?" Sasha chuckled. "Any moron would. The only question is where to get the half million bucks."

After that he unloaded a ton of technical information on me about the model he and I were going to "see." The problem was, he kept asking my opinion. Evidently, I'd become something of an expert for him. The fact that I'd "seen" it gave me tremendous weight in his eyes and inarguable advantages. He asked me about its specifications, the history of its making, and all kinds of other nonsense that I had no notion of, naturally. When the situation became critical, I tried to distract him by changing the topic.

"Listen, how's Petrovich doing? Did they ransom him from Chechnya?"

But Sasha was as stubborn as an ox.

"The hell with Petrovich. Who cares what happens to him? If they haven't ransomed him they will. You have to tell me something else..."

And it would start all over again. He would tell me something, then ask more questions, I would nod, and when I had no other choice I'd start rattling on about nothing. I had to hold out for another twenty minutes. There was just a short way to go until we got to the spot I was planning to take him to. According to my calculations, at that time of year it ought to be deserted.

"Hey, no one's here," Sasha said, hopping out of the car. "Where've you taken me?"

"They'll bring it soon," I promised.

I was getting quite a kick out of my stupid trick. For some reason he believed me. He must have really wanted it to be true. Once again I felt rather inexplicable pricks of conscience.

"Here?" he asked again and looked around.

He was quite right. I'd chosen a dodgy spot for a Ferrari. We'd driven off-road pretty far into the forest and now had parked on the shore of a small, weedy pond. To our left loomed clumps of dried reeds.

"They don't want any publicity. You know how much that baby costs."

"No fucking shit," Sasha said, walking closer to the water's edge. "Look. The whole thing's covered in ice already. Did you like breaking it when you were a kid?"

He tapped his heel across the shining surface.

"Careful," I said. "God forbid you fall in."

"Bullshit." He gave a wave of the hand and kept banging at the solid ice, which was unexpectedly sturdy for this time of year.

Looking at him, I suddenly thought that this was very strange on my part, to bring someone here for what I planned to do to him and then be worried about his getting his feet wet. It's always like that with me. All kinds of stupid stuff gets into my head at the most crucial moments.

"Hey, you know what this is like?" he said suddenly.

"Meaning?"

"Well, look. You and I come here, outside town, to this abandoned spot. Well, it's fall, and there's this pond and the trees have already dropped their leaves. Remember?"

I didn't understand what he was talking about.

"Come on!" He gestured impatiently. "*Seventeen Moments of Spring.* Stirlitz. Well?"

I shook my head.

"You must remember. Durov was standing right by the water there, and Stirlitz suddenly pulled a gun."

My heart went cold.

It can't be, I thought. Has he really guessed?

"Well? Remember? There was this exact same lake, and trees, and these same reeds. Remember?"

I shook my head again.

"What's wrong with you! How can you not remember? Durov was standing with his back to him. Like this. And Stirlitz pulled his gun and fired while this guy was yakking nonstop. Remember? Listen, you think they filmed it right here?"

I was speechless. How could he have guessed about my gun? Or was this just a coincidence?

"I think I read that they shot it in the Baltics." Sasha kept talking. "But who knows? Maybe they just wrote that bullshit in the newspapers. I definitely remember this little lake. I saw the whole film four times. Durov turned out to be this rotten dude, and Stirlitz decided to mess him up. Because if he didn't mess him up, he was going to rat out all the good guys. Remember now? There he is over there."

I just didn't know what to say to him.

"And Stirlitz picked him off from there. Right from where you're standing."

"Yeah, yeah," I finally got out. "I think I remember now."

"Well then, you see?" He clapped his hands in delight. "You've got to agree, it's the very same spot."

"Yeah…looks like it…"

"Quit the 'looks like' shit! It's the exact same spot. I'm telling you for sure."

"Yes," I said. "It's the exact same spot."

"There, then! And you had doubts."

He was so overcome he slapped himself on the thighs and jumped onto the ice with both feet.

I don't know why he did that. Maybe he's a very emotional person. And maybe he felt like finally breaking the unyielding ice armor. I don't know. He probably liked seeing things all the way through.

Whichever it was, the next second he was up to his knees in water and looking at me with frightened eyes. It occurred to me that we could have hardly ended up in a more comical situation. Now my whole plan was taking on shades of a Charlie Chaplin silent movie.

"I'm screwed!" Sasha hollered at the top of his lungs. "I fucked up!"

It was odd that he should be so surprised. If someone jumps on the ice with both feet to break it, either he succeeds, and then, naturally he inevitably ends up in the water, or else he doesn't, and then why jump at all, you have to wonder?

This human projectile kept yelling while standing half a meter from shore, and I felt like walking up and knifing him to get him to shut up. Only a vague sense of guilt kept me from violence. I'd willed this idiot here. If it weren't for me, he'd be sitting in a warm place right now, counting his money.

"How can I drive the Ferrari now?" he shouted from the water. "They won't even let me in the car! I'd muck up their whole car!"

Two minutes later he was sitting in the backseat of my SUV, squeezing out his socks, and I was pouring the water out of his soaked boots.

"Let's hurry up," he rushed me. "Or else they'll come now. And my feet are frozen solid. At least shut the door. You're standing there with your shoes on."

I felt as though a little more of this and I was going to explode. I was sick of him. My plan was probably a little on the slippery side. And not just because this jerk now had wet feet.

"Let's go!" he went on. "Look, my fingers are turning blue. Look, they're all bent up!"

I threw him his boots through the open door. Maybe a little harder than I needed to.

"Hey, watch it!" he exclaimed. "You nearly got me in the head."

"Listen." I finally got down to the point. "I wanted to ask you one thing here."

"What?" he exclaimed. "Talk louder. The radio's blaring. Do you like those pieces of ass from *Sparklers*?"

"Turn it off, why don't you!" I couldn't restrain myself. "Turn it off if you're not listening."

"Great pieces of ass," he said, turning it up. "Especially the tall one. She's always got her belly button poking out from under her shirt. A great fucking belly button. I get off on that."

"I wanted to ask you about your store."

"Meaning?" he muttered, holding his leg up over his head to tie his long shoelaces.

"You haven't been in charge there long, have you?"

"No."

"Who was before you?"

"Damn it, my lace is tangled," he grumbled. "Some goon. Why do you give a fuck?"

"I just do. Humor me."

"I never tried tying wet shoelaces before. They squeak like elastic. I'm fucking getting pneumonia here."

"What happened to him?"

"Who?"

"The goon who was in charge at the store before you."

"He died."

"And you inherited his whole business?"

"Not quite." Sasha grinned. "I had to press a few levers. He was a creep too, that guy. I'm glad he bought it."

"And he didn't leave anyone behind?"

"Me!" he shouted.

"No, well…relatives…heirs…"

"He left one rat and one baby rat." He tapped the floor with his foot. "But I settled things with them. Listen, there's still water in my right. You didn't pour it all out."

After what he said about Marina and little Misha, any pity I'd had left evaporated. I didn't care what he thought anymore. He deserved what had just happened to him. Every person has to answer for his actions. As a deeply religious person, I was sure of this.

"Listen, maybe I can turn the radio on now?" he said.

"Turn it on," I replied, and I lowered my hand into my pocket for the gun.

---

"God damn, great piece," he said admiringly. "Like a real one! Where'd you get it?"

"It is real."

"Oh come on, quit it. Where would you get a real one? It's probably gas. Let me look."

He reached out, not taking his admiring eyes off the gun.

"Well, give it here. What's with you? I can't reach that far."

"It's real."

"Okay, I believe you. Let me look."

"It's loaded."

"Let me look. I'm telling you."

"There's just one cartridge missing."

"Listen, come closer. I don't want to get out of the car. All that muck will stick to my wet boots."

"It's loaded with live cartridges."

"Damn, why do you keep harping on that? You think I've never held a gun? Especially since, by the way, it's a gas pistol anyway. Wait up, I'll get out now."

"Don't," I said quickly.

"Why not?"

"Stay where you are."

"Meaning?" Childlike surprise flashed through his eyes.

"Look."

I aimed the gun at a crushed Fanta can lying under a tree and pulled the trigger. The drum turned smoothly, the shot rang out, and the can flew off about ten paces.

"No fucking joke," Sasha Mercedes said slowly. "And you're not afraid of cops? They're pulling people over like crazy these days."

"I'm not afraid of anything."

"Let me look," he said, and he leaped out of the car.

"Stop!" I shouted, aiming the gun at him.

"Hey, watch it!" Sasha exclaimed. "That thing's loaded."

"Exactly. I was just telling you. Put this on."

I tossed him what I'd stopped for at Children's World.

"Handcuffs? What, have you lost your mind? Quit it and let me have your gun."

"Stop right where you are!" I shouted again. "Don't move!"

"What's with you, are you crazy?"

"Put them on!"

"I'm not going to put anything on. Go fuck yourself."

"Put them on," I repeated very quietly, and I raised the gun to the level of his forehead.

"But what for?"

"Put them on, I'm telling you."

"Fuck a duck," he cursed, clicking the handcuffs on his wrists. "These are kind of weird. What's the idea? Have you lost your mind?"

"Don't jerk your arms," I warned him. "Stand still."

I was afraid he might break them. If only he knew I'd bought the handcuffs for him at Children's World! A very good imitation. I wonder what kind of children they make toys like that for?

"Well, what next?" he said. "Why the fuck are you doing all this?"

He looked pretty foolish in the handcuffs. True, I'm afraid I didn't look all that smart with the gun either. I can imagine what our little twosome looked like from a distance. Too bad Marina's classmates couldn't see us. This was definitely cooler than their *Cherry Orchard*.

"Well, are we going to be standing like this for long?" he said at last. "Maybe you can quit pointing that at my face?"

But I needed a little time. I still hadn't come to my senses. My nerves were shot. My ears were actually ringing.

"Wait up," I said. "Can you stand like that a little? I'll tell you what you have to do in a sec."

That was when he guessed he'd been tricked.

---

People are strange creatures, I've noticed. Someone will believe something and later just plain not want to know anything. Even if he's standing in the forest, and there's no one around, and nearby is a half-frozen pond of God knows what depth where it would be easy to throw his stiff body, and he has a heavy, black revolver that some idiot carried illegally through customs aimed at his head. Try all you like to explain it to someone like that—he doesn't give a rat's ass. The only thing that bothers him is that he's had a fast one pulled on him. In short, he was silent for a couple of minutes, and then he said, "Well, are we going to be standing like this for long? Maybe you could stop pointing that at my face?"

"Wait a sec," I replied. "Stand there. I'm going to tell you what you need to do."

"Stop!" he hollered in a suddenly wild voice.

I'd never even heard anyone shout like that before. Maybe they taught them that in the army.

"Stop!" he shouted again, as if once weren't enough.

The joke was that he and I both were standing there practically without moving. So who he was shouting "Stop" to was a complete mystery.

"Stop!" he shouted a third time, which I thought was definitely overkill, so to speak.

"What's with you?" I asked. "Why are you shouting? You could be quiet for a while. My ears are really ringing as it is."

"Why did you drag me here?"

"Wait a minute and I'll tell you everything."

"You dragged me here especially to put these irons on my wrists?"

"Stand still or I might accidentally pull the trigger."

"You set me up!"

"So what?"

"There is no Ferrari?"

"Where am I supposed to get a Ferrari in the forest? Think about it."

"I won't be able to ride in it?"

"Maybe some other time."

"You promised me I could drive a Ferrari!"

In despair, he kicked the tree trunk and immediately grimaced in pain. For a second I actually thought I would have to shoot him after all. He just couldn't calm down. I had no idea how seriously he'd take all this. The gun scarcely worried him anymore. He kept kicking my SUV, and I started getting seriously worried he might break a leg or my car.

"Hey, quit it!" I shouted to him. "Give it up. It's time to go."

"Oh, go to hell!" he shouted, turning toward me. "Creep!"

Real tears were shining in his eyes.

"I got my feet wet because of you!"

He kept cursing nonstop, so in the end I was forced to get out the masking tape and tape his mouth shut. I couldn't listen to him forever.

Actually, pretty soon it became clear that I shouldn't have done that.

As soon as we came out on the Ring Road he started making strange noises. When I was a kid in the village with my grandma I heard the same noises when her old brass samovar would start to boil. First you had to throw in all kinds of wood chips, which my cousin and I picked up all over the yard, and then they would start to sputter, cloaked in bitter smoke. Sasha Mercedes was sputtering almost exactly the same way now. He was sitting with handcuffed hands and taped mouth in the front seat of my SUV and sputtering like my grandma's samovar.

At first I decided to ignore him. I was so sick of his sorry-ass obsession. First he refused to go, then he fell through the ice, then he nearly dented my bumper because I'd tricked him about the Ferrari. How else was I supposed to drag him away from that lousy store, I'd like to know? But no, that wasn't enough! Now he'd decided to sputter. Hatred was bubbling up in me stronger and stronger every minute.

But he wasn't limiting himself to just samovar sputtering. Evidently, in order to get me really mad he soon started rolling his eyes. He went quiet for a moment, turned toward me so I'd get a better look, and then rolled his eyes back, which were as red as a black guy's. I don't know how he managed to fill them with blood, but I found it really repulsive.

"Are you going to quit this circus of yours or not, damn it?" I finally shouted.

Anyone would have shouted the same in my place. There is a limit to anyone's patience. Who would enjoy seeing all this?

"Quit it, I'm telling you! If you don't stop it, I'm going to whack you on the head with this crowbar."

But he kept turning his head and bellowing something through the tape.

"Shut up! I'm sick of you, you idiot!"

I didn't know what to do with him. I was reluctant to beat him with a crowbar, of course. He'd been unlucky enough today already. Anyway, the blood would probably have stained the seat.

Finally, he started to quiet down and I thought, Well, thank God. We didn't have more than fifteen minutes to go.

After a brief silence he suddenly wheezed and collapsed to the side. My side, moreover. He fell on me with his whole body so that we nearly rear-ended a dark blue VAZ-8. I don't know how I managed to hold on to the wheel. I was bathed in so much sweat, you'd think I'd worn a fur coat into a steam room.

"Hey, have you lost your mind?" I hollered, braking on the shoulder. "Have you completely lost your senses or something?"

He didn't react at all and kept leaning on my shoulder. I had to strain to push him off.

"What's with you?" I said when his head thudded against the window. "Can you hear me?"

He rolled his eyes senselessly, barely giving any signs of life.

"Hey, what's with you?" I was suddenly worried. "Are you okay?"

He looked dully first at me, then into space.

"Can you hear me?"

He didn't answer.

"How do you feel?"

Suddenly I realized he was dying. I saw it in his eyes.

I'd expected all kinds of things this morning, but honestly, I was definitely not prepared for this. A hundred percent not prepared. A million percent. A billion, if you want.

———

"What, can't you breathe?" I shouted like a crazy person. "Can't you breathe? Hey, can you hear me?"

I slapped his cheek as hard as I could.

"Look at me! What's the matter with you? Can you see me?"

He tried to focus on me, but I realized he wasn't going to be able to. He was slipping away from me.

"Breathe!" I shouted, and I ripped the tape off his face. "Breathe! Come on, breathe! Breathe deeper!"

The tape ripped off with such a horrible crack that I thought it had taken a piece of skin with it. But Sasha Mercedes didn't even shudder. Obviously, he barely had any notion of what was happening to him.

"Asthma," he wheezed. "The tape...You shouldn't... Allergy..."

"You have asthma?" I shouted. "Asthma? Why didn't you warn me?"

An idiotic question, of course, but at that moment I had nearly lost it completely. Murder had not entered into my plans.

"Hey! Hey!" I continued shouting. "Don't check out! Listen to me!"

He wheezed and rolled his blood-filled whites again.

"Medicine! You must have some kind of medicine! What do you take? Can you hear me?"

"At the store..." he hissed. "Kirya knows."

This was a total bummer. As I understood it, without medicine he was going to kick the bucket very soon, and then his death would rest wholly on my conscience. Actually, my conscience wasn't the biggest problem here. Where was I going to put his body? My armpits were soaking wet instantly. On the other hand, what could I say to Kirya? "You know, there was a minor glitch. I taped your boss's mouth shut, and now he's dying. Quick, show me where his medicine is." Was that what I was supposed to tell him?

"Listen," I shouted again. "What's it called, this medicine of yours? You have to tell me. Maybe we can buy it at a pharmacy."

But he wasn't responding anymore. He was just rolling his eyes and wheezing like a busted electric kettle. That sound alone gave me gooseflesh. How was I supposed to know what to do now? I didn't work in an ER.

"Kirya knows," he suddenly wheezed again. "Ask Kirya... Help me..."

So it turned out I had to save his life. Moreover, he obviously didn't have much time left.

---

"But where is he?" Kirya asked me immediately. "Where did you leave him?"

Personally, in his place, I'd hardly have taken such a deep interest in geography.

"Give it to me, bring me the medicine! He's in a very bad way."

"Here it is," he said, appearing from the shed a minute later. "I'll go with you. Where's your car?"

Oops! This was yet another twist I hadn't prepared for.

"Wait up, wait up!" I said. "Where do you think you're going?"

"With you. Hurry up."

"You're not going anywhere."

I couldn't let him leave the market gates and see his precious Sasha Mercedes in my car, unconscious, with a bloody face and Children's World handcuffs. I can imagine how he'd rearrange my face then. And not just my face, more than likely.

"What do you mean I'm not? Come on, let's speed it up."

"Go fuck yourself! Who are you to tell me what to do!"

He was stunned, clearly not expecting that reaction. He wasn't the only one! I hadn't expected it myself. But what other choice did I have?

"What?" He must have thought he'd misheard me.

It was all right, I'm not proud. I could repeat myself.

"Go fuck yourself, punk! You'll be giving orders in the morgue!"

I may have overdone it with the morgue bit. Actually, what was important now was to keep him off balance. Especially since he still had the medicine in his hand.

"Give it over!"

"What did you say? Did you call me a punk?"

"And who else? You're a natural-born punk. Only on top of everything else, you're stupid. Because if you weren't stupid, you would have given me the medicine a long time ago and not pestered me with your stupid questions."

"You shithead, you are so fucked!" he bellowed, finally coming to his senses.

I realized the critical moment had come. Losing now meant losing everything.

"Just you try," I said as calmly as possible. "Then in twenty minutes your boss is going to cash in his chips, and screw it if I'm going to tell you where to find him. And afterward, they're going to be all over you for his death, because you made the wrong decision, punk. I don't think Nikolai Nikolaevich is going to let you off so easy for Sasha's death. You'll have to answer for the mess. So why don't you give the effing medicine over and go back to your counter. Where I can see you, punk."

I held my breath waiting for his reaction. My life was now entirely in his hands. I couldn't read a thing on his broad, heavily fleshed face. You had to be a butcher to read faces like that.

"Why can't I go with you?" He finally came out with his doubts.

It was a good question. At least for me. The answer was that I wanted to get out of here under my own steam. Meaning, feet first.

"Because I don't want you to."

Now I could humiliate him all I wanted. This behemoth was caving. Fortunately for me, he was afraid of his superiors. Actually, I think I already said that.

"But why?"

He was trying to observe the decencies. Evidently, it was important for him to justify himself to himself. But I decided not today, and definitely not at my expense. I felt no pity for him.

"Because you're just a flunky. And I only let decent people into my car. Flunkies are supposed to run errands. They don't ride around in my car. They do their flunky thing. It's bad enough I'm wasting time on your boss. Because in principle this has nothing to do with me. An ambulance should come deal with things like this. Hand that crap over."

I wanted to call him a punk again, but this time I refrained. Who knows how badly he really feared his superiors?

When he was handing over the blue vial, though, I was able to read a thing or two on his face. It said that this was not our last meeting. It wasn't written very clearly, but I was able to make it out. Even on faces like that, a thing or two sometimes shows through.

---

"Well, how're you doing?" I asked Sasha when he had come around a little. "A little better?"

"I thought that was it," he whispered barely audibly. "I've never had it that bad before."

"Did you see a long tunnel? A bright light and a white door at the end?"

"I didn't see jack shit."

"Don't swear," I said.

"Why?" He was so surprised he even managed to hold his head normally.

"When you swear, the angel flies away from you. Weeps and flies away."

"Yeah?" He goggled at me as if he'd heard the voice of God.

"Definitely. It only comes back when you've stopped swearing."

"Is that right? How do you know?"

"This guy told me. He works in a church."

I couldn't admit I'd just made that up. It just came to me, all of a sudden.

"No, I didn't see anything," he said again, and he lowered his head on the seat back.

"How did the army ever take you with your asthma?"

"I didn't have it then."

"You mean you got sick after?"

"No. When I broke my leg that spring, they shot me up in the ER with some…crap."

He stumbled over that last word and looked at me.

"Listen, were you telling the truth about swearing?"

"That the angel flies away?"

"Well?"

"A hundred percent sure. Someone very reliable told me that in secret. And when the angel flies away, you're left completely defenseless."

"Now I get it," he muttered barely audibly.

"What do you get?"

"Oh, I was wondering why all this"—he stumbled again—"shit keeps happening to me."

"What shit?"

"I never have any luck. Just when it looks like I'm on a roll—wham!—there's always some glitch. Either I break my leg, or I pick up this asthma, and now, hell, there's you and your cannon."

He stopped to think for a second and looked at me with alarm.

"Can I say *hell*? Or will it fly away?"

He looked very concerned.

"You can say *hell*," I allowed.

"Good," he sighed with relief. "Or else I thought I couldn't do squat."

"So where did you get your asthma?"

"I told you, they stuck the wrong needle in me in the hospital. And it gave me an allergy. And then it all turned into asthma."

"You're so young."

"Did you think only old people got asthma?" He grinned. "I heard about these people I know whose three-year-old kid died."

"Shut up!"

"Seriously. He got sick when he was two and at three he was already dead."

"Goddamn."

"So you shouldn't have stuck that stuff to my mouth. It made my allergy kick in."

"I didn't know."

"And my face is all bloody."

He raised his hand to his face and cautiously touched his lips.

"Did you beat me or something?"

"No…it's…" I didn't find the right words right off. "The tape really stuck."

"Took the fucking skin off with it."

"I guess so."

For some reason I seemed to be trying to justify myself to him.

"Well, what are we going to do now?" he said huskily. "Why did you start all this?"

"What?" I asked, though I'd heard him perfectly well.

"Why the fuck did you set up this whole racket?"

"I need money," I said after a brief pause.

"Money? That makes sense. Everyone needs money. Were you thinking of kidnapping me?"

"Something like that."

"Cool. No one's ever kidnapped me before. How much do you need?"

"I need…" I stumbled again. "I need fifty thousand."

"Dollars?" he clarified.

"Yeah."

"Cool. Where am I supposed to get that much?"

"I don't know. You have a store."

"I get ten percent off that store. The rest goes to Nikolai Nikolaevich."

"Well, let him pay."

"It would be cheaper for him to blow us both off."

"Well, I don't know then. I have to come up with something. Basically, these aren't my problems. You tell me the telephone number and I'll make the call and ask for the money."

"Just like that?"

"Exactly."

"And what if I open the door right now and just walk away?"

"Then I'll shoot you in the head."

He looked me right in the eyes.

"You'd really shoot?"

"I'm not a hundred percent sure. But you can try me. Are you a gambler?"

He licked the blood from his upper lip.

"Not so much."

"Fine," I said.

"Not so fine. I wonder why Kirya didn't come with you."

"He intended to."

"Yeah? What happened?"

"I didn't take him."

"And he listened to you?"

"Not right away."

"You turn out to be one cool character." Sasha grinned. "It's usually hard to convince Kirya of anything."

"Each person requires an individual approach."

"It's best to approach him from behind with a crowbar in your right hand."

"There are other ways."

"He's going to kill you."

"I already figured that out."

"No, he's seriously going to kill you. Dead."

"To do that, he's first going to have to find me."

"He's not going to back off now."

"That's all right. We'll muddle through somehow."

"So why do you need that much money?"

He was asking too many questions.

"I want to open my own business."

"Too bad you didn't come work for me at the market. I would've paid you well. But now Kirya's going to kill you."

"So I heard."

At first I'd planned to tape his eyes shut so he wouldn't see our route. But then I just lowered his seat and threw my jacket over his head.

"Lie quietly or it will fall off."

"What do I care? Let it," he muttered muffledly from under the jacket.

"Then I won't be able to let you go."

"You'll kill me or something?"

"I don't know yet. I haven't thought that far yet...I just couldn't let you go."

"Then no amount of dough would be enough. How long do you plan to hold me?"

"I don't know yet. That doesn't depend on me."

"I see," he said. "Listen!"

"What?"

"Thank you."

"What for?" I was amazed.

"For not taping my eyes shut. It would have torn my eyebrows off all to hell. You wanted to, I bet."

He was quiet for a while, but then I heard his voice from under the jacket again:

"Listen, can you say *damn* or not?"

"I think you'd better not."

---

When we drove up to my building, I had to take the jacket off his head. I couldn't take him from the car to the front door looking like that. You never knew who might look out a window at just that moment. There was a risk he'd remember the building, naturally, but I'd been winding around the outskirts for so long that the only way he could find the place later would be by chance.

"Only be a little more careful with those handcuffs," I said, cuffing him to the radiator.

"Yeah? What's the deal?" he asked warily.

"They aren't quite the usual ones. You can see they've got a slightly different shape."

"Yeah. So what?"

"So nothing. It's just that if you jerk hard they'll explode and carry off my entire kitchen."

"What do you mean explode?"

"Right here under this little thing, there's a detonator hidden."

"You've got to be kidding."

This time he obviously didn't believe me right off.

"Try it. Jerk harder and you'll see. I don't have anything to lose. If you don't care either, then go ahead."

He looked carefully at the handcuffs and then shifted his mistrustful look to me.

"This is bullshit. Where did you get these? I've never even heard of these."

"This FSB man gave them to me. I helped him with his son. Remember the kid I dragged along to Petrovich's for the going-away party when you and I met? That was his son. And up until last year the handcuffs were top secret. That's why you've never heard anything about them. But now the special services are getting another model, so these are old hat now. But you should still be a little careful with them."

"What other model?"

I had to think of something, and fast.

"They're going to be even cooler. They inject poison. Potassium cyanide. Violent edema of the lungs, and you suffocate in fifteen seconds. It's like pouring five liters of water down your throat."

I'd probably never lied that baldly before.

"Consider yourself warned. Try squirming a little less. Don't even try to reach the phone. It was shut off a long time ago."

He licked his lips and suddenly smiled.

"What's with you?" I asked.

"I've seen a thing or two."

"What have you seen?"

My heart went cold. Did he really remember the route? No matter how much I bluffed about this, I definitely had no intention of killing him.

"Well, remember you were asking about the light in the tunnel? The white door at the end, and all that stuff?"

I caught my breath, relieved.

"Was that when you started turning up your toes?"

"Mm. I just remembered for sure. I saw it as clear as I'm seeing you."

"So what was it? Angels?"

He paused and smiled again.

"I won't tell you."

"Why?"

"Balls! That's not swearing, is it?"

"No, it just refers to a part of the body."

"Okay, up that other part of your body. I'm not telling you a fucking thing."

---

When I got to Marina's dacha and asked whether I could spend the night with her, little Misha threw a ball at me. I caught the ball and tossed it back. We horsed around like that for five minutes or so while Marina watched us, shaking her head.

"Well, what do you think?" I asked, when Misha had run off to the far trees after his ball.

To be honest, I'd thrown it there on purpose.

"You know." She shrugged. "Why ask?"

"Yeah?" I said.

She didn't say another word on the subject all evening. We made out on the porch in the dark, silently, until Misha went to sleep, and then she took me to her room.

## Winter: Mikhail

I never expected it all to turn out this way. Not the part about abducting that moron Sasha Mercedes, but about suddenly winding up at Marina's dacha. That is, of course, I wanted to end up at her dacha, but no one could have guessed it would happen exactly the way it did. What I mean is, because the prisoner was now sitting in my apartment. And most of all, that it all worked out on its own. Sasha was sitting in my apartment, and I was staying with Marina at her dacha.

From time to time, I'd make the trip into Moscow to check up on him and see Sergei. Because of the financial crisis, Pavel Petrovich had started having problems, and he had absolutely no interest in me. Sergei didn't want to know about anything but his computer either, so I could once again calmly go about doing whatever I wanted. And I must say, there were things to do.

Sasha's bosses didn't want to pay for him. The bummer was that I'd overestimated his persona. He turned out to be an ordinary employee who no one needed on principle. No one wanted to shell out for him. I'm not talking about fifty thousand—they wouldn't even pay a thousand for him. Deep down, I understood them. Even I was ready to spit on the whole business, but I still didn't know what to do with my captive. I told Marina I had a relative from Siberia living in my apartment who'd come to Moscow to make money, but instead he'd started drinking heavily. I didn't want her to decide she wanted to meet him.

Actually, I shouldn't have worried about that. If she did have any desires, they were all connected to her own life. She had ceased to be concerned altogether with anything that was happening past the last line of pines growing in front of the train station. For her, the rest of the world with its trains, scandals, and political murders no longer existed. This was obvious from her calm gaze, her movements, how she answered my questions and Misha's, how she made up his bed in the evening and folded his sheets into the drawers of the large, antique cupboard. Personally, I felt exactly the same way. Sometimes I even forgot I had a captive living in my apartment.

The first time this word occurred to me, by the way, I was actually amazed. It didn't suit poor Sasha at all. I was bringing him medicine and feeding him Marina's soup, and he was telling me stories about the army. It's funny, but he had in fact nearly stopped blaspheming. He watched a lot of television and then told me about various fights in the State Duma. I wasn't cuffing him to the radiator anymore. I would just give the security rim lock three turns and leave. He would never risk climbing down from the twelfth floor. Actually, sometimes I got the impression he didn't really want to escape. I don't know why, but I had a strange feeling. Maybe he'd gotten used to sitting in one place in that army of his.

We didn't do anything special at the dacha really. We would walk to the station and back and rehearse. I would play with Misha. In the evenings, Marina would tell him fairy tales before he went to sleep, and I would be amazed at how many she knew.

"I don't know them," she said one day. "I'm making them up."

"On the spot?" I was amazed. "As you go?"

"Yes. Basically they're all the same. A good prince first gets into trouble, but then he always finds his princess."

"Yesterday you were telling a story about a brigand. And the day before that about the White Wolf."

"So what? It's all the prince anyway. The main thing is that he finds his princess."

"You could probably write a children's book."

"I'll give that some thought," she said, and she touched my face.

Sometimes I felt so strange because apparently I now had a family. Not just a family, but a whole family with a real child, as if we'd had him from the very start. True, he was Marina's brother, not her son, but there was no difference at all in principle. I suddenly started feeling kind of like his father too. It's silly, of course, but I really did. I mean, the love there and all that stuff. In the mornings you wake up and suddenly remember where you went to bed the day before. At first that made me feel very strange. As if I'd tricked everyone. Not in the sense that I'd pulled a fast one or taken someone for a ride, but in the sense that you've pulled a low card, and you're bluffing, and all of a sudden they believe you. Meanwhile, no one is even mad at you. You're lying in bed in the morning, watching the snow fall outside, and in the next room Misha is playing with his toy trucks. I liked stoking the stove too. I never thought I could like something so much before. Marina always made pancakes in the morning. They were awfully tasty with strawberry jam. But Misha liked them with cherry.

A month and a half went by like that for us.

"What lousy weather," I said, entering the apartment and shutting the door behind me. "My jacket was soaked through before I could get to the door. Don't you know that's bad for your skin?"

"Is yours Turkish?" he asked.

"You're Turkish. I bought it in Italy. After I was released from the hospital, Pavel Petrovich paid me a nice fat bonus. Like a prize for medicines."

"They probably have plenty of Turkish ones there too."

"Oh, go to hell," I swore with no offense meant. "It was a brand-name store. With all the bells and whistles."

"Then nothing's going to fuck it up. So it's raining again?"

"Go to the window. You've gotten awfully lazy."

"What's the point? It's been so long since I've been outside anyway. So your weather doesn't matter to me."

"There's never been a winter like it before in Moscow."

"There's been fucking everything in Moscow before."

"Well, it's definitely never rained in late December. Wouldn't you know, it may well be the end of the world. Lots of people are talking about it in the metro. They say we only have a year left."

"What's the temperature?"

"One above."

"Then it is the end of the world. What else do they say?"

"They say Yeltsin's going to die soon."

"They've been saying that for years. What else?"

"By February the dollar will be worth thirty rubles."

"Now that's more like the truth. What else?"

"The Russians are going to reach an agreement with Hussein and kick the Americans' ass."

"Then it will definitely be the end of the world. What else?"

"The Kremlin's nothing but gays."

Sasha frowned.

"Well, I don't know. They look like regular guys on TV. Well fed. Satisfied."

"And gays are supposed to look hungry or something? Is that it?"

"Well, I don't know. Some look different. Not hungry necessarily. But, you know, not very satisfied. As if they needed something else."

"It's obvious what they need."

"But those guys in the Kremlin, they have everything. They're living the high life. That's why they're so fat."

"In the metro, people say there's going to be some throat-slitting there soon."

"No one's going to be slitting their throats. They're the ones who want to slit people's throats. In Chechnya did you see any real helter-skelter? I wish someone had said something to them. They looked into it seriously—with planes and guns and tanks. Those guys have scope. No comparison with my Nikolai Nikolaevich. Though he's a very solid guy on his own level."

"I'm tired of your solid guy," I said, going into the kitchen. "Why didn't you eat the soup again?"

"He's not paying up?" Sasha asked.

"He doesn't even want to discuss the subject."

"What did I tell you? He's probably got fifty guys like me. You think he's going to pay fifty grand for each of them? If so, he'd have had all his guys abducted a long time ago. He'll just replace me with someone and forget me. Someone else is most likely cutting the cabbage at the market instead of me already."

"Kirya," I said, fishing meat out of the soup.

"What do you mean, Kirya?" He was definitely surprised.

"Why so surprised? He's your pal."

"Well, yeah…Only…That's why I'm surprised."

"That your pal took your place?"

"I took him on out of pity."

"Oh, that."

"He's dumb."

"Stop it. How smart do you have to be there?"

"Not much…But still…"

"Basically you're just mad."

"I don't know," he said with a deep sigh. "Maybe I am."

"Too bad you didn't finish the soup. There's still a fuck of a lot of meat left."

"Did you bring the medicine? I've run out."

"There's not going to be any more medicine."

"What do you mean there isn't? Why? What, have you decided to finish me off right here? I'll croak without medicine. I have asthma."

"Hey, wait up," I said. "Why are you so excited?"

"Fuck excited. He tells me he's not bringing me any more medicine, and I'm not supposed to say anything."

"I'm letting you go."

He was so worked up that he didn't even understand me at first.

"What? What did you say?"

"You can go buy your own potions. As it is, they've stunk up the whole apartment. Only I'm not giving you money for it. Don't even ask. You know how much I've spent on you already?"

"You're letting me go?"

He couldn't seem to believe his own ears.

"Well, yeah. Yeah. I'm letting you go. If you want, I can say it again. I made a lousy kidnapper. I'm sorry I took you captive."

That was idiotic, about taking him captive, but I wasn't exactly in my element either. It's not every day you release hostages.

"In short, you can go. The door's open. If you want, you can finish the soup first."

"Fuck your soup."

"Well, if you don't want to, don't. Go right now. There's a bus stop right across the street. You just have to walk around to get to it."

"I don't have any money for the bus."

"And so it begins," I said, and I got change out of my pocket.

For some reason he didn't look very pleased.

"Maybe you'll at least let me collect my things?"

"What things?" I said, amazed. "Everything here is mine."

"Meanwhile, I've spent a month and a half in this apartment."

"But it's my apartment. Now I'm going to be staying here."

"Yeah?"

"Of course. What did you think?"

"I didn't think anything. You're just behaving like a pig."

"I'm behaving like a pig?" There were no bounds to my amazement. "I'm letting you go. You can go to the four corners."

"And did you ask me?" There was indignation in his voice. "Did you ask me? You always do what you feel like. You thought you'd take a hostage and bam! You got a gun and held it to someone's head. The ransom didn't work out and bam! To hell with you! You think you're the only one with problems? Or is everyone just supposed to solve your problems? What about the fact that I've lost my job? Maybe I won't have anywhere to live now, even!"

I was a little upset by his energy.

"What do you mean nowhere? You mean you were living at the market?"

"Where else? If I hadn't landed in the hospital last spring, I would have left Moscow a long time ago. I have family in Ryazan. My mama works at the post office. But I hung around the hospital for the summer and then Nikolai Nikolaevich let me loose on the market. And now Kirya's living in my pad."

"You mean he doesn't have anywhere to stay in Moscow either?"

"Before, he rented a room at Three Eighth of March Street. Ten minutes to the Dinamo stadium by bus. But what the fuck does he need that apartment for now?"

"Good God, that's funny."

"I wouldn't call Kirya exactly funny."

"Well, I don't know," I finally said. "You can stay here for now. Maybe something will turn up."

"It can turn up twenty times over," he mumbled, but more amiably now. "Do you know how much housing costs in Moscow now?"

"I'm not giving you any money."

"No one's asking you to. Though, when you think about it, you should, of course."

"Listen, you've really lost your mind."

"I didn't force you to come to my place with a gun. And also you lied to me about the Ferrari."

"And I've been feeding you for free for a whole month. In times like this, that means a lot."

"I could have fed myself easy. And anyway, it's a month and a half, not a month."

"All the more so."

"You've kept me locked up like a prisoner for a month and a half."

"I told you you could go."

"I don't mean that."

"What then?"

"I might have had plans for that time, by the way."

"What, you want me to apologize to you?"

"I wouldn't mind. But that's not the main thing now."

"What is?"

"Tomorrow is New Year's."

"So what?"

"What so what? I doubt you're going to celebrate it alone in this empty apartment."

"You have the television."

"Stick it…you know where."

"I'm supposed to bring you a tree or something?"

"Fuck your tree."

"So what do you want? Tell me straight."

"I want a New Year's like regular people."

"Meaning?"

"A party, fun. I haven't seen anyone but you with your ugly face for a month and a half."

"Where am I going to get you a party? Have you completely lost your mind?"

"Well, you're going somewhere."

"You're fucking crazy! I'm not taking you anywhere!"

"Then I'll go and bring Kirya here."

At that, his eyes narrowed and turned into tiny slits. Evidently he had decided to give me a scare. But I was prepared for tricks like this. I had a nasty surprise up my sleeve for him in this case.

"Just try. They're nearly sure there that you decided to cash in on this business and arranged your own kidnapping."

"You're lying!"

"Check it out. I have a cell in my car. You can call them right now. We'll see how long it takes them to drive over and deal with you. Are you sure you can convince them? It doesn't much look like you and I are enemies. I'm afraid they aren't going to believe you. Especially since I don't plan to keep quiet either."

"You're playing me. You're always playing me!"

Naturally, I was playing him. Especially since my phone was in my right pocket, not my car. What idiot leaves it in his car? I just needed to play for time and at the same time press my attack. I knew he would quickly surrender when attacked.

"Check it out. We could go down in a minute. Only, just in case, I'm getting into my SUV and making myself scarce, and you're going to have to make tracks on the bus. I already gave you change. I think there's even enough for the metro. If you can get off the bus after three stops, consider yourself lucky. They're definitely not going to shoot in the metro. There are a hell of a lot of cops there."

"Damn!" he hissed.

"So you'd better put a lid on it. You won't be able to prove anything to them anyway. And if you run, then they'll definitely think you're the only one to blame. You have no other choice left. The smartest thing to do is to get on that train and go to your mama's in Ryazan."

"Damn!" he said again.

"What, it's so bad in Ryazan?"

"I just asked you about New Year's." He sighed deeply and dropped his head, upset. "You could just have said no but you had to start scaring me...You spoiled my whole mood."

"You asked for it."

"I just didn't want to be alone here all night tomorrow."

Suddenly I felt sorry for him.

"Well, you want me to bring you champagne?"

"You and your champagne can go to hell. You'll hold the money against me later anyway."

"Whatever," I said. "Maybe I'll stop by tomorrow too."

"Go to hell," Sasha repeated, now without any malice.

When I went downstairs, the phone in my pocket rang. It's a good thing I was already outside. Actually, I probably would have wiggled out of it even then. Poor Sasha was so fucking easy to play. Especially since lately I'd gotten awesome in that respect. It was hard to catch me flat-footed now. I don't even know what could seriously catch me unawares.

"Yes," I said, opening the door.

"Listen, has Marina called you lately?" I heard Sergei's voice.

"Marina?" I repeated, and froze without even getting behind the wheel.

"Well, yeah...I just thought...It's been nearly six months... Hey, can you hear me?"

"I...can hear you...Yes, yes, everything's fine."

"You've kind of dropped out of sight. Maybe you can stop by? We could talk."

"I had a few things to take care of...Fine. I'll stop by tomorrow, in the morning...We can talk."

"Happy New Year."

"Yeah, yeah, you too," I said. "Tomorrow at eleven, okay?"

"Okay." He hung up.
What the fuck, I thought.
Other than that, my mind was drawing a blank.

---

I arrived a little before eleven. I don't know why it turned out like that. I just couldn't sit still any longer. I got up very early and left the dacha before Marina and Misha woke up. I really didn't feel like talking to either of them. It's not that I'd suddenly taken a dislike to everything. I just knew that I was going to lie, and I was going to lie specifically about them. It even made me a little sick to my stomach. Not a lot, but in general, in a mild way. I always get sick to my stomach when I'm nervous or just worked up. At school, before exams, I was always nauseated. I never actually threw up, but I felt woozy and nasty in general. I cut out before they woke up. I had no desire to talk to them, knowing I was going to lie about them. About how I hadn't seen them for a long time, and all that jazz. For some reason, it felt as though it would be like saying they'd died. That was probably what was making me feel sick.

"Well, how goes it?" Seryozha said without turning around when I walked in. "Lots of people walking around with New Year's trees? Did you see Father Frost?"

"Not that many," I answered. "Everyone has artificial ones now."

"I've got plenty of Santa Clauses here."

"What's that?"

I took a step and looked over his shoulder.

"It's Paris."

There was a public square on the screen.

"A movie or something? A video?"

"A video. It's the Internet."

"Did you hook it up to a television?"

"No, I just found this site where they get information from video cams all over the world. The cams are hanging on the central squares of all the capitals. A New Year's trick. Cool, huh?"

"Is there one in Moscow?"

"What do you care about Moscow? Look out the window and you'll see."

"Yeah? It never occurred to me."

"Look, here's Buenos Aires. It's still night there."

"And hot, probably."

"You said it. The Santa Clauses are going to be sweating. See, there he goes!"

"That's odd," I said. "It's so hot, and he's in a fur coat."

"He's not going to go around in a T-shirt and shorts."

"Why not? And what is he doing loafing around at night? It's still the night before there. Or the night after?"

"Look, it's Tokyo now."

"Good-looking tree. I don't get the ornaments on it."

"When we were kids we made the ornaments ourselves."

"What for?" I said.

He finally tore himself away from the monitor and looked at me.

"We had a fir growing in the yard at our dacha. My father and I would take sand molds...You know, those little fish and little stars?"

"Yes."

"We'd fill them with colored water and freeze them. The main thing was to put in the thread. Afterward, it froze inside, and we hung the ornament on the tree by it. It was pretty, and they hung for a real long time. By March, there were only threads left on the tree."

"What did you color the water with?"

"Watercolor paints. The best was the blue. Like real icicles."

"Did you ever try licking them?"

"A couple of times." He smiled. "My tongue stuck. They had to lift me up so we could pull the ornament off the tree."

"Did it hurt?"

"And how." He smiled again.

"Look," I said. "Someone's waving."

"It's Naoko."

He turned quickly to the screen.

"Who?"

"Naoko. A girl from Japan."

"But who is she?"

"I don't know. I just met her half an hour ago. I was surfing the Internet and happened to run into her. She was the one who told me about this site. Then she said she'd go to the square and wave to me. She lives somewhere close by. Look, she's kind of attractive."

"Not bad," I agreed. "You could fucking collect people all over the world like this."

"Yup," he said.

"And they could wave to you."

"What for?"

"I don't know. For fun. Is she going to wave like that for long?"

"She doesn't know we can see her. She'll probably stop soon."

"She just did. What time is it there?"

"Almost night, I think."

"That means they'll greet the New Year before us."

"Well, yeah. They're in the East."

"I get it," I said. "That's good."

"In what sense?"

"I don't know. It's just good in no sense."

I was feeling a little better now. He was obviously in no hurry with his questions.

"I'm really not in any kind of mood for some reason," he said with a sigh.

"Well, let's lift that mood."

"Oh, I don't mean that."

"What then?"

"Well, you know, there's this mood on New Year's. Like in *Irony of Fate*."

"Aha," I said. "In the old days we always used to eat tangerines on New Year's. Whenever I smelled them, my head would start spinning right away. You know, Father Frost, presents, and all that. It was awesome. Now they sell tangerines year-round. I can't even remember how they're supposed to make you feel."

"Are you in a New Year's mood?"

"Me?" I shrugged. "I guess so. Why do you give a damn?"

"Well, I don't know. There should be some kind of... feeling."

"Why?"

"Well, it's that kind of day."

"What kind?"

"I don't know...Special."

"It's a regular day," I said. "Only afterward there are always lots of dishes to wash."

"What's your special day then?"

"Mine?" I paused. "I don't have special days."

"Not at all?"

"Virtually."

"And you never feel different?"

"Different how?"

"Not like usual."

"And how do I feel usually?"

"Well…"—he was a little confused—"like ordinary."

"Ordinary gets me high."

"Is that right?" He was silent for a moment. "Then you're very cool."

"Meaning?"

"People don't like their usual lives. Too gray."

"You think?"

"Ask anyone."

"I think they're lying," I said.

"What for?"

"They're afraid of jinxing things."

"Jinxing things?"

"Well, yeah. We're secretly crazy about our life, but we give each other the business about how sick of life we are. It's a self-defense mechanism. You shouldn't believe people when they complain about life. In that case, you either have to run them off or give them money. But under no circumstances believe them."

At that moment I suddenly thought, Oops! What am I doing? Too much philosophy.

Actually, I had good reason. Seryozha had completely forgotten that he'd wanted to ask me about Marina. So I was rejoicing.

"How can you not believe them and give them money?" he asked in amazement.

"How else? I'd even say you should never do what you believe."

"How's that?"

"Very simple. What you believe will happen anyway. Otherwise it wouldn't be true."

"Yeah?" He looked at me with increasing astonishment. "What would it be then?"

"Oh, I don't know. A users' manual. You don't believe a washing machine is going to wash the laundry."

"What do you mean I don't? I do."

"No, you don't. You know for certain. See the difference? Believing and knowing. After all, you know it was made especially to wash laundry. Why do you have to believe it? Here you're following the manual. But when you start talking about belief, normal belief, I mean with all the trimmings… Well, when you believe…There, only asses are going to follow instructions."

"So you should only do what you yourself don't believe?"

"That's it. After all, someone has to. It's not going to get done by itself."

"But that's ridiculous!" He looked at me, smiling.

"Nevertheless. At least your conscience is clear."

He shrugged and stared at his computer. True, you could tell he didn't care. Meanwhile, something happened to him for the first time since we'd met. He was looking at the screen but thinking about something completely different. A second later, I realized I'd have been better off if he hadn't.

"You mean, if I *believe* that sooner or later I'll see Marina again, then I shouldn't do anything to make that happen? I shouldn't try to see her?"

He turned around and looked at me.

Now I didn't know what to tell him. Why the fuck did I ever start this conversation? I never got a decent grade in philosophy at school.

"You think it will all happen by itself?" He was still waiting for an answer.

"Such bizarre examples you cite," I mumbled. "It's just a theory, after all."

"She hasn't called you?"

"Marina?"

Now that was one idiotic answer. I'm a hundred percent sure I shouldn't have repeated her name. Who else could he have been asking about!

"Well, yeah, Marina. Has she called you since we got back from Italy?"

"No," I said slowly and uncertainly. "Not really."

"How's that, not really? Has she called or not?"

"Basically, no."

"I don't understand you. How can she not 'basically'?"

Even I didn't know that, so I just shook my head as if my ears were ringing. "It happens. Out of the blue, I get this ringing in my ears."

"Why are you shaking your head?" he asked warily.

"My ears were ringing. Really bad. I can't hear you very well even."

"I was asking you about Marina," he repeated, louder. "Have you seen her or not?"

"Not," I replied quickly.

It's good he asked "or not." His "not" for some reason really helped me say my own. That happens too. You lean on somebody else's word and then—hop!—you jump to where you need to go.

"That's too bad." He immediately lost interest in me. "For some reason I thought you knew something about her."

"That's odd," I said, and I tried to look surprised.

It's a good thing he wasn't looking. Because I didn't do a very good job of it.

"You really don't know anything about her?"

"Oh, no, I don't know anything about her. She hasn't called, I haven't seen her, and no one's told me anything about her."

"Too bad," he said again.

"And how," I said.

We both fell silent.

"I didn't even think I was going to miss her so much. I tried calling her, but they gave up their apartment for some reason. There are completely different people living there."

"Imagine."

"It all turned out so idiotically for us in Italy."

"You shouldn't have taken her along," I interjected and stopped short.

After all, it was actually my idea for Marina to come to Italy with us.

"You think so?" He looked at me. "I don't know…I think it might have been even worse without her."

"Worse?" I was actually a little surprised.

"Well…I'm not talking about your wound now."

"Ah," I said. "I did think you were talking about my wound."

"In what sense?" he said cautiously.

"Well, you know, the bullet might not have hit my collarbone. It could just as easily have taken my head off."

"You do know I wasn't shooting at you."

"Yes, yes. Don't get bent out of shape."

"This has nothing to do with you."

"Yeah, I know. Why did you get so wound up?"

"Maybe you think I was jealous of you and that's why I shot you?"

"Why would you be jealous?"

"You were sleeping in the same room with her."

"Yeah?" Suddenly I was a little shaken.

The conversation seemed to have taken a wrong turn.

"Weren't you? And probably in the same bed."

I didn't know what to say to him.

"The same bed? Weren't you?" He looked me right in the eye.

Turning away now would have meant giving myself away lock, stock, and barrel.

"There wasn't another bed in your room, was there?"

"There was…this sofa in the foyer…"

"And you slept on it? Every night?"

"Well…basically…yeah."

I'm afraid I wasn't very convincing.

"Every night?"

Why the fuck did he have to repeat his dumb questions?

"Until you shot me in the collarbone."

"I told you I wasn't shooting at you. You were the one who came at me."

Now that was awesome. I really did like this kid. Like an idiot, I offered up my old, aching bones to the bullet, and now he was blaming me for not letting him scatter my brains all over the goddamn Italian hotel. Good kid. Gratitude was obviously the last thing I could expect from him.

"Of course, I was the one who came at you. I'm sorry it turned out like that."

"What, were you mad?" he asked a minute later.

"Oh no. Why should I be mad? It's all good. You were trying to show off, and I got in your way. Anyone would be angry in your place."

"That's not quite the point." He even gestured out of impatience.

"It's not? What is?"

He turned away and said nothing in reply.

"What is? Huh? Why don't you say something? If you're not going to talk, I'm leaving! I wanted to visit with you before New Year's!"

"The point is that I was miserable without her," he said in a muffled voice, not turning away from the computer. "You can't even imagine how miserable. You shouldn't have got in my way that time."

"I could see the bullet right up against the firing pin," I said slowly.

"That's what I'm talking about…You shouldn't have got mixed up in it."

"So," I said slowly.

To be honest, I didn't think he was serious. But who knows with these teenagers? Either they're guffawing all the time or they're sitting like that, with their back to you, at a computer. It's a good thing I'd taken the gun away from him at least.

"It's true you haven't seen her?"

He shouldn't have asked me that.

"Is it true? Why don't you say something? You're all over me and then just like that you're silent."

"I am not."

"You're not silent? Then what are you doing?"

"I'm thinking."

"What about?"

"I'm thinking about what you asked."
"And?"
"No."
"Are you sure?"
"No."
"Meaning you're not sure?"
"No. I haven't seen her."
"Good." He sighed deeply. "If you do, tell her...Though, all right...Happy New Year's...Well, and basically..."
"Happy New Year." I tried not to look at him.

I was standing like an idiot in the middle of the room turning my head from side to side.

"It's true, I didn't shoot you on purpose then."
"You already said that."

I stood there another minute, then turned and walked out of the room. What other choice did I have? I couldn't stand there forever.

---

On the landing in front of my apartment, it took me a long time to get the key in the lock. It wasn't that it was so small or the key was so big, but I was so lost in my own thoughts, I wasn't really thinking about what I was doing there. It happens sometimes. You pick something up because you needed it a minute ago, and the next minute you've clean forgotten why you picked it up, so you stand there like a moron, turning it in your hands, but at the same time you're not even surprised because you're thinking about something else. And when a couple of minutes pass you quietly start figuring out what's what. That's what's called booting up. Especially since I was also holding a bottle of champagne.

I finally opened the door and stepped into the apartment. Sasha moved toward me from the half-dark vestibule. I was about to say hello when he raised both arms over his head and struck me with something heavy. The next moment I fell right at his feet. There were cross-trainers directly in front of me. My cross-trainers. Great, I managed to think. He's already wearing my shoes. Who knows where this is going to lead?

It's not many times I've lost consciousness in my life. I mean, come crashing down like this so naturally and lying like a blockhead in the middle of the room. In school, of course, I liked to play with key chains. I'd tighten them on my neck, count to ten, and so forth, but that wasn't the real thing. Naturally, we fell on the hall floor. One time my friend busted his head so bad they had to call an ambulance. But actually getting conked out—that had never happened to me before. Not counting getting shot in Italy, naturally. But that goes without saying. When you're shot point-blank, it's not like you have any other choice. You slam onto your back, or whatever, and roll your eyes back. This time it was completely different. No one had ever hit me in the head this hard, really. I used to think about how hard you'd have to strike someone for him to pass out. Like Tyson does when those knees start wobbling and they're retreating all over the ring until they fall down dead. Now it turned out that it doesn't take a Tyson. A Sasha Mercedes wielding a stool is plenty. Though I still don't know which one's tougher. If you smashed Tyson in the head with a stool, his knees would probably start wobbling too. But maybe not. Who knows. He's like an ox. Hardy, and all glossy. Black guys are pretty solid usually.

"Why the fuck did you put this rag on my head?" I said, opening my eyes after ten minutes or so probably. Actually, it could have been more. I don't keep track of time very well unconscious.

"There's blood," he replied. "I got scared."

"It stinks of soup. Where did you get it?"

"In the kitchen. I just washed your pot. There's no more soup."

"Damn," I said, and I threw the rag as far away as possible. "Couldn't you have grabbed a towel from the bathroom?"

"I didn't think of it. You fell so fast. I thought you were dying."

"You probably cracked my skull."

"Does it hurt a lot?"

"You have to ask, you snake?"

I tried to rise and immediately clutched my head.

"Forgive me, Misha! I thought Kirya had found me!"

"Kirya? What does he have to do with it? Being alone here has made you stupid."

"I'm telling you the truth! Someone came here from him last night. They spent half an hour trying to pick the lock. They couldn't open it. Otherwise they'd have finished me off already. And then they would have gone after you."

I thought I must have gone a little overboard yesterday, frightening him with showdowns with Kirya.

"How could he have found me? Damn, my head is killing me now! I'm going to have a concussion because of you."

"No kidding, I'm telling you." He leaned toward me and flapped his arms agitatedly. "Who else is supposed to be mucking around at your door? They would have slit my throat and then waited for you. An ambush."

He said the last words in a sinister whisper. Apparently, he had contemplated this subject fairly seriously.

"Fine, fine." I winced. "Let's say they've found us. They saw you leave the store with me. They must have tracked us down by my car. I'll have to replace it."

"Yeah, no kidding, I'm telling you," he rattled on agitatedly, but I gestured for him to shut up.

My head was positively splitting. His voice was resonating inside my skull like claps of thunder. Especially when the freaked-out dumbbell who smashed me in the head with a stool was hollering right next to me.

"I'm not staying here alone," Sasha said, leaning even lower toward me. "They'll come back today, and then they are definitely going to get your door open."

"Wait up," I said. "Where are you going to go?"

"With you."

"With me?" My head actually stopped hurting for a second.

"Where else? It's your fault I don't have anywhere to go now."

"You've lost your mind."

"Then get out your cannon and sit here all night with me. I don't want to talk to them by myself. Ultimately, this is your problem. You're the one who set me up, you snake."

"I set you up?"

"Who else? The bogeyman or something?"

Suddenly it occurred to me that he could have cooked this whole thing up just to be able to celebrate New Year's with me. I wondered whether he had the intelligence for improv like that. I'm talking about cracking me with the stool so convincingly.

"You'll stay?" He gave me a challenging look.

"Go to hell," I muttered, trying finally to get up.

"I already have. You're one tough guy. I've got all these problems because of you and now you're sending me away. No, no kidding, one tough guy."

I made it to the armchair and looked him straight in the eye. Was he lying to me or not? I was so used to constant lying that you could hardly surprise me if this retard decided to score a few points for the other side.

Was that really it? I thought, looking at his silly, stupid face.

"Where's my champagne?" I finally said. "Smashed?"

"In the refrigerator. What the fuck do you want champagne for now?"

"Open it. Maybe it'll make my head stop hurting at least."

"A little vodka's better for your head," he said from the kitchen now. "Especially since it's my bottle. You brought it here for me."

"And you cracked me over the head in spite of it."

"Why'd you have to take so damn long opening the door? Why were you mucking around with the key in the lock so long?"

"I got to thinking," I said softly.

"What?" he shouted, slamming the refrigerator door.

"Nothing. Up yours!"

"You're being crude, Misha," he said, entering the room, bottle in hand. "And you don't have champagne glasses."

"I'll drink from a water glass."

"You can drink out of your hands. I'm still not in any kind of New Year's mood."

"I'm sick of your New Year's mood."

"I'll bet you're getting ready to go somewhere."

"I'm so sick of you."

"You're sick of me?" He looked at me eloquently and took a long pause.

"Are you going to open it or not?"

"Drink your own champagne. I hope you choke on it!"

He pulled the cork so abruptly that half the bottle spilled right onto the floor.

"Good thing I don't have a carpet," I muttered, and I drank nearly a whole glass in one gulp.

The champagne wasn't bad.

"Happy New Year," Sasha said, turning away from me and rubbing his foot in the puddle.

"Get ready." I sighed. "You're coming with me. Only you're going to stay in the car all evening."

"Does your TV work there?" he asked, cheered up.

Maybe he isn't lying, I thought. Who wants to greet the New Year in someone else's SUV?

---

In fact, I really don't like holidays very much. You're always expecting something from them, and you never get it. Oh, I mean, in the sense that you have fun, and there's drinking and girls, but if you're honest about it, it never ends up the way you thought it would at the beginning. I don't know why, but you're always expecting something else. It's hard to explain. Not Father Frost, of course, but something, I don't know…new.

It used to be okay. When I was still little. It always turned out like I'd expected. Maybe the right time has just passed. Who the hell knows when it comes to time. Something's changed. Even drinking doesn't seem as interesting anymore. I could have gone to bed and slept through the whole

New Year's. Especially when my head was roaring louder than a moped motor.

Everyone at the dacha was already good and cranked up. Ramil and Repa were disentangling the string of lights. Marina and one of her classmates were cooking croquettes, and little Misha was doing his best to get in the way of them both. The smell of the croquettes immediately turned my stomach. I summoned my courage and told myself it would soon pass. At least in the kitchen I couldn't hear the wild sounds of the Prodigy as loud.

"Cool music," I said, shutting the door to make it quieter.

"I want you to meet Lida." Marina nodded toward her friend.

"We've already met." Lida smiled. "I saw you at the institute."

Personally, I didn't remember her. But that didn't matter. If we'd met, then we'd met.

"Hi," I said, trying not to wince from my headache.

"Prodigy went out of fashion a long time ago," she continued. "And anyway, this is teenager music. Everything always happens with a slight delay for Ramil."

"Yeah?" I said, and I looked out the window.

I couldn't care less about Ramil or his music.

"Why did you park your car on the road?" Marina asked.

I had to think of something, but my head felt like cast iron. That was quite a wallop he gave me. My head was more like a cannonball. Load the cannon and fire it at the moon. I read that once, as a child, in Jules Verne. Or someone else. It was *Professor Dowell's Head*. I think that's how it went. A bodiless head lay in some glass drawer spouting all kinds of drivel. I could use that head right now. Even without a body.

"Listen, I don't know," I finally said.

"How's that, you don't know?" Marina looked at me in surprise. "You don't know why you parked your car on the road?"

"Yeah, I don't. I just parked it there, that's all. I decided not to drive through the gates. That's not allowed?"

"No, no," she said slowly. "It's just kind of strange."

Of course it's strange, I thought. If you only knew who I had sitting there.

"It's better to park the car closer to the house," this Lida butted in. "Last year some people I know had their brand-new Renault stolen. They just got it from France. They left it on the road like that, and when they woke up the next morning, it was gone. The police refused to look for it."

You're all I need now, I thought woefully.

I don't know why, but I had more than a headache now. It felt as though that idiot had battered my entire body with his stool. Even my knees had started hurting. Could he have damaged my spine?

"How do you feel?" Marina frowned, concerned. "You don't look so good."

"I feel fine. I just have a slight headache. I spent all day running around town. Buying everything."

"I'll give you an aspirin. By the way, you didn't forget the whetstone, did you? The meat's impossible to cut."

I remembered I'd left it in the car. I'd tossed it on the backseat and forgotten it. That jerk was probably sitting next to my whetstone right now watching that game show, *Field of Wonders*. Just the show for him. Handing out New Year's elephants for free. No gift wrapping, though.

"Let me get it," this Lida suddenly said.

I'd known her all of five minutes and she'd already managed to eat me alive. I wonder what she would have thought seeing poor Sasha in my car, full of his New Year's mood.

"I'll get it myself. It's not hard."

"Okay, then I'll go with you. My head's starting to hurt too."

Pushy, I thought.

Now Marina looked at her in surprise too. She could scarcely have expected a temperament like that from her friend. It's always like that with friends. They always surprise you at the most inopportune time. Personally, I've never understood why anyone needs them.

"You know, I'd rather do it myself. It would be unfair to leave Marina alone with these croquettes."

"I can find you another aspirin in my medicine cabinet," Marina told her. "Want it?"

This Lida made a very interesting face.

"I'm allergic to pills."

I didn't stick around to hear about her allergy. To hell with these complicated female relationships. I'd rather watch a soap opera on the subject. At least you can turn it off whenever you want.

"Well, how is it there?" Sasha asked when I opened the car.

"You could at least leave me alone. Sit there and keep quiet, please."

"I was just asking."

"And I was just answering."

"You're in a pretty foul mood, I'd say. Today is New Year's, after all."

"Mention New Year's one more time and I'm taking you back to the apartment."

"All right already. What's got you so mad?"

"If your head was screaming like mine is, you'd probably be swearing at everyone."

"I don't blaspheme anymore."

"Yeah, I've noticed."

I couldn't seem to find that stupid whetstone in the dark.

"I didn't hit you on purpose," he said after a pause. "Word of honor."

"Thanks. That makes me feel much better."

"I thought Kirya'd come."

"You already said that."

"I didn't hit you on purpose."

As I was climbing the front steps, it suddenly occurred to me that Sergei had said almost the exact same thing this morning. I mean the "on purpose" part. Who knows, maybe he wasn't lying. When you crack someone in the head, the easiest thing is to convince yourself you didn't do it on purpose. It might not come out quite naturally, but on the other hand, your conscience quits bothering you. Cheap, but good. Like the free gifts on *Field of Wonders*. I do wonder, though, who actually does pay for them. Someone probably gets hit in the head with a stool too.

They dealt with Listyev, no joke, may he rest in peace. Afterward, more than likely, they probably told themselves, "Oh, we didn't do it on purpose."

"Maybe you could sharpen our knives at the same time too," this Lida said in a very sweet voice. "There is an obvious shortage here of male strength."

I wasn't about to tell her what her obvious shortage was, of course, but if Sasha Mercedes had stopped swearing, then I had to get a grip too.

"What do you mean, 'at the same time'?" I asked.

Somehow, I didn't feel like being rude to her, really.

"Sharpen this," Marina intervened suddenly. "We're all out of time. Everyone's going to be sitting down at the table soon."

Ultimately, it wasn't like this sharpening of knives was my idea.

"Tell me, Mikhail," Lida raised her voice a minute later. "How did you meet Marina?"

Here we go again, I thought.

"Hand me the salt, please," Marina said.

She obviously was not about to help me out. I had to bear this on my lonesome.

"We were making croquettes together."

"Ha ha ha," our Lida laughed. "I appreciate a sense of humor in a man."

Her laughter nearly killed me. Not that she sounded like a hyena, but it wasn't far off. My Marina had enchanting girlfriends.

"Now tell me"—this girl would not let up—"what do you appreciate most in us?"

"In you?"

I evidently said it in some special tone that flustered her.

"Well, not me personally...but women in general."

How can I put it without insulting her? I thought.

"Almost done?" Marina asked. "I don't have anything to cut the meat with. Hurry up."

"What I value most in women," I said in my most idiotic voice, "is intelligence, independence, and kindness."

Now she had to lay off. After that, any normal person would realize her leg was being pulled.

"That can't be," she cheeped. "Do you really pay any attention to those aspects of the female person?"

I realized I'd lost. This was a clinical case. She could only be cured in a locked facility.

"It's true," I said. "I never lie."

"You don't?" Her eyes rounded. "You have some kind of principle? Do you practice Buddhism?"

I was longing to say it was more like Stupidism, but, thank God, I refrained. In principle, I try not to be rude.

"Incredible." She kept trying to polish me off. "I've never met a man before who consciously rejected lying. Marina is awfully lucky to have you. How do you manage to avoid lying? Sometimes men simply must."

You can't even imagine how much, I thought.

Out loud I said, "I make an effort of will."

"An effort of will? How is that? Something like autosuggestion?"

"Well, an amateur, obviously, would put it exactly like that." I could feel myself getting carried away.

"How would a professional put it?"

"Here, a special system of training is very important. Tibetan monks developed a special set of exercises in the late seventeenth century."

"No way. Tell me about it."

I stole a look in Marina's direction. She was standing with her back to me, chopping vegetables. Her back didn't express anything special. I wondered how much she was prepared to put up with.

"Basically, it's a matter of a special…"

At that moment, the kitchen door flung open and Misha ran in.

"Careful!" Marina exclaimed. "Don't knock them over!"

He swept past the crystal glasses set out on the table and ran up to me.

"I want to go in the car!"

This was below the belt. I thought we'd already exhausted the car topic.

"I want to go in the car! I want to steer!"

"Mikhail parked the car outside the gates," Marina said in a stern voice. "Don't bother us. Go play with Ramil."

"Ramil told me to go sit in the car."

Today was obviously not my day.

"I'll bet you broke an ornament on the tree."

"Only two."

"I'll let you steer tomorrow morning," I said. "We don't have time now."

"Let me, I'll sharpen the knife for you," Lida offered. "Take him for a little ride. Such a marvelous little boy."

"A marvelous little boy." Misha repeated what she'd said in a happy voice.

I thought it was too bad I'd told her about the Tibetan monks. She didn't deserve that.

"No cars." Marina came to my rescue. "It's time to sit down at the table."

I breathed a sigh of relief.

"Listen, you've got someone sitting in your car," Ramil said, peeking in the kitchen.

After that everyone fell silent and looked at me. Even Misha's face expressed interest. Now I definitely didn't know what to say. I can imagine what I looked like at that moment.

"It can't be," I forced out. "It must just look like it."

"Go out yourself and take a look. You can see right from the outhouse."

"Did you close it up properly?" Lida interjected.

I am so sick of you, I thought woefully.

"Why don't we go sort this out?" Ramil offered.

Marina was looking at me in silence and thinking something.

"You just thought you saw someone," I repeated. "There's no one there."

"Thought I did? We haven't even opened the champagne yet. Wait up, I'll go out again right now and look."

Ramil walked out of the house and we stayed standing where we were. For a whole minute no one said a word. Marina kept looking at me closely.

"He's sitting there," he said, coming back in a minute later. "I'm telling you, there's definitely someone there. Why don't you believe me? I'm telling you the truth. Go take a look for yourself if you like."

I can't remember ever getting myself in a more stupid jam. Why do these things happen at all? There you are in the middle of the kitchen at some dacha on New Year's Eve and everyone is looking at you like you're an idiot, but most of all, you feel like an idiot. Your fondest wish is to be anywhere but here this very minute. At the movies, for instance. Or the library. Holding a book by Dostoevsky. *The Idiot*, for instance.

"Oh, that must be Sasha," I finally got out.

"Sasha? What Sasha?" Marina's eyes narrowed slightly. "Why is she sitting in your car?"

"It's not a she…It's a he…Alexander…A man."

"Yeah?"

Her expression didn't change. She was silent for a second.

"Why didn't you bring him along? Why did you leave him on the road? Were you planning to go somewhere? Is he waiting for you?"

"It is New Year's, after all," Lida chimed in. "Are you really planning to do business on a night like this? Stay. Don't leave us alone."

Evidently she felt lonely surrounded by four people. I wonder what she'd say if there really was no one left with her.

"I'm not going anywhere. He's just sitting there because… he can't come in the house."

Now I had told the pure truth. Even I felt good.

Lately, this was an extremely rare occurrence. It was like an obsession. You lie and lie without end.

"He can't?" they all chorused. "But why?" They had such astonished faces that I nearly started to laugh. That is, I mean, even in this situation I thought it was funny. Never before had I seen several people open their mouths in amazement simultaneously. Misha's mouth wasn't open. He was licking the icing off the cake.

"Why can't he?" Marina repeated.

"He's allergic to fir trees. He could easily die. An ambulance wouldn't come here."

The part about the allergy was great. Again I hadn't lied. Telling the truth was such a pleasure I couldn't stop myself.

"A month ago he nearly kicked it. If it weren't for me, he'd be dead and buried now."

I felt like I'd sprouted wings. Never before had I had such satisfaction. You say it and you know it's true. It's an inexpressible feeing. I would tell the truth my whole life. It was as exciting as falling in love for the first time.

"Wait up, but he's not going to sit in your SUV all night," Marina said indignantly. "Is that the only reason you brought him here?"

"But we can't bring him into the house," I objected, quietly rejoicing in the brilliance of my position.

"What do you mean, we can't? We'll take the fir outside and air out the house."

Now, that I hadn't expected. I had not taken her practical nature into account. Marina is one of those people who never relents.

"Okay, but today is New Year's Eve." I finally said the cursed words myself. "How will we do without a tree?"

"That's just it, it's New Year's Eve. Do you want us to mock a human being? Why did you drag him here at all?"

Now that was a good question. Too bad I couldn't answer it honestly.

---

Sasha himself may have been the most surprised of all.

"Don't worry," Marina reassured him. "We've already taken the tree out."

"Oh, I'm not worried," he replied, still swiveling his head from side to side.

Evidently, he was trying to see who else was standing in the dark around the car. Maybe he was looking for me.

I waved so he could tell who to focus on. He nodded and finally got out of the SUV.

"At first I thought you wanted to settle a score with me," he said, with a stupid laugh. "I look, and there's this crowd hanging around the car."

"Did we scare you or something?" Marina asked. "Did you take us for criminals?"

"How do I know what kind of people are hanging around in the dark? I look, and there's someone hanging around."

"Where are we going to get criminals here? They're all in Moscow. Celebrating New Year's. It's already nine thirty."

"What do you mean, nine thirty? The car clock says it's nearly midnight."

"Oh, I forgot to warn you," I said. "It's on the fritz. It's fast. I can't seem to get around to fixing it."

"Real cute." He harrumphed. "And I was just about to celebrate the New Year. Because of you I would have celebrated it with people in the Urals."

"Nothing would have happened. You would have celebrated it twice. That's even more fun."

"Come on, let's get back to the house," Marina suggested. "It probably doesn't smell of fir there anymore. I opened all the doors wide. Now we'll have to heat it more."

Some sixth sense told me that this idiot was just about to blab something about the fir. I took a step toward him and elbowed him as hard as I could.

"Hey, what's with you?" He hissed from the pain.

"Nothing, let's hurry up. After all, you were the one who wanted to celebrate New Year's with people. See? Father Frost granted your wish. Did you believe in Father Frost when you were a kid?"

"Take off your coat," Marina said when we walked into the house. "It's still chilly now, but it'll be warm before long. We have a very good stove. Ramil, did you close the porch door?"

"Right away," he called back.

"Quickly, take off your jacket." She turned to Sasha. "You must have been freezing in the car. You know, I think I've seen you somewhere. You have a very familiar face."

"Sasha appears on television from time to time," I said quickly.

"He does?" Lida's voice was languid. "What do you do there?"

"The weather report," I answered again.

"What channel?"

"A few." I kept answering for him, realizing I was talking total rubbish.

"But not Channel One?"

"No, not One…That requires knowledge of a language."

"English?"

"Any European language."

"How odd." She shrugged. "Why do they need a language? And why a European one specifically?"

"How do you know all these things?" Marina began.

"I…was curious."

"Looking for a job or something?" Repa intoned.

"Something like that. But Sasha was luckier. They took him, not me."

"Why do you keep speaking for him?" Marina said. "What are you, his agent? Do you really do the weather report, or is our Mikhail joking again?"

"Why 'again'?" I said.

"Yes." Sasha smiled, bewildered. " 'Rostov Province is expecting a little snow' and so on…We do the weather…I mean, we report it."

"I see," Marina said. "Well, take off your coat. Why are you standing there? Let me have your gloves."

"No!" I shouted nearly at the top of my lungs. "He can't take off his gloves."

They all looked at me as if I were crazy. I had to think of something, and fast. I couldn't let Marina see his tattoo. That would easily give him away.

"He has…scabs all over his hands from…his allergy. So the doctors fill his gloves with a special ointment…It's important he doesn't take them off at all. Just when they're changing the bandages."

Everyone looked warily at Sasha's hands. He himself gave me a dazed look.

"Is it really that serious?" Lida asked, alarmed.

"But how does he appear on television?" Marina said.

"He's on medical leave right now. But when necessary they use computer graphics. You know, like in *Forrest Gump*... They used a computer to make it look like this one actor didn't have a left leg, but in fact his left leg is even bigger than his right. I was watching the Cannes film festival afterward. He showed the leg to all the reporters there, to anyone. Just his leg. But in the movie, he doesn't have a leg. A shell tore it off in Vietnam."

I tried to carry on just to distract them from his gloves.

"Well, fine." Marina finally shrugged. "Leave them on, if you like. Only eating will be awkward."

"Eating is never awkward." Sasha grinned.

*I should have come up with another profession for him* flashed through my mind. They don't smirk like that on television. What a fool I am.

"Can you tell us what the weather forecast is for tomorrow?" Lida cooed.

"Absolutely," Sasha answered.

I could tell he was coming around.

All evening he was exquisitely happy. For a while Lida even stopped pestering me and focused her attentions almost entirely on that jerk. He simply melted in the rays of her concerted attention. She said she was a nurse and, with the face of a tenderhearted woodcutter, kept serving him salad Olivier. An hour later I started calculating when he'd get sick to his stomach. But I had it wrong. Either I fed him badly in captivity, or else this pushy Lida had some secret. One way or another he swallowed huge portions of salad without any obvious injury to his health. The champagne did nothing to hurt his excellent mood.

Unfortunately, this idyll could not last forever. Fairly quickly, poor Sasha used up his entire vocabulary, and energetic Lida clearly began to lose interest. From where I sat, it reminded me of the halting of a nuclear reactor. Not immediately, but step by step, the fire in her eyes began to dim, and more and more often I caught her glancing at me. Very soon the danger signs were confirmed. Now I experienced the contradictory feelings of a talented doctor who has made a very difficult diagnosis. On the one hand, he's pleased that he was right; on the other, he's in despair because his worst fears have been vindicated.

I was also lucky that the critical moment came right at midnight. What with all the flurry with Bengal fire, firecrackers, and fireworks, I was able to avoid her for nearly a whole hour. But afterward, when everyone had calmed down and gone back to the table, there was no more salvation. She turned her whole body toward me and with a predatory gleam in her eyes began to badger me about "what makes a real man." This was obviously quite an exciting topic for her, since she believed there were hardly any real men left in Russia. From what she said I gathered that a small remnant of them could still be found in Santa Barbara, but in order to go there you had to have a sponsor who, unfortunately, would also more than likely have to be a man. But since there were no more real ones left in Russia, then Lida was obviously faced with a vicious cycle.

Basically, I was trapped for just a little while, and as soon as Marina went to put Misha to bed, I signaled to her that I would wait for her by the porch. If this had gone on even another ten minutes, I would have strangled poor Lida without the slightest pity. Sometimes I can well understand why Othello dealt so harshly with his Desdemona. Jealousy is far from the sole motivation. It's just that Shakespeare probably didn't write everything. He didn't have it in him to write the real truth.

"Where did you dig her up?" I asked Marina when we were already sitting in the car and I had a chance to catch my breath after the longest kiss in my life.

"Why did you have to make fun of her?"

"But she's a fool."

"Just because someone's stupid doesn't mean you have to make fun of them. It's not their fault."

"Yeah? That never occurred to me somehow. Are you angry at me?"

"Only a tiny bit."

"Thank God."

At this, the misunderstanding over Lida was exhausted. At least, I hoped it was.

"Listen, about your Sasha," she whispered. "Admit you lied. He's no television announcer."

"Of course," I replied in the same whisper. "In fact, he's a criminal and a murderer. And he's not taking off his gloves because he wears them when he's planning to strangle curious little girls. Like Othello. Have you ever dreamed of playing Desdemona?"

"Oh, you." She laughed quietly. "Can you talk seriously for once?"

"On New Year's? What, have you lost your mind?"

I leaned in and kissed her again, the longest kiss in my life. I liked kissing her like that. I heard her breathing through her nose.

"You bit me," she whispered, gasping slightly. "Now my lip's going to hurt."

"I didn't do it on purpose."

"Next time I'm going to bite you too."

"Listen," I started talking after a brief pause, surprising myself. "What went on in Italy between you and that minister's son?"

"Matteo?" She laughed. "Nothing at all. We just rode around and he told me about his life. He probably fell in love. How do I know?"

"How could he have told you about his life if you don't understand a word of Italian?"

"Well, at least I think he was telling me about his life. In fact, he always talked a lot and I liked listening to him. You know how beautiful Italian sounds? Especially since sometimes he translated it all into English."

She smiled, remembering.

"What, are you jealous?"

"Of course not," I said. "I was just asking. It just came to mind somehow."

We fell silent, staring at the tiny television screen.

"Everyone's on a diet now," she said. "It suits her much better, don't you think?"

"Who's that?"

"Dolina. You mean you didn't recognize her?"

"Why is she singing in English?"

"I don't know. It's some New Year's concert. All the Russians are singing in English."

"Strange idea."

"I think it's good. Did she do well?"

"I can't tell. Russian singers don't do anything for me."

"No, I'm talking about her losing weight."

"Oh, in that sense. Of course, she did. You mean she was really fat?"

"Stop pretending. You really don't remember?"

"No. I remember that Demis Roussos was fat. Also Seryozha Krylov, and also Luciano Pavarotti."

"What's the matter with you! You're yanking my chain on purpose. Just like Lida."

We fell silent again.

"And on the yacht?" I said.

"What on the yacht?" She looked uncomprehendingly in my direction.

"Dima said that on the yacht you and that Matteo were shut up in the captain's cabin for a long time. The two of you. Without anyone else."

"Who is this Dima?"

"Pavel Petrovich's man in Florence. Remember, he dragged those art books to our hotel room? The fidgety guy."

"What does he have to do with all this?"

"I don't know. He just told me about it. After all, you weren't especially hiding from anyone."

She looked thoughtfully out the dark window.

"Still, you're jealous."

"I don't know…Maybe yes…I don't really understand what that is."

"Right here. Does it hurt?" She pressed her palm to my chest. "As if it tickled? And chills run down your spine."

"Yes," I said. "Only I don't understand—"

She covered my mouth with the same palm. My lips could feel her fingers trembling.

"To hell with him," she whispered.

"Who?"

"That lousy Dima."

We were both silent for a long time. Damn if I know what I was actually feeling. True, I don't have a very good sense of that. I did have kind of a bad feeling suddenly, but I wouldn't say I was put off. I just realized unexpectedly that her past had become a part of my life, and everything that had happened to her even before we met now affected me.

---

"Look," she whispered, tugging my sweater. "There's a car there."

Far off in the darkness, I saw a foreign car moving slowly between the trees. Its lights were out.

"But who could it be? You mean we have neighbors?"

"Of course not," Marina said. "No one's spending the winter here besides us."

The car stopped. I looked hard to see who would come out of the car, but no one did.

"That's odd," I said. "Let's turn off the television."

"You think we should hide?"

"I don't think anything. It's just better to sit in the dark for now."

"Maybe we should go back to the house then?"

"Wait a sec," I said. "Someone's coming out."

Five men got out of the car. They were talking about something, and then one of them headed in our direction.

"Misha," Marina whispered.

"It's all okay," I said. "Just sit quietly. Maybe they'll go away."

The person was coming closer and closer to our car. He was carrying a large square bag in his left hand.

"Why is he walking this way?" Marina asked, concerned. "What does he need?"

"Wait, we'll know everything soon enough."

The man was two paces away from us.

"Quiet," I whispered to Marina. "Don't budge."

The car's windows were tinted, but I still thought it was better to sit without moving at all.

The man stopped by the front passenger door and pressed his face to the window. I'd never been examined so close-up. For a second I was even tempted to flick him across the face.

Finally he drew off to the side, and I lost him from my field of vision. Judging from the rustling behind me, he had moved back somewhere. Evidently, he'd decided to walk around the car. A second later he appeared on the side where Marina was sitting. I felt her tense. Then she recoiled toward me with her whole body.

"Easy, easy," I whispered barely audibly right in her ear.

"I'm afraid," she mouthed, almost without a sound.

Meanwhile the person had disappeared somewhere below. Evidently he was doing something with his bag. The next second I caught the strong whiff of gasoline. When he stood up straight, he was holding a small gas can. Stepping aside, he started splashing it right on my car.

Now there wasn't a minute to lose.

The scariest part was that he wasn't on my side.

"When I say go, jump out of the car and run to the house," I whispered to Marina, who was frozen stiff. "Do you understand? Do you hear me? Do you understand or not?"

"I...understand."

"Shove him as hard as you can and run. Can you?"

"I don't know..."

"You absolutely have to knock him down. Then I'll be able to run around the car."

"Okay..."

"Can you?"

"I'll try," she whispered.

I found her hand in the darkness. It was as cold as ice.

"The main thing is to knock him down."

"All right."

"All set?"

"Yes."

"Wait another second...Wait...Go!"

She jerked the handle convulsively and pushed the door open as hard as she could. At that moment, the man with the gas can was shifting from foot to foot and leaning slightly forward. I don't know what he was trying to get a look at there, but it wasn't the best moment in his life. The door struck him full force in the face, and he flew back a couple of paces. Marina leaped out of the car and for a second froze in front of his motionless body. I managed to notice all this with my peripheral vision while I myself was moving at top speed past my radiator.

"Run!" I shouted. "Run fast! Don't stand there!"

The other criminals were already racing in our direction from the foreign car.

Marina shuddered and rushed toward the house. At that moment I found myself next to the man lying on the ground. He raised up and grabbed me by the left leg. I nearly fell down next to him but I kicked him in the head with my free foot and ran after Marina. The main thing now was to reach the porch faster than the criminals.

---

Afterward, thinking back on everything that happened that New Year's, I often reproached myself for my imbecility. If I'd stayed in the car, everything might have gone differently. Those jerks would have run after Marina, and I could have run them down in my SUV like rabbits. Then the whole story would have unfolded completely differently. Many problems could have been resolved directly that New Year's Eve.

Nevertheless, everything happened exactly as it did, and I didn't stay in the car but jumped out of it like a fool and ran after Marina toward the house, where our friends were still making merry, suspecting nothing.

"Cut the lights!" I shouted, running into the house and bolting the door behind me. "Cut them quick!"

Marina, her face white as a sheet, dropped to the floor beside me.

"What's the deal?" Ramil asked in surprise, holding a shot of vodka in one hand and a pickle on a fork in the other. "We already set off the fireworks. And now we're all out of them."

"Cut them!" I repeated.

At that moment, shots rang out outside.

"Oh! Someone else is setting off fireworks!" Repa intoned. "Let's go take a look at who's come."

I rushed to my room, dove under the bed, and began digging feverishly in my bag. My gun was supposed to be on the very bottom. I'd been so afraid Misha might find it.

"What's with you?" Ramil said when he saw the weapon in my hand.

"Those aren't fireworks," I muttered, dropping to my knees before the front door. "Those are no damn fireworks, guys."

I stuck the gun barrel under the door—there was always a small opening left there—and squeezed the trigger. Everyone shuddered at my shot, and Lida let out a sound more like a squeak.

"Misha, have you lost your mind or something? There are people there!" Ramil exclaimed.

"They have to know we have a weapon," I said, catching my breath a little. "If they know that, maybe they won't barge in right away."

"What's going on? Can you explain properly?"

"Cut the lights!"

"It's criminals," Marina said in a quiet voice. "They wanted to set fire to us in the car."

"You've lost your mind!"

I wasn't listening to anyone anymore. Running from room to room, trying not to show myself in the windows, I turned the lights off in the whole house. No one had so much as budged from the table. Everyone was numb.

"Turn off the tree lights too," Marina whispered, pointing to the corner where the holiday tree had stood.

At that moment, from somewhere in the darkness, we heard Sasha's voice.

"I told you they'd find you, but you wouldn't believe me."

"What, you think it's Kirya?" I said.

"Who else? Or have you stepped on someone else's tail too?"

"What Kirya? What are you talking about?" Marina interjected. "What, you know the people who attacked us?"

"Wait a sec," I replied. "I'll explain it all to you later."

"Later when? Tell me what's going on right now!"

There were shots outside again.

"If I were you I wouldn't sit there at the table," I said. "Some stray bullet could fly in and that would be the end."

"Wait," Ramil began again. "You mean you're serious? They really are shooting live ammunition?"

"Go out and check, if you like."

"Where should we hide?" Lida peeped. "Will they kill us? Will they kill us all?"

"What do they want?" Repa intoned.

"I don't know what they want," I lied. "The local toughs must have decided to have some fun."

"Maybe they won't kill us all?" Lida squeaked again.

"Naturally. They're going to drop you off at home. Just don't forget to tell them your address."

Outside, there were two shots in quick succession.

"Better to stand near the windows," I said. "Press up to the wall and don't stick your head out. They'll be afraid to climb into a dark house. They don't know how many of us are here."

Crouching, I made my way toward the door again and shot into the dark a second time. To be honest, I really didn't feel like hitting anyone. It's nasty to think you pull the trigger and a hole appears in someone's body. Bones break, flesh pokes out. I remember that all too well.

"Just don't stick your head out," I repeated again. "They might just be trying to scare us. They'll shoot a little now and then…"

At that moment the window Repa was standing next to flew apart with a crash and something heavy fell on the floor right at my feet.

"A grenade!" Sasha exclaimed.

I looked in the darkness where this small, round object was lying and suddenly I heard my heart beating. Could that really be how it's going to happen? I'm going to vaporize right now?

I shut my eyes and filled my lungs with air.

Five seconds passed, but deadly silence reigned all around as before. *I haven't died yet, have I?* flashed through my mind. But maybe…

"It's just a rock," someone's voice said.

"My God," Lida squeaked. "I nearly pissed myself I was so scared."

"Next time don't forget your diapers," Repa intoned.

I heard Misha crying in his room.

"Go to him," I told Marina. "It's dark there, after all. He must have gotten scared."

My voice was shaking a little. I even had to cough twice. I'd never had a hand grenade fall at my feet before. Even if it didn't turn out to be a grenade.

"Listen, commander," Sasha Mercedes whispered next to me.

I shuddered because I hadn't noticed him come up.

"What?"

"I'm telling you, let me go out to them. It's Kirya, after all. I'll go out and feed them a line. Maybe we can figure something out."

"What, have you lost your mind? You think he's going to be figuring anything out now?"

"He'd rather not set his buddies up for your bullets either. After all, he doesn't know you only have one barrel."

"And you want to go tell him?"

"You idiot. You held me in your apartment a whole month and never did understand a damn thing."

"What was I supposed to understand?"

"That not everyone is made of shit."

"I thought you stopped swearing."

"That's not a swear word. Not only that, I recognized your girlfriend at first glance."

"So what?"

"So now I know why you signed on for this thing. You weren't after Nikolai Nikolaevich's money for yourself, were you?"

"No."

"There, you see? The minute I saw your Marina today, I immediately understood everything about you."

"What did you understand?"

"None of your business. Your girlfriend's problems weren't because of me, of course. Other people made that decision. But I took the blame because I was the one who had to take her papa's money from her. So no matter what, I'm the one who should go now. It's plain this whole mess is because of me."

"You don't have to if you don't want. You've already paid for your mess-up."

"What do you know about my mess-ups?" He even chuckled a little. "You should be thinking about your own. You're going to have to answer someday too. So hold your fire for now. I'm going to try to shout to them from the window."

"Hold up...," I said.

But he just brushed me aside and ran over to the other wall like a swift shadow.

"Kirya!" The next second his voice rang out. "Kirya! Listen! Don't shoot! It's me, Sasha! Don't shoot!"

In the deathly silence, his voice sounded unnaturally loud. Misha had stopped crying, so there was the sensation that Sasha was shouting through a megaphone. Or maybe it was because we were in the forest. The acoustics were completely different from in town.

"Sasha, is that really you?" a voice came from outside.

"Of course it's me. Who else?"

"How do they know him?" Lida asked in a loud whisper.

"They used to be in Pioneers together," I said. "The young mechanics club."

"Wait up!" Sasha shouted out the window. "Don't shoot! I'm coming out!"

Not a sound came back.

"Can you hear me? I'm coming out!" Sasha repeated. "Can I?"

The forest was as silent as if everything there had died.

"Maybe they left?" Lida whispered hopefully. "They recognized Alexander and just left?"

"They left twice," Sasha muttered. "They're trying to decide whether to let me come out or not."

"Why do they need to decide? They're your friends."

I could barely keep from sending this Lida outside instead of Sasha. That's how sick of her I was.

"Come on out!" came from the forest. "Only come out alone. Slowly and so I can see your hands."

"I'm coming out!" Sasha replied. "I don't have a gun."

"Close the door behind me," I heard him whisper. "Or they might come in while I'm out."

"They're not going to do anything to him?" Ramil asked when Sasha's steps fell silent somewhere by the currant bushes.

"We'll find out soon," I replied.

"Maybe we should quietly climb out the window on the other side and beat the holy crap out of them?" Repa suggested. "While they're talking there."

It wasn't a bad idea, but I had no idea how many men Kirya might have brought along. Not only that, one blow wasn't going to solve the problem anyway. You fended off these jerks and others would come. Kirya was hardly going to calm down if you just beat the crap out of him. That could drag on forever. Or until they caught me for sure.

Sasha was gone about twenty minutes. All that time we looked out the windows in silence, trying to figure out what was going on outside. At some point, I even thought they'd actually left, but naturally that wasn't the case. I remembered Kirya's face and realized he was not the kind of guy to come to a stranger's dacha on New Year's Eve to sort things out and then have a talk with his former boss and calmly leave. A simple conversation was obviously not going to satisfy him. He was hardly one of those people you could convince with words. I'm afraid even fists were far from being able to convince him. A cudgel, maybe. Or a tire iron.

By the time Sasha got back, I personally was totally wound up. The thought that I had put Marina and Misha in danger was driving me crazy. I peered into the darkness and feverishly tried to figure out what I was going to do if they did decide to go on the attack. With my remaining bullets I couldn't stop more than two people. I simply didn't want to think about what would happen afterward. I started feeling sick to my stomach when my thoughts inched close to that. Getting a firmer grip on the gun's handle, I started taking deep breaths and thinking about totally irrelevant things. Still no sound from outside.

"I wonder what time it is?" Ramil said suddenly.

"What?" I actually shuddered when I heard his voice.

"I said, how long have we been sitting here like this?"

I looked at my watch but couldn't see a thing.

"I don't know. Twenty or twenty-five minutes maybe. What of it?"

"Oh, nothing," he went on in a whisper. "It's just that I think…"

"Quiet!" Repa interjected. "Someone's coming."

We leaned toward the windows and a moment later I too could make out the figure approaching the house.

"Who is it?" Ramil asked.

It was hard to tell. The man was walking very slowly, and his head was dropped low.

"Is he searching for something there?" Repa whispered.

"Or hiding his face," I said, feeling my right hand get all sweaty from the tension.

I even thought for a second that the gun might slip out of it.

"I'm afraid," Lida murmured, and this time I wasn't mad at her at all.

"Who is it?" Ramil repeated.

I raised my gun and aimed at the man's head.

"What, you're going to shoot him?"

"Mikhail, it's me," the person said at last as he walked up the stairs. "Open up. I'm frozen stiff as a dog."

"I nearly killed you," I said, letting Sasha into the house. "Why did you take so long to identify yourself?"

"Just wait," he replied. "Close the door quickly. I'm telling you—I'm frozen through, damn it."

"Well?" I turned to him as soon as the door was firmly shut.

"Do you have somewhere we can talk freely?"

"In the room."

"No, way too many people there."

I realized we were going to have a serious conversation.

"Let's go into the kitchen. No one will hear there."

"Hey, wait," Ramil protested. "What about us? What, we're supposed to sit here totally clueless?"

"There's no threat to you," Sasha replied. "Mikhail will explain it all to you later."

But I didn't. Why did they need to know about all this? The less you know, the longer you live. Kirya had lots of cop friends on the roads. One of them had spotted my SUV, which plied the same route nearly every day, passing a highway patrol post on the way out of Moscow. After that, chasing me down had been just a technicality.

# Winter: Sergei

## January 6, 1999

It's going to be a bad year. Three sixes upside down.

My father said someone blew up Vorobyov's SUV yesterday. I say, That's great. How interesting. And he says, You know what happened there? I say, How am I supposed to know? Lately he's been very busy. I barely see him. And he says, Mikhail nearly died himself. He survived by pure chance. He hadn't had a chance to reset the clock in his car. It was fast. So the explosion happened two hours early. He was still asleep. But whoever planted the bomb was evidently counting on him sitting in it. They just didn't check the clock. Evidently, they hooked the device up to the clock in the SUV and set it for eight in the morning. But it went off at six. Can you imagine what luck that was? I say, yeah. And he says, Are you listening to me at all? Turn off your computer. I say, I'm listening to you very closely. You were telling me about Vorobyov. I'm sorry all that happened to your car. He says, What does the car have to do with this? They might have killed him. I wonder who needed that? You have no knowledge of this, do you? I say, What? He says, Listen, turn off your computer. I'm talking to you about serious things now. I answer him, I can't shut it off right now. I've been downloading this stupid file for half an hour. You want me to start all over again later? And he says, Leave the file be. I'm asking you in plain Russian. Do you know anything about this business or not? I say, Or not. He says, Stop the clowning. They might have killed him, after all. I say, But they didn't. He's a lucky guy. Then he says, You're a strange one. I say, I know. Wait, look, I think I've got the whole file. Definitely. Now let's see what's inside it. He says, And the most interesting part is that they bombed the car outside of town. Did you know Mikhail was staying at someone's dacha? I say, What? He says, Stop messing around with your computer. I say, He asked me for my gun. My papa fell silent, and then he says, That one? I say, What other one? I don't have any others. He says, You should have given it back to me. I say, Apparently he needed it more. Why, do you? And he says, Stop talking like that to me. All in all, this is a strange business. So he was aware of the danger. Was he being threatened or something? I say, How am I supposed to know? He borrowed it a long time ago. It was the fall. November, I think. He says, And you didn't ask why? I say, I was shy. He says, And the dacha? I say, In what sense? He says, Whose dacha is it? Why is he staying there? I say, You're asking me? And he says, Well, you used to drive out in that direction too at one time. I say, Which direction? He says, Lyubertsy. Didn't you used to go to Kuzminki? I say, Wait up, wait up. He says, What? I say to him, Where is this dacha? He says, Just before you get to Ramenskoye. I went there with the police. I say, And who lives at the dacha there? He says, That's what I just asked you. I say, Was anyone there? And he says, Why are you shouting? You shouldn't get upset. The doctor strictly forbade that. I say, Who was with him at the dacha there? He says, Now calm down. There wasn't anyone. There were lots of toys in the house. But Mikhail said he was living there alone. Everything around there is basically abandoned. It is winter after all. There's no one at the dachas. Just the homeless. I say, Yeah? And the toys?

### January 7, 1999
In the morning I went to Marina's. For the twenty-fourth time. The same thing all over.

No one knows anything. The old man died. Marina gave up the apartment. Her neighbors don't want to talk to me anymore. I kicked their door. They said they'd call the police. I kicked their door a few more times. Children started crying inside and I left.

I don't give a damn about their police.

### January 7, 1999 (evening)
After dinner, my father said he'd told his bodyguards to go with Vorobyov. He says he refused at first. I wonder why that is. Maybe he likes having his cars bombed? Or is he the Terminator or something?

### January 8, 1999
Someone's staying in Vorobyov's apartment. I heard the person drop a glass there. Maybe not a glass. I don't know. I just rang the door and whoever it is dropped something there. Something broke. Then someone walked up to the door. But the person didn't open it. I even heard him breathing. I said, Vorobyov, open up. It's me. Don't you recognize me? Whoever was standing behind the door didn't say anything. I stood there a little while and then left on tiptoe. I heard the glass tinkle on the floor. I hope he cut himself.

## January 8, 1999 (evening)

My father doesn't want to say where the dacha is. He says, You shouldn't go there. I say, Why? He says, You're supposed to avoid stress. I say, Who said? He says, The doctor. I say, Your doctor can go hang himself. And he says, You shouldn't think about suicide. I say, I'm not. He says, You just said it yourself. I say, What did I say? He says, That the doctor can go hang himself. I say, That's not thoughts of suicide. That's thoughts about your doctor. I would just enjoy seeing him hanging from the ceiling. In his striped socks. He says, What color? I say, What? He says, What color should the socks be? I say, Do you really think I'm crazy? He says, Absolutely not. It's just that the doctor told me to write down your color visions. It's important what color you picture to yourself most often. I say, Your doctor can go hang himself. And he says, You shouldn't go to the dacha. The danger from the stress is too great.

## January 9, 1999

It's not Vorobyov at Vorobyov's apartment. This morning my father said that Vorobyov was coming to see him at his office. At twelve. They want to pick out a new car for him. At twelve ten, I was at his door. I rang the bell and listened. At first I couldn't hear anything, and then I realized someone was standing right opposite me. I could hear breathing. Then someone looked through the peephole.

My father said, Why do you go to his place? I say, He's got someone staying there. He says, So? What difference is it to us? I say, Why doesn't the person open up? He says, Listen, how many of your pills have you not taken? I say, You and your doctor can take them yourselves. He says, Seryozha, this is the best specialist. The entire State Duma goes to him. I say,

Why? He looks at me and says, Well, you know, everyone has their problems. I say, What about you?

## January 10, 1999
I didn't go up to Vorobyov's, I just sat in the courtyard, in the kiddie sandbox. I watched his windows. Whoever is living in his apartment is significantly shorter than he is. That person flashed by the kitchen window twice. It's not Vorobyov.

This person's too short. I wonder who it could be.

## January 11, 1999
There were two of them today. Vorobyov and this second person. I know the first was Vorobyov because his car was parked by the front door. My father gave him his Mercedes. He used to drive it himself. Vorobyov's his favorite employee now. He's driving my papa's Mercedes.

## January 12, 1999
Today, there were two of them again. Once they went up to the window together. And I hid under the metal mushroom in the sandbox. Papa's Mercedes was by the front door again.

## January 13, 1999
Vorobyov wasn't home, so I went upstairs. I stood by the door and listened. The television was on inside. I rang and the television turned off. Then someone walked up on the other side. Very quietly. We stood there for a couple of minutes, and I said, Open up, Marina. I want to see you. But no one opened. Then I said, Why won't you open the door for me? What did I ever do to you?

## January 14

I don't want to write "1999" anymore. Nasty number. It makes me furious.

Like three cobras. Three cobras with puffed-out hoods.

Today is the old New Year's. My father said, What can I give you, son? I said, New pills.

I downloaded a few more photographs of Audrey Hepburn from the Internet and put one on my desktop. To hell with my father. Let him try to guess. On the other hand, every morning is going to start with her now. Turn on the computer, and there's Audrey. I get gooseflesh even, they look so much alike.

I'm eighteen now. That means I can get married. If I find someone.

Maybe she'll open the door for me after all? I'll go one more time today.

## January 16

Yesterday morning, one of father's bodyguards, one whom he'd told to keep an eye on Vorobyov, stopped by. After my father let him go, I called him into my room. At first he didn't want to, but I said my father wouldn't find out. I promised to give him a hundred bucks. For five minutes' conversation. He said, But only five minutes. I asked how Vorobyov was doing, and he said he didn't know. Vorobyov had refused protection a week ago. They'd only ridden with him for one day. One day and another half day after that. I asked where they'd gone, and he said nowhere special. You know, around town, to his place, and to the dacha. I said, Where they bombed his SUV? He said, Well, yeah, where else? Absolutely. I say, Was anyone there? He says, Well, absolutely. I say, Who? He says, I don't know. Some people. I say, Lots of people? He says,

Well, absolutely. I think, Why does he keep repeating, "Well, absolutely?" But I ask him, Was there a girl there? Again he says to me, Well, absolutely. I say, What was she like? What did she look like? And then he looks at my computer and says, Like that. In the car, he kept repeating that Pavel Petrovich was going to kill him for this. When I was tired of listening to him, I said I'd give him five hundred dollars. He said, Do you have it on you? I said, Look, and he whistled. And I said to him, Watch the road. Or we'll both get killed. Then he said, We won't get killed now. We'll get there like kings. And he stopped saying, "Well, absolutely." He just whistled the whole way. And I didn't give a damn anymore.

When we walked up the front steps, Marina was standing inside. She looked at me through the window and didn't say anything. And I looked at her. We both stood there and I just couldn't open the door. I couldn't reach out. I looked at Marina and couldn't push the door. And she looked at me on the porch. Then the bodyguard said, Well, maybe I should go? I told him, Yeah. But he kept standing behind me, and I couldn't open the door. Then he said, You promised me another hundred for talking to you at your house. I gave him the hundred dollars, and he said, I'm out of here. And Marina stood and watched us on the porch. Watched me talking on her porch. With the bodyguard.

Then she went to the door and pulled on the handle. I said, Hi. She said, Hello. I say, Look, I've found you. And she says, Yes, exactly.

## January 17

I couldn't finish writing yesterday. I really don't know why I'm writing this. I just am. As if that would make it better. Or won't it? I don't know.

There. We stood like that on her porch, and then she said, Come inside. I'm glad you've come. I said, Me too. She said, Come on in. I said, Thank you. Where's Misha? Suddenly I got scared. I thought she might think I was asking about Vorobyov. But I wasn't. She said, He's fine. He's playing in his room. And I said, Ah.

Then we sat in the kitchen. In silence. That is, I sat, and she made breakfast. She peeled potatoes. I watched her. Then I heard a car in the yard and thought, Who's that? But Marina started peeling potatoes even faster. The door opened, and in walked Vorobyov.

I said, Hi. But he didn't say anything and just looked at Marina. Marina stopped peeling potatoes. I said, Look, I finally found Marina. She turns out to be staying at the dacha. Vorobyov stood by the door and said nothing. We must have been silent like that for a whole minute. Then Marina said, Great, Misha, what brings you here? And she looked at him. He said, Yeah, well, I was driving by. She said to me, Mikhail stops by from time to time. Rarely. When he has the time. Then she said to him, How are you doing, Mikhail? But Vorobyov looked at her and didn't say anything. Then he got a package out of his bag and said, Here's why I stopped by to see you. I got up early on purpose. She said, Oh, how interesting. What do you have there? He said, A dress. She said, What dress? He said, The black one. Remember, you bought it in Italy last summer? I wanted to bring it to you on New Year's, but I forgot. I had a lot to do. Now I decided to come especially. Take it. It's yours. Marina said, I can't take it. It's expensive. And he looked at her and said, No, take it. What, I got up so early for nothing? Then little Misha ran into the kitchen. And Marina said to him immediately, Come here. I have to cut your nails. He said, I don't want to. And she said, Come here. Who am I talking to? And Vorobyov and I looked at them. She took out the scissors and started cutting his nails. And we were all silent.

Misha looked at her, and looked, and then started wincing. She said, What's with you? He said, It hurts. She said, Don't lie. And she pulled his arm very hard. Twisted it, even. It was hard for him to stand like that so he started drawing closer to her and standing on his toes. And she was cutting his nails and silent. There were tears in his eyes, but he was afraid of her, so he tried his hardest not to cry. And she was evidently cutting very close. But he put up with it. Only he was crying now. But he was trying not to loudly. And he was wiping his face with his free hand. Vorobyov said, What are you, a fool or something? Let go of him. I told you, I stopped by because of the dress. Let the kid go. I won't be coming here anymore.

And he went out.

She dropped the scissors on the floor and started looking out the window. Then I said, It's time for me to go too.

But Misha was standing next to her and crying.

When I went out on the porch, Vorobyov was kicking Papa's Mercedes. I'm checking the wheels, he told me. But he wasn't kicking just the wheels. He was kicking everywhere. The doors too. And the radiator. Well, he said, want me to give you a ride home? Because it looks like your bodyguard abandoned you. I said, I'm taking the train. Where is it? And he said, Don't show off. Get in the car.

I got in, and he said, You'd better buckle up. We'll be going fast. God forbid you should smash up again. I said, What, are you in a hurry to get somewhere? And he said, That's not the word.

We pulled out on the road and he opened the throttle. I'd never ridden that fast before. Just on the computer. But obviously he didn't care. He was leaning slightly forward and had his eyes locked on the road. To the side, the trees were whizzing by.

I said, Maybe we could take it a little easier? And he said, What? I said, We're going to crash.

He looked at me and floored it. I thought, I shouldn't talk to him. Better he watch the road instead. The way he turned his head toward me, it didn't look as though he planned to turn it back. I said, Why were you staring at me? He said, It's nothing. I said, Look straight ahead. Or we'll both get killed. He smiled and slammed on the brakes. The car went into a spin. And he was still looking at me. We were spinning in the middle of the road, and he's looking.

Finally we stopped. Silence all around. A forest in snow. We were stopped crosswise to the road.

I said, Well, what now? He said, Nothing. We just stopped. Want to talk?

Then he suddenly looked to the side and said, Your bodyguard didn't abandon you after all. Pavel Petrovich has tightened the bolts on their brain. I looked in that direction and said, That's not our car. I came in a different one. Then he said, Yeah? Great, how interesting. Who besides you and me goes to a dacha settlement here in winter?

And his knuckles turned white at the edges. The steering wheel under them creaked slightly.

Then he started up and drove forward slowly. And he was looking very carefully in the rearview mirror. He was waiting for that SUV to pull up closer. Then he obviously saw something and cheered up tremendously. He said, Well, aren't we in luck. It's great they turned up right on time. Just fine fellows. Well, let's do it, boys. Let's settle all our problems right now. Once and for all. At one fell swoop.

And he leaned on the gas again.

I said, Who is it? He said, Don't be afraid, Seryozha. You'll find out everything soon enough. We really are in luck.

The SUV started picking up speed too, and pulling closer little by little.

Vorobyov pulled out on the highway, and the speedometer read one hundred twenty kilometers per hour. I told him, They're not dropping back. And he laughed and said, These guys won't drop back, Seryozha. And that's actually very good. It's good they won't drop back. They're exactly who I needed today. I'm just singing I'm so happy.

The speedometer read one hundred thirty now.

Finally he turned onto a side road and said, Well, this is it. Prepare yourself.

I dug my feet into the floor and grabbed on to the handle.

Vorobyov said, See all the monuments flashing by along the road? Someone cracks up here every year. Instant death. It's a straight road. But the forest, you see what it's like. The least little skid—and that's all she wrote. Crazy fast. Well, hold on. There's going to be one marker more now.

He jammed on the brakes and turned the car crosswise to the road. The SUV was approaching from his side. I thought that when they rammed us they might not get as far as me. But Vorobyov was going to get smeared over the whole car.

He opened his door, took the gun out of his pocket, and fired twice in the SUV's direction. Without getting out of the car.

At first nothing happened, and the SUV kept flying in our direction. But then it swerved a little, and rocked, and started skidding into the trees. Huge, straight pines. Thick as columns. Whoever was in the SUV was evidently trying to straighten it out, but nothing was working. The road was slick. A second later they were pressed right up to the line of trees and started hitting small bushes. The SUV started swerving from side to side and finally smashed head on. The car stopped dead in its tracks. A second later, a spark leaped from underneath and a fire roared up around it.

Vorobyov closed his door and said, You should have buckled up, jerks. I was so damn sick of them.

I looked at him and said, We have to pull them out. And he said, No point. The gas tank burst. The diesel's already burning. It's just about to blow.

I jumped out of the car and ran toward the SUV.

Vorobyov yelled, Lie down, fool. And the SUV blew sky high.

I was standing next to them, but there was nothing left to do. Vorobyov walked up and said, It's Kirya. I recognized his jacket. Nice jacket. Too bad it burned up. All right, time for us to make tracks. The cops will be here any minute. These freaks probably have a fucking arsenal on them. I say, You killed them. He said, They killed themselves. Let's make tracks. Go on, get in the car fast.

When we'd driven away, I said to him, Are they the ones who bombed your SUV? He smiled and said, Your papa's, not mine. I said, All the same. He said, No, and now it doesn't matter. I said, And they are? He looked at me and said, What, you want to know the truth? I said, Yes. He said, Well, listen. And he told me they came for him on New Year's Eve, but he decided that if they left he'd come to them himself. That second. But he didn't. Then they planted the bomb.

Well, as for the clock, he said, you already know that trick. Did Pavel Petrovich tell you? I said, Yes. He said, So you can see for yourself, I had no choice. Or would you like me to be burning up in the forest there now? Huh? Would you? Tell me, Seryozha. I said, Lay off. He said, No, is that true? I said, What did they want from you? He said, Now that's a completely different story. You're better off not knowing about that. I say, Who's staying in your apartment? He looked at me and then suddenly starts laughing. I say, What's with you? And he says, So that was you who scared Sasha Mercedes? I say, What Mercedes? But he keeps laughing and says, So you're the reason I can't get rid of him? Every day he says Kirya's come for him. He's running me ragged. You're the reason he's afraid to go outside. No, damn, that's great. I'm sending him back to Ryazan today. On the first train. I swear to God I am.

And he's laughing and just can't stop. He's laughing and I'm looking at him. I'm sitting and thinking, What about Marina?

# Winter: Little Misha

I told them, Put me down. I like to stand on the floor myself. They did and started taking off their coats. I walked over to the wall. Father Frost was hanging there with a red stick. I took him. Marina said, Give him to me. It's a thermometer. I wouldn't. She said, You'll break it. Then the big man up high said, Let him play. It's nothing terrible. But Marina said, He might cut himself. And she knelt down to me. Give it to me. We'll hang him back on the wall. I said, It's a toy. Marina said, No. I said, Children are allowed to. She said, It's a thermometer. It's someone else's. The big man up high said, Let him play. Marina straightened up and I couldn't see what her face looked like. The big man did. He said, Come on, little one, let's take off that jacket. Marina said, You won't be able to unzip his jacket. The zipper catches. The big man said, We'll buy him a new one tomorrow. Won't we? And he knelt down to me. What kind of jacket do you want? You want us to buy you one with Mickey Mouse? Right here, on your back. Do you? He had a big face. An old face. Not like Marina's. Like Papa's. When he was sick. The big man said, Why are we crying now? You don't want a new jacket? Well, if you don't, we won't buy one. We'll keep this one. Do you like your old jacket? Marina said, He's probably tired. It's late. He usually goes to bed early. Tell me, where is his room? The big man straightened up, and I couldn't see what his face looked like anymore. He said up high, Well, now he's calmed down. Seryozha, take the boy to his room. He'll be fine there. Can he fall asleep alone? Marina said, I'll sit with him. Seryozha said, I'll sit with you too. Marina took off my jacket and said to me, Stop it. Here's your Father Frost. He didn't go anywhere. Why are you so wet? Are you hot? I said, Yes. And I need to pee. The big man said, Why does he always whisper? Marina said, He's shy. The big man knelt down to me. Let's go, I'll take you to the bathroom. Marina said, You'd better show me. He won't go with you. The big man said, Is that true? You won't come with me? I said, Yes. He said, Why is it you're always whispering? I said, I don't know. He straightened up and said, He really does look very tired. Go on, put him to bed.

Then I peed and they took me to a room. It was dark there. And the bed was too big. Marina said, Don't be picky. Where are they going to get a child's bed? Seryozha said, We can buy one tomorrow. Marina took Father Frost away from me. They sat in chairs and waited for me to fall asleep. It was quiet. Then Marina said, How did you explain it to him? Seryozha said, I didn't. I just said this was the way it had to be. I raised my head, and Marina said, Sleep. Are we going to have to sit with you all night or something? Then I fell asleep.

And the next day I worked.

The big man shut himself up in his room and wouldn't let anyone in. I went up to the door and pushed it, and it opened. The big man said, I'm working. Then he turned around and said, Ah, it's you. Come in. Don't be shy. I walked up to his desk. There were lots of papers there. He said, See how much work? I'm snowed under. I said, Marina doesn't like being snowed under either. He said, Yes? What else doesn't she like? I said, When Misha doesn't come to the dacha for a long time. The big man put me in his lap, and I saw a black thing. It was shiny. You couldn't see it from below. But the big man saw it always. He had a tall body. He said, And did Misha stay with you at the dacha for long? I said, Yes. Five years. Until New Year's. Then his car blew up. He wound it up too hard. Marina says you shouldn't wind your toys up too hard. They break. The big man said, Careful there. You'll fall. What are you reaching for? You want the stapler? Well here, take it. It staples papers together. Let me show you. He clicked the black thing and two papers stuck together. Stuck at the corner. He said, Want to try? I said, Yes. Then Seryozha came and said, What's he doing here? I said, I'm working. The big man said, Wait, wait, don't staple that. But Seryozha said, You never let me come into your study when I was little. The big man said, Stop it. And I said, Stop it. Then the big man laughed.

But Marina didn't laugh. She was sitting in her room and not laughing at all. She was just crying. And I told her, Don't cry. My fingers don't hurt anymore. It's all better. We won't cut nails anymore. But she still cried. She took my hands and started kissing them. I told her, It doesn't hurt anymore. Then Seryozha came and said, Vorobyov quit. Marina stopped crying and said, I don't care. Seryozha said, He brought back the car and the money. And Marina said again, I don't care. Then I said, Who's Vorobyov? And Marina said again, twice, I don't care. I don't care. And she started crying again.

Then she stopped playing with me. She wouldn't play a single game. Not "tickles," not "guess where it is." I told her, You just sit there and look out the window. Or cry. When are we going to play? She said, I'll play with you later. I said, Don't lie. You're always lying. She looked at me and said, Is that true? I said, Yes. I want to go to the dacha. It's bad here. When is Misha coming?

Then I was already asleep and she woke me up. I told her, I want to sleep some more. And she said, Quiet, sweetheart, quiet. And she started pulling my sweater over my head. I said, It's prickly. I don't like it. And Marina said, Just don't make any noise, Misha. And she kissed me. I said, You have salty lips. And she said, Where are your pants?

Then we went outside. Marina gathered me up and told me to stand quietly by the door while she dressed. I got tired of standing and lay down on the floor. Because it was dark by the door. She didn't turn the light on in the hall. So I waited for her in the dark. And I got hot. But I couldn't take my jacket off because I was lying down. She came out of her room and didn't see me at first. But then she bumped into me and saw me. She said, Why are you on the floor? I said, I'm sleepy. And I'm hot. And Marina said, Do you want me to carry you? I said, Yes. But why are we talking in a whisper? And then she said, We're running away.

It was dark outside. In the subway, they told us the transfers were shut down now. We got in an empty car and then Marina poked me and said, Little one, wake up. I opened my eyes. Suddenly it was light, but I wasn't in a bed. She said, Come here. I'll carry you. And we went outside.

It was cold. Marina was walking very fast, and I was bouncing in her arms. She said, Don't bounce, please. You're heavy as it is. I said, Okay. And we went into a warm building. Then we took the elevator and stood next to a door. Then the door opened. But I couldn't see who opened it. Because Marina was holding me facing her. I saw her face. When the door closed, her face was scared. As if she'd broken a plate and was afraid now. I'm always afraid when I break a plate. And then someone pressed up from behind and I had a hard time breathing. And Marina started crying again. And I said,

You're squeezing me. Let me go. But they stood there like that. And I saw someone else's hand on Marina's head. The hand was petting Marina as if she were a little girl. And I thought that was funny. I turned around in her arms—and it was Misha. And then I said, Hi. Where have you been so long? We missed you so much.

## Winter: Pavel Petrovich

Dear Lena,

You know lately I've had these strange feelings. Completely new for me. Unexpected. Even now, I'm writing this letter and I can distinctly see you reading it. You're sitting by the window in an old armchair and the fireplace is burning to your right. Out the window there's snow on the mountains. A few bare trees. And right behind them is the start of a long slope. There must be a village somewhere below. Not many people, but you can buy food. You're reading my letter and starting to frown. But then this expression disappears. Because I'm not repulsive to you anymore.

It's a strange feeling, right? I see it all as if it were a movie. I don't know where it came from. Things like this didn't use to happen to me. I worked all the time, and everything seemed fine.

You know, I met someone recently. He's very little. Only five years old. But he and I made friends somehow. He's very serious and at the same time funny. It's too bad our acquaintance was so brief. A few days ago, I was holding him in my lap and suddenly I thought that you were probably right. We should have had more little boys. Or little girls. Whichever. Just so there'd be more of them. Because, ultimately, it doesn't matter how they come out later. The main thing is that they exist. And we could have held them in our laps. Do you understand me?

Sergei asked me to find out whether he could visit you in Switzerland. He's having a tough time of it right now. I think you're the only person capable of helping him. Not only that, he's still raving over his Audrey Hepburn. He says he wants to visit her house. Will you have him? He needs your support very much right now.

I could come too. For a couple of days.

What do you think? May I?

## About the Author

Andrei Gelasimov was born in Irkutsk in 1965 and studied foreign languages at Yakutsk State University and directing at the Moscow Theater Institute. His first novel, *Thirst*, garnered the Apollon Grigoriev Award and was nominated for the Belkin Prize; upon publication in English the *Telegraph* hailed it as "a haven of both comedy and horror." Two further novels are forthcoming in English: *The Gods of the Steppe*, winner of the 2009 Russian National Bestseller award, and *Rachel*, winner of the Booker Student Prize.

## About the Translator

*Photo © Raymond Yin*

Marian Schwartz is an award-winning translator of Russian literature. She is the recipient of two translation fellowships from the National Endowment for the Arts and a past president of the American Literary Translators Association. Her translations include the *New York Times* bestseller *The Last Tsar* by Edvard Radzinsky, Andrei Gelasimov's *Thirst*, Olga Slavnikova's *2017*, and Ivan Goncharov's *Oblomov*.

Printed in Great Britain
by Amazon